Essential Saltes

An Experiment

Fictions of Don Webb

Uncle Ovid's Exercise Book
The Seventh Day and After
A Spell for the Fulfillment of Desire
Stealing My Rules
The Explanation and Other Good Advice
Anubis on Guard
The Double: An Investigation

Essential Saltes

Don Webb

St. Martin's Press New York

Essential Saltes

An Experiment

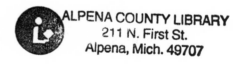

For information, address St. Martin's Press, 175 Fifth Avenue, New York, N.Y. 10010.

Library of Congress Cataloging-in-Publication Data

Webb, Don.
Essential saltes: an experiment / Don Webb. —1st U.S. ed.
p. cm.
ISBN 0–312–20302–0
I. Title.
PS3573.E1953E87 1999
813'.54 — dc21 99–22041

First Edition: May 1999

10 9 8 7 6 5 4 3 2 1

To Ragan and Clyde Haggard, William Gaddis and Gilbert Sorrentino, Stanley Jeyaraja Tambiah and David Allen Hulse, Stephen King and Prince Imam Karim Aga Khan IV, and Rosemary Webb goes this explosive mixture. Place on ground, light fuse, run away.

Table of Contents

1. A Visit to Aunt Martha's 1
2. Bowling for Books 10
3. Great Prospects 18
4. Dark of Touch: The Empty Hand 28
5. Hence Astrology 38
6. Very Interesting, but Stupid 48
7. Zeugma 57
8. Chronicles 67
9. Tea for Two and Two for Tea 77
10. Iqbal Tells His Stories (Again) 87
11. Kriegspielhaus: Both Kin and Kind 97
12. Lamed in the Notebook 108
13. Mom at the Wedding 119

14.	None but the Hopeless and the Bored	132
15.	Seeking a Sacred Space	145
16.	O Night Our Mother	158
17.	Perhaps Rex Knows Something	171
18.	Tzuris of Orfamay	184
19.	Queer Deaths and Odd Closures	196
20.	Revelations of Norman Papin	209
21.	Sparkler 451	222
22.	The Finale Rack	231
	About the Author	245

1 A Visit to Aunt Martha's

Many years later, as he was to discover that someone had stolen his wife's cremains, Matthew Reynman was to remember the night he discovered the link between fireworks, masturbation, and black women.

It had of course been on the Fourth of July. It was 1980. Matthew would be turning sixteen in November, but it was not November yet. It was, however, Halloween. It was always Halloween in Aunt Martha's house. Matthew's mother and father had foisted him off on his maternal spinster aunt. *They* were having a good time in Armonk, New Mexico; Matthew was in the poorly air-conditioned home of Martha Scott in Doublesign, Texas.

The house was large, much bigger than Matthew's own home. He was used to having a bedroom of his own, his brothers all having gone to college and finding their way in the world, but the bedroom he had here was larger, with twelve-foot-tall ceilings. This was how houses were cooled at one time, high ceilings so you could invite the air inside to swirl around. Aunt Martha had sealed her house tightly. Although the air-conditioning helped, the window units weren't strong enough to make things really cool, and the air was so thick in the house that Matthew's watch had stopped a few hours after he had brought it into the house. Or perhaps it still worked but the hands moved so slowly that a tick could not be measured. It matched the real movement of time in the house, Matthew decided.

July the Fourth was an important holiday for Aunt Martha, not because of American independence, but because it was the birthday of Nathaniel Hawthorne. As she rocked back and forth in her antique rocker (one of the few things not orange and black in the room), Aunt Martha informed Matthew on the Importance of Hawthorne whilst Sophie, the lynx-eyed black maid, served lemonade in her pumpkin-colored livery.

"Hawthorne was important. He was the first great American writer and he chose the topic for American writers—death and horror. It was because of Europe, you see. Writing is always centuries behind reality. The Americans were writing about the Dark Ages, they were caught up in that death during the birth of their own land. Hawthorne wrote the best stories about witchcraft: 'Young Goodman Brown' and *The Scarlet Letter*. Who would forget that comet that lit up the sky with the letter A for Angel? Do you know how he died? For two years before his death in 1864, he began to age rapidly, he would write one thing again and again, the number sixty-four. He was trying to write about the future, but he didn't know that the future is fiction."

Aunt Martha rocked back and forth, glad that she had aided in her nephew's education. She looked far more youthful than her years. It was because of the house, she said. It was hermetically sealed against the outside world. Matthew wasn't a good judge of age, but he would have guessed hers at thirty-five, about twenty years younger than the calendar would have shown. But Matthew wasn't thinking about Aunt Martha's age, nor about the firecrackers some boys on the block had set off that morning by lighting them with a magnifying glass. He was thinking about Sophie's cunt. He had caught a glimpse of it a week ago while she ascended the stairs. A darkness within darkness more inviting than blackness between the stars, which, like every good science fiction–reading boy, he had no doubt that Americans would someday colonize.

He would think about Sophie's cunt until he would have to excuse himself to the bathroom on the second floor and whack off.

Even the bathroom had Aunt Martha's Halloween collectibles in it. Orange parade lanterns from the thirties stared down at him as his thumb and fingers jerked back and forth. You put a candle behind the painted glass of the jack-o'-lantern face. Black Bakelite cats arched their backs in anger as he pulled and prayed and thought of Sophie's pussy. Two jack-o'-lantern-headed dolls dangled on the wall across from the toilet, their loose legs somehow picking up the rocking of his frame.

Years later when he was at college at the University of Texas at Austin, he was to write a paper comparing Buddhist and Dominican monastic practices which he would entitle "Black and Orange Don't Necessarily Mean Halloween."

As he neared climax, he heard a voice outside the bathroom door. A thick sultry voice that said, "Honey, don't waste all of it."

The shame. The surprise. And he went off like a rocket.

He was as still as he could be. He thought it was Sophie's voice. He hoped it was Sophie's voice. He feared it was Sophie's voice. He tried not breathing, he wanted to be so quiet. He was afraid that his heart was beating too loud.

After an eternity (or at least a good minute) he swung himself off the toilet seat and pulled up his pants. He would dab up the evidence in a moment, but he wanted to see if it was Sophie. He opened the door very gently. No one in the hall. He ran out (as quietly as he could run) to his aunt's bedroom, the storage room, the nice guest bedroom, his bedroom, and the solarium. No one was on the second floor. He didn't know how Sophie could have gone downstairs so quickly.

He went back to dab up the evidence, flush the toilet, and make his way downstairs. Sophie was dusting the candy containers from the display case near the front door. Currently she was working on the black-and-white eleven-inch figure of a cat lady with removable head. She smiled at Matthew.

"You're a sweet boy," she said, and he was simultaneously sure that it both was and could not possibly have been her voice at the bathroom door above. He went on into the parlor, where his aunt was still rocking. She was launching into another speech:

"Halloween is largely thought to be an Irish holiday because of Samhain. At Samhain all the fires on the face of the earth were extinguished, and people went to the underground places where the *file*—that's Irish for Druid—lived. They kept the hostel fire going—people brought that fire back to their homes. That was fire from another place and time you see, not subject to the law of fire of this earth. Do you know the law of fire here, Matthew? It goes out. That's the law. So they had to get fire from another world, from the underworld. They thought that time, Samhain, was not part of regular time. The dead, for example, were able to come to people's homes and visit them. The Irish pickled the heads of their dead, Matthew. That way when they came to visit, they had a way of talking to people. They weren't afraid of their dead relatives. But some of the dead they couldn't control—these were scary to them. So they stayed home. The Scots—all of them, not just our relatives—are descended from the Irish. They have the same myths and fears at a deep level. They knew that the dead were out and about on Halloween. But with the coming of science, and the electric light—which banished all but the most persistent ghosts—the Scots began the custom of 'guising, going out in disguise, in the 1850s. It became the practice here around the turn of the century. You know, very early Halloween decorations actually show things like thistles and plaid caps and the like. I have a few examples I'll show you tonight, unless you want to go to the fireworks down by the lake, in which case I'll show them tomorrow night."

"No, ma'am, I'd rather stay here."

This was not because Matthew wanted to be even a minute in Aunt Martha's house, but because the local boys (particularly the Simms kids next door) had treated him very badly last year, beginning with such little tricks as taking him on a snipe hunt, and ending with what might have been an attempt to drown him in the well in Aunt Martha's backyard. Partly it was because Matthew was a new boy in town, but mainly it was because of the fear everyone had of Martha Scott, believing her to be a witch.

And as good Americans they had to hate witches.

Of course a year had turned and they might have an entirely new attitude, but Matthew knew he could get a better view of the show from his window on the second floor, which looked lakeward.

"Oh, good, I'll have Sophie make us some hot dogs and I'll put on my Boris Karloff record."

Matthew knew then that if he ever heard the "Monster Mash" one more time, he would be in hell. Hell was surely repetition, repetition.

"I was thinking of watching the fireworks show from my bedroom actually," said Matthew.

"Well, in that case, I'll be sure and send Sophie up with a couple of bottles of pop."

Matthew thought just how much he would like her to send Sophie up.

"Now you remember, dear, don't open your window. It spoils the air-conditioning."

"Yes, ma'am."

He knew it would spoil far more than the air-conditioning:

he had heard his mother and father speak about his aunt's beliefs.

He was thinking how much he would like to have Sophie sent to his room. He had touched one once. Last year on a speech trip. Heather Anton's. He needed to distract himself quickly so he forced his interest on a four-sided paper lantern with tissue inserts that stood on a small table next to his aunt's orange divan. Each panel was decorated with cat and bat or pumpkin and owl and a verse. When the candle was lit, it threw the verse and cat/bat/owl/pumpkin silhouettes on the walls. The verses read: "SPOS'N THE WITCHES BEGAN TO WITCH AND YOU DIDN'T KNOW WHICH WITCH WAS WITCH? WELL—, SPOS'N / SPOS'N A PUMP-KIN PUMPED HOT FLAMES FROM A PLACE *YOU* KNOW, WHAT NOBODY NAMES? WELL—, SPOS'N / SPOS'N A GREAT BIG BUG-A-BOO REACHED OUT ITS LONG SHARP CLAWS FOR YOU? WELL—, SPOS'N / SPOS'N A H'ANT APPEARED TO YOU AN' AN OLD BLACK ROOSTER UP AND CREW WELL—, SPOS'N."

He couldn't see much point in "spos'n" any of these things except they did rid him of the telltale hard-on.

The rest of the afternoon passed quickly into evening due to television, the one-eyed serpent who devours time.

Sophie brought the phallic franks around seven in the evening, and Matthew watched the cars on the way to the lake. Many had the popular "J. R. for President" bumper sticker. God how the world loved Texas and Texas loved herself, people driving down to Yewston to see the Galleria and then on to Pasadena to ride the mechanical bull. *It was all stupid,* thought Matthew, *stupid.*

There was a group of men burying pipe in the ground on the side of the lake closest to Aunt Martha's house. The pieces of pipe were about two feet long and ranged in diameter from about three inches up to six. They also buried some cardboard tubes that looked almost a foot across. The pipes pointed upward and Matthew realized that they were cannon, the mortars for the firework shells. A couple of women were separating small cardboard spheres with fuses on them. It seemed to Matthew that fireworks shouldn't look so much like cartoon bombs, but like rockets. He really liked the idea of women, of women not afraid to face death and darkness. The women were loading the shells into ice chests, which they placed in a line parallel to the cannon. One of the men got out a tape measure to see if the chests were far enough away from the cannon. No, not far enough, and they moved them a couple of feet to the west.

There were people gathering across the lake at the pavilion. There was a big barbecue feast, brisket and beans, and many of the ladies of the community had made pies. Matthew began to realize that he had chosen the wrong place to watch all of this in the Godlike point of view of the sealed room. He thought about cracking the window open to hear more, smell more, but he knew that would fail to keep the outside world at bay. He realized that this house was exactly like the *file*'s underground hostel. Time didn't happen here, but he wondered where the fire was. His aunt had all those jack-o'-lantern-looking things, and any number of Halloween lanterns, but no fires.

He wondered if Sophie were somehow the fire.

He wondered why she wasn't wearing panties. He had never seen a woman not wear panties.

Maybe his aunt *forbade* her to wear panties.

Well—, spos'n.

Well that thought was an instant erection. There were all sorts of guilts and forbidden thoughts in that constellation from the shame of the South to the hot fire through which men see women loving women. It was another telltale moment. To think of such heat involving an older woman relative was wrong somehow, and the ebony-and-ivory vision of the two burning bushes somehow rubbing together like a Boy Scout's sticks was surely not far from the fires of hell. He fought off his masturbatory urge with a great willpower and strained to hear the speaker that was accounting the founding of Doublesign. The words were too fragmentary, too muffled by wind and distance, but catching the occasional phrase, the verbal palimpsest, he gathered that the town had had another name, that it had been named Salem, Texas—but that since it was so small there was a joke that you saw the same sign coming and going. In other words the sign saying Welcome and the sign saying Good-bye were on the same pole. A Stephen King fan, Matthew had hoped that the town would actually be named 'Salem's Lot, and that being such a good story, he decided he would tell it at Tascosa High School next year. Over the years he would tell the story enough that it would become true in his mind, and no doubt true for the listeners to his tales, and set up for the ghostly encounters he would have in Doublesign years later.

The next speaker was a man with a loud voice that began, "Next to of course God, America is what I love best. . . ." Matthew found his speech dull. He was one of those people that would vote for Reagan, J. R. being unavailable. Matthew by heredity was a Democrat. His family were Democrats in one of the most conservative towns in America, the only part of Texas that had voted against LBJ, so LBJ took their air base away from them. Matthew's parents weren't Democrat so much out of social conscience, but out of pure contrariness. Both Elaine and Herman liked going against the grain. They didn't even see it as a virtue, more just as a property of life in themselves.

The night darkened, and a black woman began to sing the national anthem. She had a great church voice that boomed out like a thousand southern gospels. When she started singing, the men lit some kind of red flare in the fireworks field. Two of them walked over to the cannon.

It was at that time a sound, possibly a moan, possibly the sound of Aunt Martha's old refrigerator starting up again, hit Matthew's ears. It was sufficiently unintelligible as speech to serve the purpose of communicating directly to Matthew's imagination the desired cue that there must be some link between Martha Scott and the lynx-eyed maid, and his zipper was off with so much friction that it would have started a fire in the dry grass around Doublesign.

Out it came to be worked. When the woman reached "the rocket's red glare" the two men touched the fuses of two shells in the cannons. They shot up three hundred and four hundred feet respectively and produced great red chrysanthemums, but Matthew's sense had all shifted to the inner sight.

He wasn't watching a moment later when the national anthem had ended. One of the three-inch mortars had been buried at a slight angle, the white titanium salute within shot toward Aunt Martha's house, and coupled with a freakish gust of wind the baffled pyrotechnician would be talking about the very night the alchemist stole Matthew's wife's ashes, shot directly at Aunt Martha's house.

With an amazing report, it exploded, shattering the windows on the west side of the house; at the same moment Matthew likewise exploded.

2 Bowling for Books

He was so happy the night of the big party.

He hadn't had anyone in his house since Haidee had been murdered, and he had been afraid that he couldn't be a host anymore.

But the party had gone well. He felt warm and happy. He had real friends in the world.

These people really cared about him.

Then he saw that his wife's ashes were missing.

And everything stopped for a long time.

One of them, one of his friends, had taken her ashes.

He looked at the very, very empty candy holder in which he kept her ashes.

It was next to the bowling trophy.

The party had happened because of bowling.

He felt as if everything in his life was a big joke, leading up to this absurd situation. Bowling and books and ROTC and Haidee's murder, and now a great laugh-track moment—her ashes had been stolen by one of his "best" friends.

He hadn't been allowed to go to the all-night bowling party when he was a senior in high school.

Seniors at Tascosa High School were entitled to a supervised all-night party at the local bowling alley. Matthew had bowled exactly once before, at a similar get-together for Navy ROTC, where he had earned his "Most Gutter Balls" trophy. He prized that trophy and kept it on his mantel for life—next to his wife's ashes, in fact. He hadn't fit in much as an adolescent. His parents were old, he was in fact a sort of mistake, they had assumed that things were safe after John and didn't think there would be any more kids. In some ways this was good for Matthew because he could get away with anything—like signing up for so many extracurricular activities that he was away from home and out of school for most of his senior year—but in other ways it was bad since they didn't notice his tendency to fat, to bookishness, and to having weirdo friends. The first led to his diabetes as an adult, the second to his profession, and the third to his salvation.

But despite the fact that Matthew longed for an all-night party—at least the comic aspect of his bowling would ingratiate him to his classmates, ironically the last time he would see them—the death of Aunt Martha drew the family to the town of Doublesign. They left the afternoon right after he got out of school. It was a ten-hour drive from Amarillo, and they checked into the Hotel Mirabeau B. Lamar in the decaying center of town. Matthew fell asleep on the stiff and none-too-clean sheets and dreamed of bowling with ten little men. The dwarves became angry at Matthew for winning the game, and so they put him to sleep for twenty-two years and when he awoke all of his friends were forty and well-to-do and wouldn't give him the time of day and since he didn't know what time it was he was caught on the street after teenage curfew and since he still looked like a teenager the cops caught him and started shaking him and shaking him and then he woke up because Elaine was shaking him. They went to the funeral and they hung around because Aunt Martha had several natural-gas wells and the family wanted to see who she left them to envisioning their fortunes in clean-cooking endless blue flames, but she left them all to Sophie. Sophie walked over to Matthew during the reading of the will and gave him a box filled with Halloween treasures. Sophie was wearing a floor-length black dress with a little bit of orange piping. She looked old-timey somehow, as if she had just stepped out of a nineteenth-century engraving. She handed him the box, mainly full of glass candy holders, and said, "Martha said she wanted you to have these." Matthew was to see Sophie only one more time in his life, but later received a picture of her from an unexpected source.

Matthew later chose one of the candy holders to hold his wife's cremains. Many of his friends thought this was in poor taste, but Matthew knew that Haidee's presence in his life had been sweeter than honey, and he had no more appropriate holder. It was a serious and solemn jack-o'-lantern, more ovoid in shape than spheroid.

The friends he had invited to the party were his customers at the New Atlantis. Austin is a terribly literate town, and used-book stores do well. The amount of ink spilled in Austin is terribly great; as famous writer Brad Denton once said, "I can't spit out my window without hitting a published author." Bradley was a customer at the New Atlantis, but not invited because of his spitting.

Matthew did invite his two closest friends: Yunus Iqbal, a bail bondsman (of Pakistani birth and the Nizari Ismaili faith), who loved mysteries and poetry; and Selma Sacks, who worked in the bank across the street from the New Atlantis and read nothing but history.

None of these people had ever bowled in their lives, and Matthew felt that he could take them with ease. He offered some pretty nice prizes, signed mysteries by Austin's best-known mystery writer, Rex Hull. Matthew was going to give five books to the person with the highest score and three books to the second highest.

He looked over the books as he drove to the bowling alley. *Night Music* (1990), the story of a dream detective who is able to solve mysteries by sleeping in the yards where the murders occurred. *The Last Gleam* (1991), a historical mystery in which Francis Scott Key discovers the murderer of George Washington. *In Lieu of a Title* (1992), a very literate mystery wherein a man, convinced his next-door neighbor is writing about him in his novel, kills the author and finishes the novel. A fan is later able to piece the whole thing together by clues inadvertently left in the book's last chapter. *Distant Drums* (1993)—here Hull stepped out of the mystery genre and wrote a *Heart of Darkness* sort of thing set in Brazil. *Little Gardens of Happiness* (1994) was a pseudo-cozy set at the American Wildflower Research Center in Austin, Texas. *Dad's Last Pitch* (1995), a baseball-mystery crossover. *Anubis on Guard* (1996), a historical mystery set in the time of Ramses III involving the Harem conspiracy. *Souvenirs of a Damnation* (also 1996), the short-story collection which was the only Hull Matthew hadn't read. He had picked them up at the Turkey Buzzard Self-Storage Facility. He rented two contiguous units there for his overflow books. He called it the "warehouse," after the place where his father had worked for decades.

Selma and Yunus were renting their shoes as he walked in. It is a humbling thing to put on bowling shoes in the presence of literate men and women.

Selma got the first triple. Matthew wasn't doing so well. By the fifth frame it was evident that Yunus and Selma were going to have the game. Matthew asked a couple of times to reassure himself that neither of them had ever bowled before; the Ismaili's grin bothered him.

The song on the jukebox was "If My Nose Were Full of

Nickels I'd Blow It All on You." By the seventh frame only all strikes could save him, and the song on the jukebox was "I Fell in a Pile of You and Got Your Love All Over Me." By the ninth frame Yunus was figuring out which books were to be his and which Selma wanted. As Yunus bowled his last ball, the jukebox played "Get Your Tongue Outta My Mouth 'Cause I'm Kissing You Good-bye."

Matthew handed the books over to the victors.

"So you had never bowled," said Matthew.

"I had not bowled when you asked me about the game, but I decided to practice in the time between then and now. Practice is everything, as Haidee used to say," said Yunus.

She had said that a lot. She said it the afternoon before she was shot. About an hour before. She had even said it to William Delaplace, but he had managed to shoot her having only killed one other person before.

Selma said, "To prove we are not bad winners we will enjoy Coke and hot dogs at our expense."

They enjoyed their food, or at least Selma and Yunus did. Then Selma brought up something unexpected; Matthew could tell it was one of those speeches rehearsed to sound casual.

"South by Southwest is coming up. You know your store is kind of in the middle of the activities—if you did some open-mike poetry nights and . . . ," began Selma

"Served cheap beer," finished Yunus.

"You could get some business then. You could have a party afterward, you know, bring the would-be poets to your home," said Selma.

"And get laid by young poetesses drunk on poetry," said Yunus.

"And for God's sake get a chance to clean up your house," said Selma. "I'll help if you need me."

"This is a conspiracy, isn't it?" asked Matthew.

"All friendship is a conspiracy," said Yunus. "All history is a conspiracy."

Matthew had felt very grateful. His friends were going to force a birthing on him, force him out of the book-lined rooms of his womblike home.

"All right, but no open-mike poetry. The last time there was that little riot and the metaphysical section got tossed in the street and run over," said Matthew.

"Oh yes," said Selma. "I can see that truck wasting Linda Goodman's *Sun Signs* even now and the horse taking a dump on *Journey to Ixtlan.*"

"I could get somebody to do a reading. I get a lot of famous people in the shop—Bruce Sterling, Susan Wade. I could get somebody, and we could put up flyers. Sure, it would be fun."

The jukebox was playing "I Would Have Wrote You a Letter, but I Couldn't Spell Yuck!"

Matthew sipped his diet Coke and listened to the twangs of country music and the sound of the bowling lanes. The idea of a party, a party in his home that he had kept shut up for so long, was a good idea. He actually was stacking paperback books so high in the back bedroom that they blotted out the moonlight. Moonlight so much belonged to her and she to it. He was in enough control of his pain not to have painted the windows black or something like that, but letting the books gradually cover up the dusty red miniblinds, why that was almost a natural process like the growth of a coral reef. A man can't be blamed for letting a coral reef grow. Surely it is a virtuous action in this age of so much environmental damage. The party was a good idea. He would take all the books off of the window and sell them at the shop. It was damn hard to do. Someday he might want to know about art since 1945 or Japanese history or learn how to read hieroglyphs without mystery. But the party was a good idea. No, really. He could start everything new. He could have people over to the house. God how Haidee would have hated it if she had known what he had done. He had killed the house, killed its flow. It had been so alive when she had lived, so flowing, energy circulating all the time. Living with Haidee had been like an endless spring breeze with unseen wind chimes. Not dead static air. The party was a good idea. He would meet people. He would get a chance to clean out his life. He could live down some of the bad things he had done right after Haidee's death. He could open the door. That was it, he would open all the doors and windows of his house. He'd turn on those lights in the back and people would be everywhere. He'd get the little fountain going in the back, and borrow John's lawn chairs. Yes, this would be a good time to get to know John again. That was good. He would be busy as hell for the next month, and that sounded so good to his body, to his muscles tired of sitting so still while he read his books and played with his cards, that nervous tic that Haidee had hated so. Riffle, riffle, riffle, you'll riffle your life way. He remembered when he caught himself doing it after being in jail the first time. It had scared him so much that he had thrown the deck away. But he had found another deck in a drawer in the kitchen.

"Yeah," he said. "We'll have a party. I might need some help—I'm not used to being a host."

They slapped him on his back and called him a good man.

"You guys want to hear a joke?" he said. "There was this Frenchman, this Mexican, and this guy from Austin sitting at a bar. And the Frenchman ordered a bottle of champagne. And when it came he tossed it in the air and pulled a gun out of his vest and shot it. Champagne rained down on everybody. And the guy from Austin said, 'What did you that for?' And the Frenchman said, 'Two things. One I wanted to show that I come from France, where champagne is everywhere, and two so you poor sons of bitches know that I am the best damn shot in the place.' Then the Mexican ordered a bottle of tequila, and when it came he tossed it up in the air and shot it. And tequila rained down over everyone. And the guy from Austin said, 'What did you do that for?' And the Mexican said, 'Two things. One to show you that I am from Mexico and we have tequila everywhere, and two to show you poor sons of bitches that I am the best damn shot in the bar.' Then the guy from Austin ordered a bottle of Celis pale ale. He tossed the bottle in the air and then he shot the Mexican and the Frenchman. He caught the bottle as it fell, opened it, and drank his fill. 'Why did you do that?' asked the bartender. 'For two things. One to show these poor sons of bitches that *I* am the best shot in the bar, and two that I'm from Austin, Texas, and know that it's important to recycle glass.' "

His timing was off; he would have to learn to tell jokes again in a month too. Well that's what customers were good for.

3 Great Prospects

Rex Hull had agreed to read a short story, so Matthew had to rent chairs. It was the title story from *Souvenirs of a Damnation.*

The New Atlantis Bookstore was packed. Hull read from a little podium in the front room. The story began, "He wanted to buy something sweet and light—a real version of the lie that comes through an east-facing church window on Sunday morning." And it went on to describe the doomed hero meeting a bald-headed man in a pub who sells him an elixir that buys him the illusion of true love for twenty-four hours. The woman, who is the vision of love, fades away, and the hero knows that his life is worse now. It had been bad, but it was implied that with the certain knowledge of love gone, it would be much worse. It ended with him driving away from the empty house where the illusion had appeared. The story ended with, "He had a funny feeling when he saw the house disappear, as though he had written a poem and it was very good and he would never see it again."

There was much applause and people getting Hull to sign this or that book and helping themselves to Celis on the way out into the street, where it was illegal to have them.

"Come on," said Matthew. "I'll drive you to my house." He had already taken Hull to dinner. It was part of the process.

Rex Hull and Yunus Iqbal got in Matthew's big, dirty old station wagon. It had hauled books throughout the hill country, and its shocks were gone.

"So, Mr. Hull," began Yunus, "you read with such feeling. Have you had such a loss?"

"No, I think none of my four marriages were of such a type. I think true love belongs only to the imaginal world," said Hull.

"I knew true love," said Matthew. "I mean it sounds corny to say it, perhaps because such things do not wholly exist on this world, but I had true love with Haidee."

"Heidi, a Swiss girl?" asked Hull.

"No. H A I D E E from the Greek 'to caress.' She was black."

"Is that the appropriate term anymore?" asked Hull.

"I stopped playing that game a long time ago. In the dark of her touch there was happiness," said Matthew.

"A beautiful line. Is it yours?" asked Hull.

"No. The best part comes from a poet named Kalmu Ya Salaam," said Matthew.

"Are you divorced?" asked Hull.

"No. She was murdered," said Matthew.

"I'm sorry. I—I didn't know. Is this something you would rather not talk about?" asked Hull.

"No," said Matthew. "After tonight I will talk about it. I've had two years of mourning and being crazy. Talking is good," said Matthew.

The streets between Matthew's store and his Hyde Park home had many dips. The car would bob up and down like the huge boat it was on a dark sea. Sometimes it scraped bottom making sparks as its form of whitecaps. Iqbal watched

Hull with interest. He had always thought himself too direct with Westerners, but he had never seen anyone like Hull. He treasured the won books all the more.

"I have never actually met anyone who had a relative, a loved one, murdered, which is kind of odd given my line of work. How did she die?"

"She died because we talked too much in a bar after a science fiction convention. As you notice, I keep quite a big science fiction stock—the biggest in town except for Adventures in Crime and Space, the specialty store on Sixth. We always have a table at the local convention, ArmadilloCon. After the con two years ago we stopped at a local bar because we were tired and hungry. We got a pizza and some beer and we started talking to this guy from Missouri. His name was William T. Delaplace. He said he had just broke up with his girlfriend, and he doubted that he could ever find love. We talked about our lives, the woman I had lived with before I met Haidee, the bad boyfriends she had had in college. I even joked about how I had wanted to kill Shirley. He seemed to really agree with that sentiment. It was kind of creepy. Then he got normal again and talked about how he liked science fiction, meaning stuff on TV, and how he had moved here to get his past behind him, and the job he was going to get at a three-letter computer company and so forth. And we drank and told him about our favorite restaurants, and about my store, and so on and so forth. Then we got in the station wagon and drove home. I unloaded the stuff at the store the next day.

"He came in the store in about a week and he bought some stuff and told me he had an apartment. He started coming in regular. Usually on Saturday afternoons. Most Saturdays Haidee came down to the store, unless she was working overtime. He talked about his job, about his new girlfriend, who was coincidentally black, about getting his life in order. He invited us to a barbecue. We showed up. The girlfriend couldn't make it for some last-minute reason, but we accepted that. The whole thing was at the grill by his apartment's pool. He wouldn't let us up to the apartment, he said it was too messy, but there were bathrooms and stuff by the pool and we were groovin' on the fact that you could have an outdoor barbecue in December in Austin, blah, blah, blah, and William thanked us several times for the good advice we had given him about looking for love and apologized for the girlfriend. So we went home feeling really good about ourselves. How many times can you help a person out just by telling them a story?

"Christmas came and he actually got us little gifts. He bought Haidee some cheap perfume from Pennys (that she would never wear in a million years) and he got me *The Yellow Flower* by Lily Brockden. It was a big self-help book a few years ago—every used-book store in the country has scads of them. By this time of course we had begun to be messianic in our own eyes. We invited William to our New Year's bash—you'll see many of the people from that shindig at my house tonight. Except those people that left my life because of being scared of death or at the way I acted after her death. Of course we had invited the girlfriend, Daisy—we knew her name by now.

"The party was supposed to start at nine. He showed up at ten looking really embarrassed. He also frankly didn't smell too good and he was actually wearing the same shirt and pants he'd been wearing on Solstice when he gave us the gifts. He said that his girlfriend was sick with some sort of stomach flu. He kind of muttered to himself, and drank a lot of eggnog. Then he sort of hit on a couple of the women at the party. I tried to tell him nicely to cool it, and he acted ashamed. And of course my ego grew in leaps and bounds. Right after midnight he asked Haidee if he could kiss her, since he wouldn't get a chance to kiss his girlfriend tonight. He looked so sad, just like a kid that had been slapped away from the table for farting, that she said yes. He kissed—I found this out later because I got to talking about fireworks with a friend and I can go on and on—he kissed her a little too long and a little too hard and tried to slip her the tongue. So she really didn't want to see him again.

"In January when she would see him coming up to the shop, Haidee would slip into the back room. He was nice as nice could be to me, but she stopped coming down on Saturdays. It really made me mad, but William would always buy stuff. He never talked about the girlfriend anymore. I figured that they had broke up, and he had acted really badly under my killer eggnog, the recipe is a family one from Scotland, and I told Haidee that he seemed cool, and I really, really missed her not visiting with me on Saturday afternoons. Saturday afternoons are either the busiest or the loneliest times for a used-book store. I have always thought I killed her, by asking for just her company. She didn't want to come. But I resolved that I would forgive myself tonight, which is why you're getting this long boring confession."

"No," said Hull. "This is fascinating."

Matthew continued because of years of needing to speak, but he wondered if he was making his life into a rack paperback. "It was the week of Valentine's. The holiday had passed, but we still had a display in the window of romances and of classic love stories and some red tinfoil hearts. William came in and Haidee was there. And for a few minutes he just stood and stared at her, grinning like a fool. Then he started talking in a low voice about how he had never had a girlfriend, how he had been embarrassed by his lack of happiness in front of us, he had never had a job, his folks were just paying to keep him away from home, and we were the only people he had talked to at first in Austin, but after I got hostile to him in January he started talking to other people and saw other people weren't as happy we were. It was people like us that stirred up everybody, we made them expect things that they couldn't have. We were the source of all evil because our story led to desire. It wasn't fair to lead a fairy-tale life, you see we were hurting other people. Now if we stopped being happy then everything would be OK. He was talking louder and faster. I didn't know what to do. I had had nuts in the store over the years, people off the street preaching this or that, but they always run out of steam. But he got louder talking about values, the relative value of one person to ten, and how he had tried to work out the algebra of unhappiness and we were always X plus Y, and X plus Y wasn't fair, because everyone else was just Y. Y not have pain? Y not be lonely? Y? Y? Y? and then he pulled a little .38 from his pants pocket, and shot her twice in the chest. He just walked out as she slumped over. I couldn't believe it. I called nine-one-one. I wasn't even speaking English, just yadda yadda yadda, and then I held her till they came but she was dead."

This created an awkward lull in conversation. After four or five blocks, Yunus said, "Mr. Hull, I particularly liked the way you used the idea of mourning over an abode to symbolize the lost love. That is a device in classical Arabic poetry; did you use it consciously?"

"No, I just felt it was right. I guess it's a Jungian thing, sort of woman equals house," said Hull.

"That's a simplistic analysis, I would think," said Yunus. "Women, like books and stars, are liminal things. To know them one must cross a threshold, whether it is looking into a telescope—and suddenly your perception leaves the world and goes into a liminal space—the round circle of sky with its glowing gem, or opening a book and leaving yourself in its dream—I have found this very experience in reading your *Night Music*—or in looking at a woman. A house is a house, but an abode is a place where you pass out of the world into a different place, where the laws are different."

"That is great. When I explain to my audiences how I meant all of that, I will think of you," said Hull.

Everyone laughed.

"I'm sorry," said Matthew. "I hadn't meant to go on and on like I did. That was probably gruesome and horrible and you think me an unfeeling cad."

"No, really," said Hull. "It was—it sounded like you needed to tell it. I envy you your loving marriage. All of mine have been bad, and the last one—well, let's just say if you look up the word 'harpy' in the dictionary, you see a picture of Caitlin."

"Well, I wanted to tell it before the party. The party is the first time I've had people to the house since she died. I wanted to get the telling over with."

"Matthew, my friend, you should probably drive around the neighborhood a little. Drive to the 7-Eleven and get some more beer. If you want to confess, there may be other things to say," said Yunus. "It is up to you, but it will only be before the party once, you know."

"Can I say more?" Matthew asked Hull.

"Say all you need to say."

"The cops caught William that day. He had just gone to his apartment and waited there. Inside was filthy. He hadn't thrown out any trash for the whole time he lived there. It was foul beyond belief. He gave them the gun and told them years from now people like himself would be viewed as public heroes. He told them he was ready for a press conference. They hauled him down to jail. It seems that his parents had been slipping him money, but that his dad had died recently and his elderly mother was too distraught to keep the cash flowing. He was suspected in the disappearance of one Shirley Barrett, who had been his fiancée. He had split town after she had gone missing, and he was living in Austin under the fake name of Edward Dowser. William was his real name. The mechanics of his folks getting money to him was very elaborate. Apparently they had money out the ass. Since he was such a nutcase he had a cell all to himself. I knew that he would get some nothing sentence or be sent to a funny farm. I knew he would get off, and I got a little crazy. I sold my best books, the cream of my collection, to get some money to buy some information about the jail. There was a way to get past all the weapon detectors and get to William's cell with a gun. It involved being at a certain entrance at a certain time and walking in like you knew what you were doing. Don't be surprised, jails are easier to break into than out of. I hadn't fired a gun since high school. Once in Navy ROTC I tried out for the rifle team and was judged a potential danger. But I could get as close to him as he had been to Haidee. I walked up to the cell. He wasn't afraid. I told him I was there to kill him. He told me that I had clearly not processed my lesson and that he would have to kill me. It was all a matter of time, either I would understand and he could let me go free or he would have to break out of jail and terminate me, since I didn't know how to read. Those were his words—I didn't know how to read. What I didn't know was that his cell was wired for sound. There were police on me like flies. They took the gun away from me and took me to a holding cell. I knew I would get caught, but it had never occurred to me that I would get caught before I had a chance to slay him. I was there a long time and then they let me call my lawyer. The guy that handles my piddly-ass business at the bookstore. What a surprise for him at midnight. And then arraignment and that's when I realized I hadn't loaded the gun. You see it was Haidee's gun, she kept it in her nightstand next to our bed, it had been a gift from her uncle Chester, she had always kept it loaded. So bail was assessed and I had to find a bondsman, and I wound up with Yunus here. Iqbal the Bondsman. Of course he wasn't the one who came with the money, that's not the boss's job. My lawyer argued that I had never meant to kill William, that at most here was a question of soft damages, I had no priors, and the guy had killed my wife. So I got off."

"But you were going to kill him," said Hull.

"Oh yes. Maybe I haven't learned to read yet, because I still haven't stopped wanting to kill him," said Matthew. "You are the first person I've told the story to except for Yunus. It makes me feel better giving it to a stranger."

"Well, I'm not exactly a stranger. I've been shopping in your shop since it opened, what, eight years ago?" said Hull.

"Ten," said Matthew. "It was two years after we were married. I had had a convention-only business—one set of things for the book-and-paper show circuit, one for SF and mystery conventions. I had a little mail-order. Then I lucked across *The Great Free Love Trial . . . Address to the Jury, and Mankind* by Beverly Paschal Randolph, published in Boston in 1872. I found it at a little used-book store in Waco for two dollars. It is an exceptionally rare book. Randolph was a friend of Lincoln's. He was a black man who ran a mystical sex magic order called the Brotherhood of Eulis. He had been arrested for circulating obscene books in Boston in 1871, and the book was his version of the trial. It was one of the great books for free speech in America. He was a very odd fellow, taught people how to scry in magic mirrors, was a Reconstructionist politician in Louisiana, practiced medicine. I could go on about him all night, but the important thing is the book gave me enough money to buy the book stock and the first six months' rent on my building."

"Do all of you book people know stuff like that?" asked Hull.

"No, I lucked out. I had just read an article on Randolph that week. He was mentioned in this article on black erotica. I was so excited when I found the book. Everything opened for me. I even thought of naming the store after his novel *Ravalette*, but that was too weird, so I went with Bacon's New

Atlantis. It was a bad choice, because that name symbolizes progress and rationality, but it brings people looking for occult books. I do keep a collection of erotica and banned books for sale to honor Randolph for helping me out."

"And," said Hull, "you keep a big occult section for your customers. So you're sort of keeping Randolph's tradition alive despite yourself."

"I guess that's what a magician is about, keeping people enjoying the things he did after he's gone," said Matthew.

He pulled up into his driveway. The guests were parked all around the neighborhood waiting for him.

4 Dark of Touch: The Empty Hand

A few days after the party when Matthew Reynman realized, really realized on a gut level that one of his guests, one of his friends, had stolen the ashes of his wife, he made this list of them. In one of the few smiles he allowed himself that week, he thought, Now I am making my life an avant-garde novel: the list is their great convention.

Yunus Iqbal. Hair in his ears long enough to catch a moth. Age thirty-eight. A collector of the weird. Spiritual descendant of the Assassins.

Rodger Falconer. Growing paunch and declining vitality. Age forty-two. Told me about pyrotechnic funerals. Always curious about what it was like to make love to a black woman.

Doug Falconer. Ten degrees, overqualified for any job in the world. Age forty-four. Too much energy for Cow Town.

Janet Falconer. Helped a deaf choir put on a show. Age forty. Strives against nature, never helped us load or light.

Heidi Falconer. A waif at the doorway of gothdom. Nearly eighteen. Caught in the lure of the weird. Too much written on her pants.

Selma Sacks. Tight pants and low-cut blouse. Age thirty-six. Obsessed with the filth of money, with mineral salts and people that hoard pennies.

Norman Papin. Read every *Star Trek*, *X-Files*, *X-Wing*, *Star Wars*, and *Gor* novel. Age twenty-eight. Believes that he will be beamed up, fascinated with the episode of classic *Star Trek* where people are turned into Styrofoam dodecahedrons.

Anthony O'Callaghan. Genealogy became his hobby after *Roots*, discovered that he was related to me with an Irish ancestor in 1842, due to British colonial policies. Age fifty-three. Never happy I married a black woman, or that I had no kids.

Billie Sue Lovejoy. Born-again pagan thinks she is Sekhmet, the raging goddess of destruction. "The burning eye of Re." Age thirty-three. Would drown in Town Lake if tossed in because of number of amulets she carries. Does that mean she's a witch or that she's innocent?

Greg Madonia. The Lurker at the Open Mike. Age unknown, thirty-six to thirty-eight? Can't come out about his homosexuality, once tricked in the New Atlantis bathroom with

Stephen Kozalla. Can't be quiet about his homosexuality. Age ?? Tries to look in his twenties. Has a "Send Them Back to Venus" bumper sticker. Haidee said that he was so busy being gay he has forgotten that he is black.

Nicholas Askel Denning-Roy. Failed novelist, buys ten used books a week to get sentences to filch for his eight-hundred-plus-page work in progress. Age fifty-one. He had written a novel, finished it all except the title seventeen years ago. He intended to find the perfect title before he sent it off to the publishers. "Titles," he would say, "are very important. The medieval scholar Remigius of Auxerre derived the word 'title' from 'titan,' because he said it was the illuminating 'sun' of the work. Titles are the beginning of the work. You must know them to know the work, and you must know them to remember the work." Probably not his real name.

Kim Csernica. Reads every damn vampire book I get, fiction or nonfiction. Age God knows, forty? Wasn't "Csernica" Dracula's aunt's name? Dresses more and more like Anne Rice.

Rex Hull. His ego can't fit into the void you would expect of someone called King Empty. Age forty to forty-four?? Seems too interested in what's going to come next to do much.

Dallas Strauch. Named after a city where people respect the ability to buy art more than the ability to make art. Age twenty-eight to thirty-five?? This white girl was so liberal that she used to berate Haidee for not having a "Black Conscience." Haidee once told her she would "conscience her ass someday."

When they had left that night about eleven o'clock, he had felt so good. He turned all the lights off and lit candles just as he did when Haidee was alive. It had been their "wishing game." They would light candles throughout the house and then sit very very still—sometimes for minutes—then one or the other of them would get up and start walking through the house—which candle would he/she blow out first? After faking once or twice he or she would blow out a candle, and then in the touch of dark give a wish for the other. Sometimes it was to get well after a sickness, or to make up with his or her mother, or for the bookstore to do well or for WDS to do well, or for the lantana in the backyard to bloom better, or for the mountain laurel to bloom at all. Many times they got their wish, but that may have been because their wishes were so small and because they were so willing to work on everything. Nothing was easy in the early years, but they learned to work, and to talk, and that was all and everything.

Sometimes after she had been killed he had imagined that she was in the house. They were people that read a lot, so they would often read in different rooms. She liked to build a little nest in the front room where he was now, and arch around in all sorts of cat positions, which would sometimes drive him crazy with wanting her, wanting to "me-you" her. After all, why do you think they call it pussy?

But he had resolved driving home with Yunus and Hull that he would only imagine her one more time. He would do it this night, as a way of saying good-bye. He knew that he had to let her go, that he had held on too long, locking himself up. His mother, Elaine, had said to him, "If a man locks himself up, he will lose what he's supposed to keep and keep what he's supposed to lose." Elaine had locked herself away after Herman's death, but after she got involved in high school class reunions, Class of '39, she had turned both active and wise. It was odd that he would be learning something from his mother at their respective ages, and it gave him hope. Of course, now that they didn't talk anymore—he would probably not learn anything until he cleaned up her estate.

But then he had always assumed that women were wiser and stronger than men—one of his few points of agreement with Dallas Strauch.

The "wishing game" had evolved somehow; he never knew when the rules came into being. Maybe it was in the early days, that week they had no power because they couldn't pay for it. He had always had a mania for candles that he got from his aunt Martha.

Tonight's game would be played in a special way. He was going to close his eyes and listen for a sound, no matter how faint, that would tell him that she was in the back of the house, maybe the bedroom or the small den with the TV. There would be some sound, so he could make believe—make-believe always began with sound—and he would think she was back there, and then he would get up and wish her a good rest, and then he would close his eyes and make believe that he was she, and she would blow out a candle and make a wish for him, and it would be all over. He would be the sun and moon tonight, and after tonight he would be the sun.

Finally there was a click from the back of the house. It sounded like someone switching off a light. The house had been built in the fifties, a wooden frame house, so it made noises like that.

He got up and went to the blue lotus-shaped candle on the small end table with the two beers on it and the fragments of crackers. He bent over the candle and said, "I wish for Haidee a pleasant sleep before awakening." It was always the last wish they made for each other just before going to bed.

Then he closed his eyes. In the warm red light that the candles made through his eyelids, he imagined himself looking down on her ebon limbs. "The blacker the berry the sweeter the juice." She smiled, he had said it to her so often. She must tell him bye, tell him to get along with his life. She walked to the mantel where a silver taper burned in a small purple glass holder that she had bought at the Everything $0.99 store. She arched her body, lithe with the bloodlines of a thousand African beauties, over the candle, and started to blow it out, to wish him good-bye, when suddenly he saw the emptiness in the candy holder.

It was the emptiest emptiness in the world.

It was a black hole that immediately swallowed imagination, time, and space. It held him forever. Then he saw it again. It was empty. It was gone. The little metal cylinder that had held her ashes was gone.

Quick—when had he seen it last? When was the last time he had really looked at that painful object to make sure of its painful place in his universe?

It didn't matter.

Maybe he hadn't looked at it since New Year's Eve, but it didn't matter.

One of them had taken it. One of his friends.

One of his friends.

He stood there unsteady, in the candlelight, muttering syllables that almost resolved to her name, or that again almost named one of the partygoers as if he might call them back to undo his crime, as though he could recall, and summon back, a time before death had entered the world, an Eden before accidents, before even magic, and before magic despaired itself to religion.

It was after seeing in the mirror above the mantel a reflected candle burn too low and start some reflected paper aflame that he moved. He swatted out the fires with his hand and cursed the power company for leaving its bill there, and then he laughed at that. He smashed out each candle flame. No more wishes. He didn't even notice the fire on his fingers.

He stared for a long moment at the bowling trophy. Richard Brautigan. Depression and anger took him past absurdity.

He picked up the candy holder in the dark and carried it with him, as though it might suddenly gain the needful weight. He carried it back to his bedroom, where he sat on the edge of the bed and just held it for a while, hefting his loss and whispering sounds that tried to become words or names or perhaps clues about what to do next.

The next morning, after he checked his blood sugar, which was dangerously low at 55 (you get confused under 70), and fed the cat, he called the police. They thought it was a kind of joke, and they kept threatening him with obscure laws that protect law enforcement from pranks. He couldn't imagine the need the police had to be protected from fiction, when he had a real need. Eventually, after he gave his name for the twenty-second time, he was connected with a detective named Anthony R. Blick. Blick kept saying, "Mr. Reynman, Mr. Reynman, what is it now?" And Matthew kept trying to say that he wasn't having the bad behavior of the past, but Blick kept talking about bodies and mirrors, and finally the phone call ended somehow with each person firmly convinced that he was dealing with the deranged.

Matthew decided he would go to work. Perhaps the thief would regret his/her actions and return the ashes, so he left his front door unlocked. It was a Saturday. His boss in the fireworks crew, Doug Falconer, would be going back to Fort Worth, but he would bring the family by to buy some paperbacks. Doug was a great reader of mysteries and weird-tales collections. Matthew wondered if he could determine Doug's innocence or guilt by the books he bought. What books did an ash stealer read? Maybe there's been a code all those years, maybe he should like call the police, right, and say, "Hey, a guy down here just bought a copy of *Blackburn*, you think maybe he's a serial killer?" Or maybe it wasn't obvious links, maybe serial killers bought cookbooks.

It couldn't be Doug.

Of course not.

But it had to be someone. Some friend of his.

Some good friend.

Then he was woozy and realized he needed to get some sugar. This won't help. He hated the goddamn diabetes, but he couldn't ignore it. If he let it go, it would take his eyes, and that was the fate worse than death for a print addict. Of course he had peeled off those extra pounds that he had got since college, and Haidee thought it made him a better lover. He remembered the day quite well. The ophthalmologist was shining a light in his dilated eyes, and said, "Matthew, is there a history of diabetes in your family?" Of course there was, Elaine's maternal grandfather, Douglas Orne Williamson, was "borderline," and Herman's father, Dr. Matthew Reynman, was "borderline." It seemed terribly unfair that they could get him in a darkened room years later. It was at that moment he had understood what the ghost story's really about. He had sold enough of them.

He ate a little box of raisins.

The trick is to stop eating the simple sugars, despite the fact your body tells you MORE! MORE! MORE! You must wait for ten or fifteen minutes and see how you feel. If you really want to be precise you prick another finger, dab another slip, and check your monitor.

Haidee had been with him when the ghosts attacked. She was there since she would have to drive him back. When the doctor told him that about half of his right eye was marred by retinopathy and that he should see a doctor right away, it had been her not-so-gentle pressure that had made him make the appointment. Even with the threat of gathering darkness, it would take him months. She was always his strength, his power.

She would know what to do in this situation, and would have the strength to get it started. In order to find her, he would have to think like her, he would have to be strong like her. He would have to spend his days creating that art.

He felt better and he started the drive to the store.

He had forgotten that everything was a mess down there. Somehow when you get a great shock, the world returns to normal in your memory—there aren't ongoing things like your cat's ringworm, your expired vehicle inspection, the broken coffeepot.

Oh hell, vehicle registration, yeah, that's got to happen too.

He put up the charts and wondered for a minute about Doug's wife, Janet. He could see her sitting off about a hundred yards from the show they did every year for the last five years. The first two shows had been in Schertz, Texas, a little town near San Antonio with a great snake farm. The last three years had been in Doublesign. The families of the crews could sit closer than the spectators, close enough that they had to wear earplugs. It was their job to count the number of shells lit versus the number of shells that went off. You always had to find your duds. Some kid could find them and light the inner shell—the one that explodes in the air, lighting the graceful stars. Janet was the best counter. She never lost track. He could see her lit by the rocket's red glare, focused, counting.

She didn't buy as many books as Doug, mainly religious items. She couldn't be guilty.

But someone had done it.

He had been in their Fort Worth home, swum in their pool, counted Doug's degrees and certifications on the trophy wall. Doug collected degrees the way Matthew collected books; he had to be careful filling out a résumé because he could easily label himself as overqualified.

There was a cop knocking at the door.

He must have seen the expired registration. Damn!

Still an hour to opening time, but that argument probably wouldn't work.

Matthew let him in.

"Mr. Matthew Reynman?"

"Yes."

"I have what may be some bad news for you. Are you familiar with William T. Delaplace?"

"It's not a name I am apt to ever forget."

The stains were still on the floor less than six feet away.

"Um, due to a clerical foul-up his name got confused with a William Redell and he was released from Huntsville on Tuesday of last week."

Matthew felt woozy again. He sat down.

"That's it? That's all you have to say?" asked Matthew.

"No, I am supposed to tell you that we will be watching your shop and store very carefully for the next few weeks, and if you have any kind of weirdness, give us a call."

"I already called you for weirdness this morning."

"Must have been before eight, we didn't know then. The notice got sent to the Houston Police Department."

"Maybe when Delaplace shoots me the bullet will take some other bookstore owner for me."

The cop grinned. "That's the spirit, sir."

5 Hence Astrology

"When you're making your own Roman candles," Doug had once told him, "you should use candle comp instead of Chinese visco. That way you have a nice stream of golden sparks between your shots."

Candle composition is a mix of potassium nitrate, sulfur, and crushed charcoal; it acts like a fuse as it burns between the stars and salutes. In most of your commercial Roman candles sawdust is used between the salutes, and a visco fuse runs between them. Matthew had written a sonnet for Haidee comparing their love to candle composition after their first professional fireworks show six years ago.

It was not a good sonnet.

She loved it.

Love makes bad poetry better.

It is very powerful.

He had kept a copy of the sonnet for years stapled onto the wooden bookshelves that divided the poetry and history sections. Most of the bare unfinished wood had something stapled on it. Interesting news stories, or little tidbits about an author, or a cartoon. He had never signed the sonnet because he figured that perhaps his customers would ascribe its words to a Dylan or a Williams.

Three hours after the cop had told him about Delaplace, the Fort Worth Falconers came by. Matthew wanted more than anything to tell them about Delaplace, but the cop had suggested to him that this was news best kept to himself.

There is nothing harder to do than not to talk.

We talk all the time, telling each other our boring pointless tales, our lives in this regard being sadly like the postmodernist literature that Matthew could never sell except to writers like Hull who wanted to cop certain phrases for their works to attract a scholarly crowd to their genre novels, thus achieving the double score of critical and popular success, and who wouldn't love Hull's novels anyway with their high body count, sex, and gore?

We talk all the time to cast a spell on each other. The spell we cast is one of sleep. We want everyone to be as asleep as we are, so we talk, talk, talk. Even Matthew's dilemma would lure the Falconers to sleep, because they would talk about it and talk about it on the trip up to Fort Worth. By the time they got there they would have so many theories about Delaplace's location, motives, and likely manifestations that they could no longer see the real thing when it happened.

Of course the same thing was already going on in Matthew's mind. He had died a hundred times by the time they arrived, and the nature of his hundred funerals had almost removed his sense of loss of Haidee's ashes by the time the Falconers came in.

Doug wanted to buy some of Hull's novels. He had never met a writer before, at least not a fiction writer—many of his engineering friends had written books, but you didn't read those for pleasure. It might be the most gripping piece of writing ever on the topic of hydrodynamics but in the end you didn't find out who did it or why. The who and why question, the how and when question in such books were always presented fractally, you could find the answer on every page, each equation was a single wave in the ocean of engineered knowledge.

Matthew took him to the mystery section. Janet was looking for a cookbook on Slovenian cuisine. She had had some paprika schnitzel at the Lost Weekend Pub for lunch before Matthew's party. The Lost Weekend had acquired a Slovenian chef who hoped to cash in big on the coming interest in Balkan cooking. She was disappointed in her quest.

They left with the usual invitations to Matthew to come and spend time with them, enjoy the pool, and so forth. Matthew always spent the night or so before the Fourth with them, since they always returned to their home after the shoots.

Matthew had tried to think of something clever to say that might make them reveal their guilt in the matter of Haidee's ashes. They *were* awfully glad that he had had the party and that he was on his way out of his shell, they didn't seem to notice how weird he was acting, or maybe he just didn't look that weird to the outer world. It's not like there's an expression for "I think you stole my wife's ashes from my house and by the way I think there's a murderer looking for me because I tried to kill him" smile. It's pretty much one of those moods out of the ordinary.

There was thankfully a real rush of business after the Falconers had turned their car-boat back toward Cow Town.

Customers never care if you are being stalked by a murderer. They never ask, "So, Mr. Reynman, are you being stalked by a murderer? Gee, I know I hate that when it happens to me."

The customers' function is to cause sleep, to cause one's emotions to drift far away, far into the center of one's being, where then they can be kept at bay by reading and collecting.

Matthew always smiled at that class of people that classify science fiction, fantasy, horror, detective fiction, and so forth as "escapist literature"—all writing was escapist. The moment your mind seized upon the words, you escaped. This isn't a bad thing. Can you imagine a world where every minute your mind was focused on the shock and boredom of the present? That is to say, on nothing? On froth? The present is the scum of history.

Customers had saved him from pain before, especially in the weeks after Haidee's second of her three planned funerals.

The second funeral had been the worst.

It was in Tulsa. It was the funeral for her relatives, most of whom hated Matthew with the same hate that Matthew's relatives had focused on Haidee for the same reasons.

The absurd is what makes us sleep.

It is what makes us sleepwalk and turns what we see and do into nightmares.

Racism has been the greatest source of absurdity in America. Racism generated by whites is absurd and its victims have to evolve absurd behavior in order to compensate. Absurdity upon absurdity.

Their daughter, their granddaughter, their sister, their cousin had married a white man and he had taken her away and now he brought her body back and he was even going to take it away too and burn it like a cross on a lawn. It had all been a game to whitey.

And they hated him with heavy burning eyes during the funeral and the hymns in the Baptist church, and her mother had come to him that day at the hotel and begged him not to burn her body. He tried to explain that it had been her wish, but it wasn't Christian, she said, and Matthew didn't want to tell her that Haidee had long ago made a break with Christianity for what it had done to her people, so all he said was that it had been her wish and that he was going to fulfill it, and when the time came he would be burned up and their ashes would be ground down and mixed into stars shot into a starry starry night.

And Mrs. Bomars slapped him full and hard, and Haidee's two older brothers led her from the hotel room.

Matthew had never been slapped before, but it was nothing compared to the pain that he would experience that night when Haidee's younger brother and his friends came by and asked him to go with them for a drink to memorialize their sister.

It was at the second funeral that he had seen Sophie Vann. She looked older than she looked when she worked for Aunt Martha, but not as old as she should have looked. It was a strange moment looking across the sea of angry black faces and seeing her looking at him. There was a shock of recognition, and then a greater shock. He would have expected a sympathetic stare, a wise deep understanding, because Matthew belonged to an absurdist tribe that believed with all their little white hearts that blacks were not burdened with the absurdity of their white brethren, not heirs to all of the shuffled bad ideas and detritus of civilization—but somehow because of their *primitive* nature (let the scenes of a thousand *Tarzan* movies flicker in the cave)—somehow *purer* and capable of great wisdom. Blacks become the symbols of wisdom, in the supreme hope that they have won at a game that the white man realizes is absurd.

But such is not the case. The absurdity of the oppressor is greeted by greater absurdity in the oppressed, and so on ad infinitum, so that no pure daylight glance could be had.

Ms. Sophie Vann was looking at him with a mixture of pity and contempt, more he thought of the latter than the former.

She came by his hotel room after Mrs. Bomars left and before Caspar Bomars came.

"Why did you come here?" she asked him.

"I came because these were Haidee's people, her family. They had to know," he said.

"They knew because they could read the paper. They knew because they saw the body. You didn't have to show your face, you didn't have to tell them you were going to burn her body like a log, that you had already had a funeral for her for your people, that you ship her body everywhere so everybody can have their death moment."

"I am doing what Haidee wanted."

"That is between you and the ghost in your head. Leave now. The funeral home will ship the body to the crematorium."

"I thought you would understand."

"Why? Because I worked for your aunt? That was on another planet. This is the planet of broken dreams, here; you're a smart boy, Martha always said so, you know about all that."

"Yeah, I know. So I thought if I showed that I was helping out with Haidee's dream to become a shower of stars, that would show that I was on the side of the good."

"People here are tired of people trying to help out with the dreams of men and women of color. What kind of dream is that? To have your ashes shot in a firecracker? That's some weird white man's dream, no different than those people who want their ashes put in orbit. Death is for the living."

"Why are you here? Because of me?"

"The world does not revolve around you and your childish dreams, Matthew Reynman. Estelle Bomars is my first cousin. Haidee was blood kin of mine."

"I never knew, she never said."

"I imagine she said little about her family, when they rejected you. What did you tell her about yours?"

"I told her about Martha."

"Sure, everyone loves a weird tale, but did you mention your brothers, your mother and father that would sneer at me every time they deigned to visit Martha? Did you tell her about your life?"

Matthew hadn't told her these things, and wanted to know how Sophie knew.

"I knew because you knew you could not make her part of your old life, nor could you enter into hers."

"We tried making a new life."

"I tried that once, Matthew Reynman, and because of my honoring the dream of an artificial life is why I have come to you to tell you not to spend the night in town. Artificial lives don't work. You fall back into your old life. People die, or sometimes they just age and then you have to go back to the old valley where they hold a lottery every year to pick a sacrifice. You can't get away from history. You go, and don't you think I forgive you for coming here."

She left.

Matthew knew why the Bomars had come to Tulsa, Tallasi in the Creek tongue for "Old Town." They had crossed into Indian Territory by covered wagon in 1904. Tulsa drew black folk by covered wagon, horseback, foot, and rail. It was negative space—an area that existed only as a dream—it was going to be their own town, their own chance to be Americans. There were plenty of all-black towns in Oklahoma—Liberty, Langston, Bookertee, North Fork Colored, Lincoln City, Summit. They had a nice little section called Greenwood, which the white people called Little Africa. It had its own shops and schools, and it became just too much of a target, so it was burned down to teach the darkies a lesson. Now that was long ago and far away in 1921, three years before Matthew's mother was born. Tulsa's black folks are no different than any other group, they bled just as well on battlefields. But the reality of a dead dream lives in the Bomars and the Vanns, and many others who gambled on what a nonabsurd America would look like.

Aunt Martha had been right, American history had been written by Hawthorne, Poe, and Lovecraft.

Caspar Bomars came by with two male friends at sundown. Matthew knew that Caspar had come by to beat the hell out of him, but he went along anyway because some part of him wanted to have the hell beat out of him.

They took him to a pool hall where dark old men sat playing dominoes. Matthew had come from Amarillo, Texas, and knew how to play dominoes—some of the Protestant sects there hold against cards.

It was smoky and dirty.

Austin is a clean-air city and you forget what it's like to breathe cigarette smoke.

Matthew ordered a rum and Coke and hoped he could get enough of them down before the beating started.

Caspar and his friends talked about sports. They asked Matthew who his favorite players on this, that, and the other professional team were. Like many people who have made reading books into an ersatz religion, Matthew didn't follow sports closely. When he managed to name a player correctly, they smiled approvingly among themselves. They kept getting closer to him. They kept saying to one another, "See, the Man knows! He's in touch! He knows the score!" They would bump into him and touch him and help him raise his arm to drink. They kept offering him cigarettes and then as they lit their own they would toss the extinguished matches against his white skin. "The Man don't smoke you see, because he's into fireworks. Walk into a fireworks stand with a cigarette going and the whole place blow up BOOM! like that. The Man knows. He keeps score."

The old dark men played their dominoes and didn't look up.

Then Caspar asked him what he thought about a white man marrying a black woman.

This was it.

Matthew said, "Well, if they love each other . . ."

The first punch landed before the second syllable of "other" had been uttered. Matthew swung out at one of Caspar's friends, but after four or five rum and Cokes he was fighting the air. He had never been good with his fists anyway. Matthew tried to remember moves from the *Kung Fu* series, and then catching this absurdity began to laugh, which was entirely the wrong message to send. Someone came up from behind, someone not in the original party but joining on the general principle, and pulled Matthew out to the back.

He was down in the filthy alley, and they kept kicking him so that his head knocked again and again against a big Dumpster. The third or fourth kick ended his consciousness for a while, but he woke up later.

They had dragged him down the block and they were writing the words "white devil" on him with oversize red Magic Markers. When Caspar saw that he was conscious he started slapping Matthew's face, then in a moment of inspiration had everyone clear away and took a long piss on Matthew, much of the hot urine burning cuts and scrapes on his face. Matthew tried to get up, and they pushed him down again and then someone pulled his head up by the hair and let it smash down again. Then he went unconscious for the second time.

When he came to, a middle-aged black woman was leaning over him in a well-lit hospital room. His clothes were gone, and he felt like choirs of angels were singing to him. He considered briefly that he might be in heaven, but realized that it was probably morphine. His future appreciation of beat literature was vastly enhanced by this flash of satori.

"Don't try to talk just yet. Can you make a peace sign for me?"

Matthew held up his fingers.

"That's good. I'll be back in a little while. You just close your eyes, and I'll be back."

He dreamt many sweet dreams about his bookstore being moved to another planet. He and Haidee were there and looking out at a Saturn-like world. Haidee was saying something very important about the effect of the night sky on the human psyche, but Matthew couldn't quite follow her words about starry wisdom. It was some kind of wake-up call, some way out of the nightmare of history, or maybe that was some weird white man's dream about space colonization and the human diaspora solving all of our problems left over from his sci-fi days. Maybe she was saying something more, something deeper—cooking down their lives into something beautiful like a shower of stars.

The nurse came again and again, and eventually pain came, and the getting better.

He didn't press charges against Caspar. He lied like a trouper to the trooper.

When it came time for him to leave, Mr. Bomars, Haidee's father, came down and helped him get his car out of the police impoundment lot where it had somehow wound up.

He looked at Matthew a long time and then said, "I don't give a damn what they say about you. That's just talk. You made her happy."

And he smiled.

Matthew drove out of Tulsa with those teeth being the last stars he would see for his years of depression.

6 Very Interesting, but Stupid

Happiness is inevitable. Matthew knew this from fighting it for two years, but it is as inevitable as any part of the human condition. Perhaps that made Delaplace into such a bitter hero—he took on an opponent that is sure to win. Matthew remembered going to a showing of Edvard Munch prints at the Huntington Gallery with Yunus. There were all pretty grim stuff, *The Scream* by no means representing Edvard on a gloomy day. During the exhibit, as they walked around in the upstairs gallery, Yunus had asked him, "Do you suppose that Munch would wake up too happy to paint some days? That he would just say, 'Oh, this damn happiness, all I vant to paint is butterflies and little puppies, how I vish it vould go away!'?" Matthew had let his guard down and laughed long and hard at that one.

Sunday night was bad, but Monday he had a plan. A plan always gives hope. There is nothing (with the possible exception of a blow job) as good as a plan.

He would call all the people on his list and ask if they knew anything about getting a home security system installed. Firstly this might induce guilt in them, that he might go and stab them in their prayers (none of this Hamlet shit for him), and secondly if he got a good home security system, he would feel better about William T. Delaplace being out there.

They were less than helpful.

Nicholas Askel Denning-Roy had had bad experiences with a home security service because he kept forgetting his access code. If the question bothered him, he didn't show it because his compulsion to self-narrative made him tell every damn time he got locked out of his house and set off the damn alarm and eventually the neighborhood association made him move and they were a bunch of Nazis and he had a chapter in his book called "A Bunch of Nazis" in which every bourgeois matron on the board of the neighborhood association was mentioned in anagrams. And so forth. While he droned on, Matthew seriously began to suspect him of being the thief. He could have stolen Haidee's ashes in order to have someone to talk to.

Norman Papin had a variety of schemes to booby-trap one's home against burglars. He lived in a cheap house near the state offices on Lamar, right under the flight path. He said that they hung wires and bells in their backyard, and they once caught this guy sneaking into the backyard—perhaps (Norman hinted darkly) after Norman's comic-book collection. When he asked what they did with the man they "caught," Norman explained that they had interrogated him and given him coffee. He claimed to be a homeless bum, so they gave him a tuna fish sandwich and took him to the Guesthaus downtown. "We let him know what kind of people he was dealing with though. I showed him my Klingon dagger and Mike showed him his nunchakus." Matthew struck Norman from the list; although he had no doubt that Norman was clinically mad, he was sure that stealing was not the Klingon way.

Calling Billie Sue Lovejoy was—he realized as she said hello—a mistake. She offered to come put a protective circle around his house, or better still teach him how to protect it with visualized streams of rainbow energy. She protected her own property the same way. When Matthew pointed out that her house had been robbed the year before, she said, yes that was true, but that was her destiny, she was paying some karmic debt from another life. Matthew had had similar talks with other magic-using personalities. If something was good in their lives, it was their power working, if something bad happened to them—well that was good too because it was their destiny, and they would get stronger. What does not kill us makes us quote Nietzsche.

He decided to give it one more try with Stephen Kozalla. Stephen had recommendations right away. He had dated one of the servicemen of that company with the jingle you can't get out of your head, and knew all the false stuff they promised—like sensors that weren't hooked to anything or tight connections with the Austin Police Department. Stephen's boyfriend's new house was security-proofed by Brewster Ling Security, which used satellites, among other more conventional devices. If it was good enough for Ray, it was good enough for him. The idea that a security firm could get a satellite picture at the time of a break-in sounded both dubious and pricey, but the appeal of the All-Seeing Eye runs deep in Americans. Annuit coeptis. He got their answering machine a couple of times and realized that it was noon.

He needed a snack. Type II diabetics live their lives measured out in snacks. Their ideal life would be one of thirteen little snacks a day, a tiny medallion of cheese while their friends can drink malts or eat pancakes smothered in syrup. Matthew had once been so overcome with the idea that he couldn't ever eat pancakes with syrup, real maple syrup and tons of butter, that he pulled off the road and had a good cry.

Before he had the diabetes, that is to say before it was diagnosed, he used to have a whooping big pizza lunch with Selma or Yunus or a couple of bookstore owners at a twenty-four-hour delicatessen on Sixth Street. He would plow into a bagel with cream cheese or a burger dripping with fat, and those milk shakes were the nearest thing to orgasm that you could pour in a glass.

After the diagnosis he would break down about once a month and binge. Then he would refuse to check his blood for a couple of days; if he didn't see the figure it probably wasn't real.

Then Haidee caught him.

She didn't say anything.

She just used his equipment and tested her blood and wrote down the result for that day. "At least you have a fiction instead of an absence. You won't feel guilty looking back at it months from now when you get better control."

It didn't end the bingeing right away, but it did do so in about six months.

He had had to learn how to cook. Haidee didn't cook. If God had meant for women to cook, he wouldn't have invented the microwave.

All of the recipes, all the memes of cooking he knew came from the rich southern food that Elaine had cooked. He blamed his mom in part for the disease, blamed her coconut cream pies; her bacon, lettuce, and tomato sandwiches; her use of ice cream as a way of avoiding issues around the house. So he got good and mad at her again when he was diagnosed, almost as mad as he had been when she said to him that she really didn't want any pickaninny grandchildren. It had come out unexpectedly; she hadn't meant to be hurtful. She was lamenting the failure of his brother John's marriage to Cassilda Jones and his brother Paul's marriage to Terri what-was-her-name? The family would die out, it was the way things were. All the smart people didn't have kids, and all the stupid people had ten kids and eventually the future would be filled with marching morons. She hadn't wanted kids, but it was her duty. Then Matthew said that he and Haidee were planning on a family when he was able to buy a place for his shop instead of renting. Then it came out, and could never be recalled. He hadn't spoken to her since then. He supposed that she knew that Haidee was dead; after all, John had seen it in the papers with the trial and all. He wasn't talking to John or Saul or Paul at this point either.

But after the diagnosis when he just needed a snack he got in the habit of not leaving the store. He had an assistant for years, the last one being Norman, who was almost as glad for the discount as for the salary, but he had canned Norman after Haidee's death. He was glad for the extra hours it gave him at the shop. Sometimes he slept there. He would work really hard making sure that everything was swept and alphabetized and checking people's want lists, and then he could collapse about one. He would get up early in the morning and drive to his house and feed the cat. He made a lot of money because of Haidee's death.

He pulled out his snack, a crunchy rice treat.

Very few calories and not all from fat either.

And you could chew it.

Slowly and well.

While he chewed he realized that there was someone sitting in a long green car across the street. The car was down the block a little—difficult to see out of the glass door to the New Atlantis. Matthew had to sort of lean over the counter to see him.

The man would glance back at the shop every so often. It could be the police or Delaplace or just some random guy.

Being stalked—and being stalked is a state of mind: you are stalked if you think you are—being stalked is having a power vacuum applied to your life. At any moment any shadow, any strange noise, any strange silence and it sucks the power right out of you. It doesn't matter what decisions you've made or you're about to make—because he's out there. No matter how well you have managed your life, no matter what efforts you made, he's out there. It could be the best day in your life, and it ends right then.

With a sudden satori, Matthew realized that being stalked for a white man is a lot like being black. He remembered a talk he had once with Caspar Bomars. Caspar pointed out to him that when a white guy is pulled over for speeding the worst thing that will happen to him is probably a ticket. When a black guy gets pulled over for speeding, the best thing that will probably happen to him is a ticket. No matter how smart he's been that day, no matter how great his efforts, no matter nothing. Because of the man.

He thought of calling Caspar and sharing this observation with him, but he doubted it would do any good for healing their relationship. Caspar was a good guy. A friendly little spook, as Matthew always wanted to joke but never felt quite comfortable enough to do so. His name meant "guardian of the treasury," so it made sense that he was the most angry of the brothers when Matthew had married Haidee. The Bomars family went in for meaningful names. Haidee was Greek for "caress." With a Norwegian name like Reynman on the end of it, people often thought it was a version of Heidi.

He thought about walking out to the man in the car, look him over, maybe he could just walk to the end of the block—mime posting a letter in the snorkel box. Perhaps he could strike up some Chandleresque conversation with the man. Or maybe he should call the police. They would understand that he was nervous, so it wouldn't matter if he was reporting the police to the police.

Then he tried to keep himself busy, striking up stupid forced conversation with the customers that wandered in.

After a while he began to picture the man in the car as

Arte Johnson in *Laugh-In,* who used to play this Nazi soldier who hid behind a philodendron and would comment on the skits, "Very interesting, but stupid!"

Then after selling some sword-and-sorcery romances to a pair of demivirgins, he looked up and the car was gone.

By closing time, which was eight, he had forgotten about the man in the car.

He drove home in the dark looking forward to his evening walk. To fight the blood sugar he walked forty-five minutes a day. His neighborhood was well set up for walkers, nice sidewalks, post oak trees, a little park with kids playing on the swings. Walking about eight-thirty to nine-fifteen gave you a nice tired. It let you put the events of the day in order, it let you watch the turning of the seasons, and it had little gamelike aspects. He had always meant to mention that aspect to his brother John. John was a game designer. He wrote the scripts for computer games and had also designed paper games. In the first years of his marriage to Haidee, John and his wife Cassilda would invite them over to play-test some of John's games. He was very proud of a board game called Law, in which different players could try to be the first to get a bill passed by both houses of Congress and signed by the president. It took a fuck of a long time to play, which is why John had never managed to sell it, but they all hoped it would do well, be the next Monopoly. John had run a fantasy role-playing game as well, and they had spent many hours being paladins and illusionists and elfin thieves.

It wasn't John's fault. After his divorce from Cassilda, he was really weird. He would call you at three in the morning and shit like that, and he did blame Matthew for having alienated Mom. Matthew had expected his brother to take up for him. They were close in age, unlike the twins, who were a decade plus beyond John. John didn't agree with their mother's feelings, but still felt it was OK to blame Matthew.

He drank a little, he cussed a lot, and he was just weird—like many freelancers, he slowly forgot the importance of the clock in the lives of others, so the parting of the ways came about a year before Haidee's murder. John had sent a tiny wreath of flowers, far too small to notice.

Perhaps Matthew should call him up, invite him to set up a gaming section at the store. John had talked about that once. Maybe one of his friends actually did that. There was always old FRP stuff for sale in the shop—of course for all Matthew knew it might be so amusingly out of date as to appeal only to dinosaurs. Maybe Norman would know.

Anyway he should write John a little letter about the game aspects of walking—getting 10 points if you see the blonde who does her gardening in her bikini—5 points for seeing that fat guy walk his hamsters—minus 15 points for stepping in dog poop. A perfect walk was 100 points or more, and Matthew had racked up 115 by the time he walked up his driveway—the last 5 points being spotting a hummingbird drinking out of a morning glory across the street. He had seen two of them, out at almost night. The full moon was as big as a ship and Matthew paused for a moment just to take it in.

The party had opened him up, even with the fears and suspicions it had given him. He was like a foot that had fallen asleep; when blood pours in again, there is a lot of pins-and-needles discomfort, but it is alive. It is alive.

He opened the front door and walked in.

There was a light coming from the den.

There should not have been a light coming from the den.

He picked up a rock, a beautiful mineral specimen of azurite and malachite that his mother had given them as an anniversary gift, and he ran to the back.

Someone had pulled down one of his bookcases. The books were everywhere on the oval rope rug. They smelled of piss.

The lamps were turned on and there was a message written in red ballpoint across the off-white paint of the wall.

Dear Mr. Reynman,

I waited for you to come out of your store all day, till I got bored. So I thought I'll see you another time. I need to talk to you before I kill you. I've got to get some things straight.

Best,
(S) William Delaplace

7 Zeugma

The second or third time he saw Haidee she gave him a paper about the word *OK* which she had written for her freshman comp class. He had been walking her to her dorm after calculus, and talking about how you say "OK" when someone asks you how you are. You say "OK" if things are great, or if they are awful. If you asked someone dying of cancer how he was doing he would probably say "OK." Even if you're completely numb with some kind of shock, you say "OK."

It was the kind of nervous chatter that courtship is based on.

He was a junior, she was a freshman.

Matthew felt OK as he fell into the Naugahyde rocker and stared at the wall. He sat there for an hour just rereading the text. It wasn't just the threat, it was the power to come into the house and make the threat.

Haidee's paper had been based largely on the seminal study by Lorenzo Dow Turner's 1949 *Africanisms in the Gullah Dialect.* OK may be traceable to African roots. Various attempts have been made to derive OK from German, Greek, Scots, Finnish, Choctaw, or even as the abbreviation for "Old Kinderhook," a nickname for Martin Van Buren, but considering that its first recorded appearance was among Jamaican blacks in 1816, and that there was no known use among the white population until twenty years after that date, OK is very likely derived from West African languages that were forcibly imported.

It sounds like the Mandingo *o-ke*, the Dogon *O-kay*, Western Fula *eeyi kay*, and the Wolof *waw kay* or *waw ke*. All of these forms mean "yes, indeed." The O- occurs as an adjectival prefix in many West African languages. The O- means "in the manner of"; the K part means "that which has been done." The OK-like word is used as a link between sentences in running narrative or discourse. It both confirms what has been said and links it to what will be said.

The K principle is common to a lot of African religions; among the Kwa language group its similarity to the Egyptian *ka* has been noted by some scholars.

OK is a little African invocation that was popular at least five thousand years ago among Nile dwellers, and is still going strong.

Man fears time, time fears the Pyramids, the Pyramids fear "OK by you?": the question that asks another to see if your plan matches up to the questioned one's divine reality.

Matthew, although fully conscious, awakened with a start. He hadn't checked out his house! Christ.

The back door was open, and beyond that the gate that opened onto the creek. He ran through the house, checking each closet, and in a blip of insanity the refrigerator door.

Other than damage to the books, nothing seemed to have been touched or be missing.

So he went to the back door again. It didn't look to be forced. Could he have left it unlocked?

He looked in the backyard for George the cat, a big yellow tom, fixed and fat, that wandered in his dreams of royalty. He called George inside of the house, despite this normally being not allowed. He walked out and pulled the gate shut, ramming the steel bar closed. He came in and called the police.

They took a long time coming.

The urine had dried on the books, and he began wiping them off with a warm wet blue towel. He was stacking them when the police came.

They made photos, looked around desultorily and said they didn't see any surfaces that were worth taking prints from, as they had said four years ago when he was robbed. They asked all the questions that Matthew was trying to figure out. How did the burglar obtain entrance? When did the break-in occur? If Matthew had spotted the man in his car, why hadn't Matthew called the police? Could Matthew identify the car? (It was green and kind of long, he thought.) They apologized for being late: they had gone to the other Mr. Reynman's house.

"You mean John?"

"Yes, we got to know your brother pretty well last year."

"Why?"

"Well, that would be up to him to tell you. We just heard the name Reynman and went over there. He was at some kind of concert at UT."

"New Music."

"I beg your pardon?"

"He goes to the New Music Ensemble. Look, this doesn't matter. If I call you again, do you think you'll come to my house first?"

"Oh, definitely sir, we'll make a note."

"Do I need to keep this sign on my wall?"

"Why don't you cover it up with that bookcase, sir? That way it will be out of sight, out of mind, but it will be nice evidence when we catch him."

"What are you going to do tonight?"

"We'll look around the neighborhood for a while to see if

he's lurking. I doubt that he wanted to do more than throw a good scare in you. Otherwise he would have waited and killed you when you walked in the door."

"Don't you think you're ascribing a little too much logic to a nut?"

"Nuts can be very logical, sir, that's how we catch them. You only have to worry about your illogical nuts."

"How do you tell the difference?"

"Well, sir, the illogical ones we don't catch."

With calm assurance they departed.

Matthew decided the smartest thing to do was to take Delaplace at his word. Delaplace wasn't going to just kill him, he was going to talk to him first. So there would be no jumping out from behind a tree and Bang! You're Dead! There would be a conversation, probably a capture, some kind of conversation under duress.

He would get a pager, no a cell phone, tomorrow. That way he could dial 911. He should also get a gun. He knew that Selma was pretty knowledgeable about guns. He would ask her. Since this was, thank God, Texas, it wouldn't take long to get a gun.

Maybe there was some phrase, some word he could say to William that would convince him not to kill him. If he knew why William wanted to talk to him, he would know what to say.

Would he lie and say that he and Haidee had never been happy?

He didn't know if he could say that even to save his life.

He had asked her if she really thought that OK came out of Africa. She said the etymology struck her as a little chancy and that mainly she was putting it down just to piss off her instructor. It is important to piss off white people often.

"All white people?"

"All white people."

He must have looked crestfallen.

"But," she continued with the sexiest smile he had ever seen, "there are some words whose African origin is indisputable, such as 'poon-tang,' a term used to describe this."

And she caught his hand and shoved it down her shorts.

It was wet, and hot, and hairy.

He was just beginning to find his way around this unexpected garden when her roommate came in, and he pulled away quickly. It wasn't till the Friday night dance that he was able to eat thereof and discover knowledge of good and evil from this African Eve.

He put the bookcase back over the graffitoed wall, and began putting books back. He had had a persistent fantasy about his books for years, that somehow a major (unnamed, unimagined) catastrophe would strike the earth and as a result all of civilization would be lost. Except for his books (pay no mind that many of his books were paperbacks which due to the acid content were quietly working toward their own destruction—undoing the very function of the book as the dumping grounds for culture made irredeemably classic). Someone—something would find *his* books and make a world out of them. His slant on things, well at least the received ideas that he claimed to be his slant. He never had imagined violence to his books, even such trivial violence as a few ounces of murderer's piss.

The wall would probably remain written on, although covered. When people got as many books as he had they never painted again. All bare wall space became covered in books; books were an internal ivy. For public institutions of learning ivy was cultivated as a sign of the depth of the learning within—so deep was thought in these places that the actions never intruded nor burst forth so that a vegetable kingdom could grow without. For private places of learning—Austin, by the way, has more used-book stores per capita than any other city in the US of A—this greenish enterprise was handled through books, books becoming an ersatz wall. All of those words of heavy print keep you safe, and it is well known and scientific fact that a layer of books increases the insulation value of a house by as much as whatever percent you can talk your listeners into believing in.

Austin was a great town for such instant ivy. The Harry Ransom Center for Humanities Research (known colloquially as the HRC but more formally as the HRCHR, looking like a Czech verb signifying doom) had come into being to give instant culture to Austin. It held the copperplate of *Dracula*, much Keats, much Yeats, much Crowley, and tons of SF. All Matthew had done was reproduce in miniature what the city itself had done macrocosmically. The collection of Aldine books at the HRCHR is truly breathtaking; Matthew and Yunus used to visit it before Matthew's two years of solitude.

There all done, and it was only midnight.

Really he should have taken half these books to the warehouse months ago.

It was very quiet outside, only the songs of the locusts showing that this was late spring, and that they were early. The big drought the year before and then the floods this spring had upset the timing of things. Matthew tried very hard to believe that the police were out there patrolling the neighborhood, that William would be waiting for them, crouched behind a tree or a mailbox, smiling that stupid grin he would strike up in court when either side suggested that his actions were not those of a sane man.

Matthew decided that he would get out in his car and look as well. He got his new gun, which this time was loaded, and went out to the station wagon. He had no real plans of blowing William away, but it was better than just lying in the dark listening to every twig snap, or the riotous thunder of the cat chasing an opossum across the roof.

He drove up and down each block in Hyde Park.

He knew many of these people. It was that kind of neighborhood. He had conned many of them into stopping into his store at least once. The first year of business Haidee had printed up some red-and-green flyers with a "Christmas Buck" on each one, good for a dollar off on a book purchase, and she spent one weekend in November walking up and down each block sticking them in people's mailboxes.

They had both hated the Friday dance. Matthew had said that he thought "her people" were supposed to be great dancers; she had said, "Oh no, it's the white folks with Fred Astaire, we always watch the white folks fo' our dance steps." He had apologized again, and she said that some of the clichés were true. For example blacks were better at sex, because it was one of the few experiences that wasn't mediated by white reality. She was very serious, he could tell that wasn't a joke. She then told him that her roommate was visiting her folks back home in Shreveport. He began to nibble her perfect gazelle of an ear. There had been some kind of subterfuge necessary to sneak him into the dorm at night—the details eluded him as he drove scanning for signs of Delaplace—but by the time he came to her room she had lit candles and incense and she was lifting up her skirt to take off her light blue cotton panties.

She left the skirt on and motioned for him to kneel before her, and in a musky moment stepped over him and to him so that his mouth was on her wetness. He reached up with both thumbs and opened her pussy. Black women did have larger clitoris—he could actually find it with his tongue alone. At least the world of books had not failed in that learning.

She pressed hard down on his face, and for a moment he had trouble breathing, since she clearly meant to rut on his face.

He had never had a white woman take such an early interest in the action. Making love to them was like masturbation—he did all the work and as best as he could tell he got all the rewards.

She came and she came *loudly*.

When she got her breath back, she said, "I need you in me. Strip and lie down."

He was down but pointing toward the sky when she mounted him and her vagina began to kiss his dick. So he decided that was what was meant by a snappin' pussy.

He didn't last very long. (You wouldn't have either.)

She said, "That's OK, the first time is the quickest."

The first time? He had never had a woman who talked that way. Sex was always ten minutes of begging and five minutes of doing.

She kissed him on the mouth and then worked her way down; long before the time she got to his dick it was once again at attention. She sucked with skill and grace, until his toes curled. She masturbated herself while she sucked, a habit that Matthew was profoundly grateful for each and every time he saw it until her murder.

She paused once, looked up, and said, "Now I fed you, don't you be shy about feeding me."

About a minute later he proved he wasn't shy.

They snuggled for a while, and then she asked him if he had ever fucked a woman in the ass.

He was twenty-one and he had not.

So she told him how, and then got some lube. And he discovered the meanings of the words "tight" and "hot."

He had never been so fucked out, weak kneed, and satisfied in his life. Yet she continued to nibble, to rub, to hug and caress, and was rewarded with another erection, which he gave her missionary style.

"That's a good night, four fucks. One for each hole and an

extra one for my pussy. You just might do, white boy, you just might do."

He crawled to the roommate's bed and fell dead asleep. There were more tricks in the morning to sneak him out of the dorm. She joined him and they had breakfast at McDonald's, doing silly things like singing the "Big Mac" song to each other—a crucial part of their childhood. They had Egg McMuffins and bliss.

Later he departed for the Perry Castaneda Library. He had to do some research on his Flaubert paper. In *The Temptation of Saint Anthony*, he wrote, "Flaubert reveals (and implicitly criticizes) the library as the generating ground for new books. He takes that criticism a step forward in his unfinished comedy *Bouvard and Péuchet* by making the book the destroyer of reality because it is such a poor substitute for it. The two goofy Parisian bachelors Bouvard and Péuchet meet by chance and by discovering their common view on reality, which is that it can't be found behind a desk, and their common occupation of copy clerks, decide that they are ultimately in sympathy. When a rich uncle (named Ovid) dies, Bouvard has enough money to buy a small farm in Normandy. He takes his friend Péuchet along, and they begin looking for reality. They will find reality by farming. They read up on it. They fail. They try arboriculture. They fail. They try garden architecture. They read up on it. They fail. The advice in the various manuals and treatises doesn't match the real world. Yet undaunted by their successive failures, they move to text after text: chemistry, physiology, anatomy, geology, archaeology. . . . They eventually realize that all knowledge is a mass of contradictions, and they return to their former occupation of copying."

For a brief moment he worried that perhaps he and Haidee were like Bouvard and Péuchet. Their goals, his of teaching literature and hers of being a doctor, might not really be the doors into reality. Their commonalities—like knowing the "Big Mac" song—might be false commonalities. What if they were like Bouvard and Péuchet, come to the end of becoming what they were in the first place? Surely that would be the worst of all possible relationships. Change of the partners is the good, even if it is Daphne into a laurel tree.

He wrote pointing out that Flaubert didn't intend Bouvard and Péuchet to be fools. "Flaubert wrote, 'They acquire a faculty of desiring pity, they recognize stupidity, and they can no longer tolerate it. Through their inquisitiveness their understanding grows; having had more ideas, they suffered more.'

"Flaubert never finished his novel. He died suddenly of an apoplectic stroke leaving notes on an unfinished page for the conclusion: 'They copy papers haphazardly, everything they find, tobacco pouches, old newspapers, posters, torn books, etc. (Real items and their imitations. Typical of each category.)

" 'Then, they feel a need for a taxonomy. They make tables, antithetical oppositions such as "crimes of the kings and crimes of the people"—blessings of religion, crimes of religion. Beauties of history, etc. Sometimes however they have real problems putting each thing in its proper place and suffer great anxieties about it.

" '—Onward! Enough speculation! Keep on copying! The page must be filled. Everything is equal, the good and the evil. The farcical and the sublime—the beautiful and the ugly—the significant and the typical, they all become an exhalation of the statistical. There are nothing but facts—not phenomena.

" 'Final Bliss.' "

He grew tired of driving. He went home.

8 Chronicles

"You look lousy," said Selma Sacks. She had come in to thank him for the party and to show off her boobs.

"I didn't sleep well last night," said Matthew.

"Well, you know, if you're not sleeping you can always give me a call, and I'll talk to you. You could even come over and maybe we could work on some kind of stress reduction."

"I, eh, thanks. I'll keep that in mind."

"Did you get a lot of feedback from the party?"

"Oh, yes. I found out many things because I had the party. I can't thank you and Yunus enough. It was eye-opening, I mean, to know how many friends I had."

"Well, I want you to know you always have me."

"You're on the top of my list." *After all, you suggested the damn party, which is the first time I let you in my house in over two years. What did you want?*

"While I'm here, where are the Hull books?"

"You liked what you won?"

"I'm hooked. I just finished *Little Gardens of Happiness*."

"Mysteries are over there." He gestured with his left hand, suddenly inspiration-struck. "You know, I'm writing a mystery short story."

"Really?"

"I thought it would be good therapy to spend some time putting my words down. I know you can't get rich off of short stories, but I figured it would give me a nice little hobby, force me to learn to use Haidee's computer, and maybe give the store a little publicity."

"You're going to write about the New Atlantis?"

"Well, I figured I'd mention it in the stories, and then people would want to come by if they're in Austin. But I'm not very good at it."

"Trouble plotting?"

"I can't come up with a MacGuffin I need. See, I've got this guy that's being stalked and I want him to communicate with the stalker—you know, have them meet. The stalker's a nut, so I think he's apt to walk into a trap, but I don't how to contact him."

"And this is set in Austin, right?"

"Yeah."

"Well, in *Little Gardens of Happiness* there's the same situation where the lady who works at the Wildflower Research Center is being stalked by someone from her past. So she puts a personal ad in the local free paper. The stalker calls up the discreet phone service and then she calls the police."

"Did it work out OK?"

"Well, not really, but you don't want me to go into that because if you knew too much about that other plot, wouldn't that be plagiarism?"

"Well, I wouldn't want my hero to have any problems I hadn't thought through."

"In the book, it happens that the stalker has her phone bugged and knows what's going on."

"That sounds a little farfetched."

"No, the stalker's this ex–phone company guy, which lets Hull go off on these riffs about the Network."

"Well, then, presuming the stalker doesn't have access to superior forms of information, this would be a safe idea."

"Coming up with the ad would be half the fun."

Selma wandered off to the mystery alcove. Matthew restrained himself from picking up the *Chronicle*. His store was one of their free distribution places. Matthew had a secret relationship with the *Chronicle*. Years ago, after he had his falling out with John, Haidee and he had wanted to keep on playing Dungeons & Dragons. They had tried putting little ads in gaming stores for active groups, but they kept being called up by teenagers, so they did an ad for the *Chronicle*—"Looking for Adults for Fantasy Role-Playing Games"—and gave their phone number. They started getting calls from a man named Frank, who would leave boozy messages on their answering machine, "When it gets too kinky for most people I am just ready to go." Eventually Frank called when Haidee was home, she tried to explain that they were interested in an entirely different type of fantasy role-playing and suggested that Frank place his own ad in the *Chronicle*. He did, and then others did, and eventually the ads became a mainstay of the little weekly paper. Matthew had meant to mention this to the editor many times to see if he could get a free ad for his store, but the whole thing seemed farfetched.

Selma came back with *Dad's Last Pitch*. And he had a *Chronicle* in his hands before her butt was out the door. It was one of their "Best of Austin" issues. His eyes fell on the "Best Street Name" entry. The *Chron* had picked Kumquat Court (over Ferret Path, Gnu Gap, Possum Trot, Whiskey River Drive, Hangman's Court, Bunny Run, Cooing Court, Dali Lane, Cockelburr Cove, Festus Drive, Sugar Shack, the High Road, Cotton Picking Lane, Alimony Cove, Capsicum Cove, and Easy Street). Ah, here's the section on personal ads. He would have to mull this over for a while. It didn't fit in any of the existing categories, and other niceties—like whether or not to use the optional 9-point-type headline—would need to be thought out. He should probably call the police for their advice, but he felt he was going to do it anyway. As his mother had once said (although *not* while talking to her kids), it is easier to ask forgiveness than to ask permission.

There were some other customers; one said "angio-something" to his equally elderly blue-haired companion, and Matthew's mind raced back to his fluorescent angiogram, which he had had two months after his diagnosis of diabetes. The procedure is simple—your eyes are dilated, an orange dye is pumped into a vein in your arm, and a series of pictures are made of your retinas to see how much dye leaks out in a few minutes' time. Haidee had taken him, really because he was scared of how much of his eyesight might already be lost to retinopathy, but nominally because he couldn't drive after the test.

As the strobe light lit his eyes, and nausea filled his being, he grew very guilty at having killed the dream of Haidee becoming a doctor. For some reason it was all he could think about.

By the end of his senior year Haidee Bomars and Matthew Reynman had progressed so far in love that the world was not big enough for anything else and they made love anytime, anyplace, trying to reinvent it each time they did. They had the naïve belief that the power of their love, which to them was as constant and obvious as gravity, was a true force in the objective universe, so that whatever objections their families might raise (and who could truly object to an interracial couple in the eighties, for God's sake?) would pass like a cloud in the light of their love's sun. Their news was met by a distant reception from Elaine and Herman Reynman, who explained that with Herman's growing health problem they would not be able to send Matthew to graduate school. But Haidee's family was not overburdened with politeness. She was abandoning her dream. She still intended to be a doctor, but they pointed out marriage was the last thing that aids one's academic career. Of course if she were marrying a man of color, she would at least be furthering their dream—the collective dream they all had. Besides, her grades at UT had been terrible; only after she had fallen into the pit of romance had her academics suffered. Where was the valedictorian who had given the racial-pride speech? Where was the "I am going to come back to my community and give"? Their daughter was dead. (That she had had white ancestors was not to the point, nor that her brothers were lighter skinned than she.)

But it was true. Matthew knew it was true as the lights flashed into his eyes. He had killed her dream. He had killed their dream, and now years after the fluorescent angiogram he realized that he had killed her as well. She wouldn't have been in the store if she hadn't fallen in love with him. With that special knowledge that guilt brings of one's total responsibility for the fates of others and even the mechanical properties of the objective universe, Matthew was ready for William's bullet. It wasn't as if these feelings hadn't occurred before, but no matter how well banished, they needed only to have a certain name spoken to return to see him.

Speak of the devil.

Matthew had long ago decided that his announcement of his intent to marry Haidee had killed his father as well. At least helped along that disease he had caught years ago in Brazil.

The announcement was that he would marry Haidee when she had finished her bachelor's degree. Since this plan didn't get the support they had wanted, they moved to plan B, which was to get married immediately.

Matthew had his B.A. in English after all, and they had the enchantment of love—what could indeed stop them? Perhaps they would have to live in a garret downtown while Haidee finished her degree. Perhaps they would have to get scholarships of the most promising sort, but it could happen.

It didn't happen.

Matthew went to work for the largest chain of used-book stores in Texas as a buyer and spent long hours telling people just how damn little their accumulated books, records, and magazines were worth. The garret proved to be a third-floor apartment on Lamar Street next to a bus stop, which had roaches the size of small dogs. Lots of meals with John and Cassy, just like the barbecues with William, Matthew suddenly realized. He hadn't realized that he had equated William with John on some emotional level.

His father died.

His mom went into isolation and mourning for a few years.

John got his divorce.

Paul and Saul had their own troubles as the New York legal scene knew boom and bust as the Reagan years cycled through the American economy bringing ruin and relief and setting up certain long-scale tides that would chaotically create the U.S. in the next century.

And William shot Haidee.

It was his fault.

Just as the diabetes had been his fault for eating too much.

He started to fill out the ad form.

Apparently you filled out the form, and they billed your credit card, unless you were getting one of the free ads from E-mailing on a certain day or using a fax on a certain day or having a name beginning with a certain letter. The cost went to the person calling in to answer the ad. Now that was a weak point: William did not have a phone just yet. But he had a car somehow. He seemed a pretty resourceful guy. (It would be a shame to be stalked and terrorized by someone who wasn't resourceful; you mustn't be easy prey.) Then after they billed you, you called in a voice message to go along with the ad, and then people could call you up and leave a message.

This was the ad:

"Dear William, I read the message you left. I too want to talk. Let's get together. Matthew Reynman."

He mailed off the form at lunch. He closed the shop for half an hour and walked over to the central post office.

Two days later the confirmation came in the mail, and he called and left the following message. "William, I know you're out there and I've given a lot of thought to many things and think you may be right. Why don't you call me up and we can meet and talk. Then if you still have business to do, you can take care of it."

He didn't know what he was going to do when William called him. He could work out a scheme with the police to catch him, or he could go and end William's life, or he could let William kill him for the very real crimes Matthew had committed. Each had a certain goodness to it, but he tended toward a mixture of the last two. He could go armed to the meeting and try to have a shoot-out. Shoot-outs were, after all, in his blood. He was the nephew of Lullaby and Pegleg Reynman.

He had been amazed that Haidee hadn't heard of Lullaby. It was one morning after he had gotten in the habit of sleeping in her dorm room. They were watching her roommate's black-and-white TV, some Tom Mix—no, Gene Autry movie about him fighting the evil forces of some underground kingdom and she had made fun of the whole idea of a singing cowboy. He pointed out that his uncle, who had died before his birth, had gone out west to make a career in Hollywood as a western-band leader and had got really and truly involved with Japanese and Nazi spies and killed some of them in a shoot-out in rural California. At first she hadn't believed him, but as it came to be more and more clear that it was so, she at least conceded that it must be family legend. He promised to some time tell her the whole legend of Lullaby Reynman. He realized that he hadn't done this, and this was a bad thing. He had always had certain hopes for his marriage that he hadn't gotten to do. One of the first courting gifts he had given Haidee had been Sir Francis Burton's translation of the *Arabian Nights*, which he very pedantically always called by its real title of *The Thousand Nights and a Night*. It had been for sale in a publisher's discount catalog, only about $150, and money was easy to come by before they were wed. He had got the long box full of the black volumes with gold and silver titles and carried it to her dorm room on a cool December day. (It seldom got truly cold in Austin.) She found it after chemistry and he promised that they would read a story to each other every night. They got to night twenty or so, when reality cut the head off of that project, but the vow was made again and again. One night he had thought of reading aloud to her ashes, but that had struck even him as too morbid and pathetic. If he lived out his encounter with William Delaplace, he would find her ashes and do so. There had been too many unfulfilled vows in his life. Looking back, he decided that all of the happiness he had had—which he would be the first to admit was more than most men—had come from the vows he had fulfilled, and even if he did not have another really happy day, he would fulfill his vows anyway. His honor would be known by his faithfulness.

The sheet that explained how to call in for the ad he put by his work phone. It would remind him to call once a day. More than that would be obsessive.

Thursday came and he saw to his horror and amusement that the ad was placed under "Variations" as opposed to "Men Seek Women," "Women Seek Women," and so forth. He tried to visualize William picking up the free paper somewhere. If he could think about it strongly enough, maybe William would do it. That was no doubt the origin of magic, people being unable to do something about a situation so they thought strongly about it. It was either that or worry. It had to do with excess psychic energy, which is what separates us from the beasts. The brain power of a cat or a goldfish is sufficient for the job, so when the job is done the brain is done. People have an excess of the energy, so when the tasks at hand are done the brain comes back to whatever occupies it. This gift of energy is what makes or breaks people. They can use the energy to worry about things, to obsess, to tear themselves apart—which is the natural way of the world and why our lives are filled with cigarette smoke, gin, heroin, and romance novels. Or someone can use that gift to create him- or herself in art or music or just plain good thinking. People need to be reminded of that often, which is why they read books or watch TV. They like to see others using the gift, they like to think that they would be clever or creative with the contents of their minds. However, some folk—and Matthew realized that this was a very good thing (otherwise the New Atlantis wouldn't pay for his blood-test strips)—become confused in the difference between the quest for inspiration and the actual process of inspiration.

He felt better for having launched the plan to meet with William. He was hoping that the police wouldn't read the ad. He doubted that the police department had a person that read the ads in the paper, but you never knew. There were all those spy movies and novels where someone takes out an ad like "The wolves are placed diagonally on the game board" and this alerts some secret operative in the world. Christ, a real secret message would be "The Sunday morning book club will meet an hour later next Sunday."

Matthew wondered idly if you did put a message in the personals like "The game board is a box which is a building" how many people it would set off. How many seemingly normal folk lose their rules at an unexpected stimulus? What if some secret understanding of brain chemistry existed so that a book with messages aimed entirely at the amygdalae of the world could be created?

Heck, such a book might already exist. He might even have copies of it on his shelves. The real world-changing book might not be Plato's *Symposium.* It might be James M. Cassutto's *Guide to Austin* for that matter. That was a great idea for a story. Maybe his words to Selma were prophetic. Like he would have the time to write stories, if he was going to inventory his life for unfulfilled vows.

He would tell the next writer that came into the shop.

He looked up and saw Rex Hull walking in.

What were the chances?

9 Tea for Two and Two for Tea

"**Mr. Hull, I was** just thinking of you," said Matthew.

"Why do I always hear that from shopkeepers and never beautiful blondes with lots of money?" said Rex Hull.

"No, I was just thinking of a story idea," said Matthew.

"And I can write it and we can split the money because you don't have time to write it, is that it?"

"No, I was thinking you can have it. But I could give it to any of the scores and scores of writers that come through my door."

"OK, that was rude of me, give me the idea."

"I'm not sure that I want to now."

Ideas were part of foreplay: if the mood wasn't right, Matthew wouldn't share them.

"Well," said Rex Hull. "I came by to thank you for your party last week. I had meant to be by earlier, but I was too busy. I enjoyed doing the reading for South by Southwest, and if you have any April events let me know."

"April is always a bad month for the used-book trade."

"It is the cruelest month."

"Yes, not many people realized that T. S. Eliot was in the used-book trade."

"With his verse I wouldn't have thought anyone could think otherwise," said Hull.

The phone rang. A man with a Hispanic accent asked about *The Grasshopper Lies Heavy.* Matthew ran upstairs to the SF loft; Dick came and went, always a good author to have.

Matthew came back. "No sir, we're out of Dick right now."

Hull had been playing with the books on the counter, looking over the purchases Matthew had made that morning. He picked up Kenneth Kinnamon and Richard Barksdale's *Black Writers of America.* "I am going to write a mystery about a black mystery writer in the nineteen forties who can't get his mysteries published, and becomes a psycho killer for a decade, and then gets his mysteries published, and calms down, and spends the rest of his life trying to cover up his crimes, but a young graduate student with a grant goes to study the guy in the seventies, and finds out about the crimes and has to decide whether or not to turn the guy in. So I'm researching black writers of the nineteen forties."

Matthew wondered why people had to tell him why they bought certain books. It was a bookstore after all. He said, "Sounds like a good book to me."

"So what was that idea you were going to tell me?"

"Em, that was it. Exactly. It must have been synchronicity."

"Wow. I'll dedicate the book to you. It is fate. Things like that just happen that make great writing. I've got to go now and get started. This is great."

Rex Hull almost hit Stephen Kozalla, who was flying in on fairy wings.

"What's he in a rush for?" asked Stephen.

"The muse just paid him a visit."

"Oh he did, did he?"

"I get the best people in the world here."

"Well, of course you do, Mr. Matthew, look, I'm here."

Stephen Kozalla didn't usually turn on the camp like this unless things were very good or very bad in his life. Which are times to visit used-book stores.

"So how are you, Stephen?"

"Do you know someone that's looking for really entry-level grunt-work technical writing? I know of a job that just opened up. It's easy stuff, gathering some existing documents together and putting them into Word, probably ten or twelve dollars an hour."

"I don't know anyone offhand, but I'll let you know if I do. Where's the job?"

"It's at DRC, where I *used* to work."

"Oh hell, what happened?"

"In theory I am late from lunch, late in the mornings. In reality everyone is. I stay late, I always make up the time. Which most people don't. In reality the boss, who I always thought was a very tolerant guy, simply turned out to be clueless. His eighteen-year-old son started working there—mowing lawns, emptying trash cans, and other preexcutive training. The kid explains to dear old dad that I am gay. Rather like explaining that the Gulf of Mexico is wet, I suppose. Well then every day last week the old man is by the door noting when I come in from lunch. Today he tells me that I don't have to come back this afternoon, so I came downtown to get something I need for a long weekend, which at my advanced age of thirty-seven also sadly includes things to read, and I am planning a five-day weekend. Next Tuesday I will hit the cruel, cruel streets again looking for employment."

"Isn't that—," began Matthew.

"Illegal, unethical, crude, stupid, cruel, and mean. I believe your philosophical friend Selma—I can't imagine anyone marching to her—has summed this up with her deeply meaningful bumper sticker, 'Mean People Suck.' I therefore am a social butterfly this weekend flapping my gaudy wings in the hopes of raising a storm in Stuttgart or wherever Mr. Grubert's ancestors come from."

"I am really sorry to hear that."

"Don't be sorry, they probably need the rain." Stephen asked, "I know this will sound a little hokey, but do you have anything about my people?"

"Most of the gay stuff is on a shelf in the back room marked Grove Press. I had some trouble years ago with the Citizens Against Pornography when I had a section labeled gay."

"I don't mean gay, although that's my favorite form of marginalization, I meant black. Haidee used to say that I should have more of a sense of blackness because that was part of who I am. I've been thinking about that a lot since your party. And by the way, thank you for that very much, I really liked hearing that guy read."

"Readings are fun. I always hear a book read in the author's voice after I've heard the author's voice," said Matthew. "Anyway, I do have one of the most comprehensive anthologies of black writing right here. I bought it this morning."

He looked for *Black Writers of America*. He saw that it was gone. Mr. Hull, in his inspiration, had stolen it. Writers are a pain in the ass.

"I should have given him my idea," said Matthew.

"What?" said Stephen.

"Um, nothing. I thought I had something right here. What kind of thing are you interested in? Writing? History? Political movements?"

"Writing I guess."

"Have you ever read any Chester Himes? Black ex-pat wrote some wickedly bitter detective stories."

"I haven't read much mystery. I had a lover who loved Raymond Chandler."

"Why don't you look in the mystery aisle for *Cotton Comes to Harlem?*"

"That was a movie, right?"

"Yeah, but Haidee and I missed it when it was in town. Pity too, she really wanted to see it."

"Yeah, I remember it, Haidee and I went to see it. She snuck off from work and we went. Godfrey Cambridge and Redd Foxx."

"I didn't know she got a chance to see it." Matthew felt a little sad and alone.

"Oh, you know how she was. We went to those movies."

"What movies?"

"The ones she didn't think you would understand, those blaxploitation movies that were revived at the dollar houses, *Trick Baby, The Spook Who Sat by the Door, Honky,* you know."

"Oh, yeah, I had forgot."

Matthew had never known that Haidee had done any such thing. He couldn't imagine her sneaking away from work—she had never done so for him. He tried to look busy with his books while Stephen swished over to the mystery aisle.

The mystery aisle ran along the south side of the shop where the New Atlantis backed up against a bar called the Decline of the West. Matthew could see about half the mystery aisle, but part of it was occulted by true crime. He had set a round mirror in the upper corner where the south wall met the east—that is to say, the front wall of the shop. He could see the mirrors over true crime and watch his patrons. He had put this in place during the early days of the shop, because he had figured that people that read about mysteries were somehow the most likely group to steal books. In reality he discovered that it was his occult titles that grew legs and walked away. There was a class of hopeless people that felt if they only got the right name of the right demon to invoke, all would be well; perhaps they could even pay the store back with their lottery winnings. Pornography too was a high-risk category, but you had to let those people look over the goods in a certain amount of privacy or they would never buy the things. He could rearrange the store so that the mystery niche held the occult and porno classics, and that way he could watch the soon-to-be-guilty, but moving shelves of books is hard work. As anyone who lives with books knows, books have a special gravity that grows the longer they are in one place.

So Matthew watched Stephen with half an eye and kept his other eye and a half on the titles he had to put away, glad that Hull had not been even more inspired. Matthew wondered if Hull took the big book as a payment for the reading.

Matthew opened one of the volumes, a hardback ex-library SF novel. He didn't recognize the author, Austen O. Emme. *Planet of the Future Dead.* What a great title. We are all living on planet of the future dead. His eye fell on

> Until Dr. Thom's *Search for a Chemical Soul* was published during the Beletrin war, reading had offered a refugee a place where the self was absolutely inviolate. From early civilizations where scribes held sway by being able to decipher written language, to public readings where skillful or inept performers make or break their poetry in the ears of the audience, the readers have always had the supreme power to make meaning. With Thom's book, however, this inviolate state was over. Readers knew something was wrong, wrong, right at that moment, and looking up from their text they would see

Matthew looked up and watched Stephen. Stephen had picked Chester Himes's *Pinktoes* and was frowning at the text. He was also playing with something in his pocket. His black hand brought out a small vial—cremains. He was the one.

Those were Haidee's ashes. No wonder he had been thinking of her.

Stephen put the vial back in his pocket and the book on the shelf. He picked up a copy of *Shaft Among the Jews* and moved from the mirror world into plain sight.

He said, "I need to borrow the little boys' room. I'll take this." He showed Matthew the book and took it with him as though it were some kind of masturbatory text.

The rest room was behind the counter—that way Matthew could see if anyone was taking books into the rest room that disappeared under coats or shirts or slacks.

God, what does he have her ashes for?

He isn't going to do anything *in there* with them, is he?

Matthew put his ear to the door and listened and then realized that he had no idea what he was listening for.

If he accused Stephen of being the ash man, what would happen? Matthew might never get all of her ashes back. What would anyone need ashes for?

Maybe he was eating them.

Matthew took out his gun, and leaned on the door and shoved. This pulled the little wire hook-and-eye arrangement from the door and Matthew fell forward onto the sitting Stephen, who had his pants off, applying a lighter to a glass tube that was filling with smoke. The lighter burned Matthew's elbow, and as Matthew's body carried Stephen off the toilet and onto the wall, the gun discharged, the bullet striking the cinder-block wall. As Matthew dropped the gun, his face ran into the pipe, knocking it from Stephen's lips, and Matthew smelled the steamy invigorating mixture. The pipe hurled out of Stephen's mouth and struck the wall, shattering into a million pieces, some of which fell onto Stephen's bare arm and also onto Matthew's bare right hand now trying to block his own fall onto the wall, while in a brief bruising parody of a kiss their lips met and Matthew could taste the smoke inside of

Stephen's mouth. As the glass cut into Matthew's palm, Stephen began to scream, then paused for a moment as his head hit the wall. Matthew then fell downward with his elbow hitting the inside of the toilet bowl.

It had not been an auspicious moment.

"What the goddamn hell are you doing, you crazy?" yelled Stephen.

"My wife's ashes!" yelled Matthew, grabbing up the remains of the crack pipe. He was thrusting both arms around Stephen's legs.

"You're fucking crazy. You're fucking crazy. I always knew whyte people were crazy."

Stephen was trying to stand but the pants around his legs, Matthew's arms, and his angle half off the toilet were making this impossible. He bucked and kicked against Matthew, who was holding on for dear life.

"Just let me go, you crazy son of a bitch!" yelled Stephen.

Matthew's hands were getting pretty cut up with the glass. He was making incoherent cries. Some of the glass was getting on Stephen's dark legs, making little rivulets of blood. Slowly the idea was dawning in Matthew's head that perhaps Stephen had not been smoking his dead wife's remains. He could feel some of the crack high that he had sucked from Stephen's mouth.

"Wait, wait," said Matthew. "Be calm."

"Be calm? You son of a bitch, you're trying to kill me."

Stephen managed to kick Matthew off. Matthew crawled backward into the counter, upsetting the stack of books that he had purchased earlier.

Stephen stood. "As soon as I get this glass out of my pants, I am getting out of here and I am going to be sure they lock your white ass behind bars as long as the grass grows and the water flows."

"You don't understand. I thought you had my wife."

"Your wife is goddamn dead and everybody but you knows it. She's dead because she was married to a crazy son of a bitch like you."

Stephen was taking his pants off and shaking them to remove the glass fragments.

"I am going to make sure they lock your ass up for good this time, for goddamn ever. Who knows how many innocent people you've assaulted in this bathroom."

The little bells in front of the door jangled as someone entered the store.

"We're closed!" yelled Matthew. "Saint Swithwin's Day!"

"Save me from this killer whyteman, he's already tried to rape me and force me to smoke drugs."

Matthew turned to see a slightly portly man in a dark business suit reach for a shoulder harness, pull a gun, and yell, "Freeze, police!"

Even though it was a cliché, Matthew froze.

"Thank you, God!" yelled Stephen.

"You come out of there with your hands up! You behind the counter, don't even think of breathing."

Stephen came out of the rest room. He had nothing on beneath shirt level, his legs were covered in blood, glass fragments flung spangles of light. Matthew's shirt was wet, and he was crying. Matthew realized that the toilet water from his right arm had made all of his right side wet.

"Put your hands behind your head. Both of you. Now!"

The portly man walked slowly up to the counter, never taking his eyes or the gun off them.

He pulled the phone to him with the instruction sheet for the personal ad beneath it. He dialed three numbers.

"This is Blick, I am at the New Atlantis Bookstore next to the Decline of the West. I need backup now. I stopped a homicide in progress. Neither man appears to be armed."

Blick looked at Matthew.

"Mr. Reynman, I was on my way to lecture you about your little ad, and why it is not a good idea for private citizens to take the law into their own hands. But it looks like you'll have the time to write a little essay on that for me. You just earned detention in the school of life."

10 Iqbal Tells His Stories (Again)

"Do you know why Ismailis are respected in Pakistan?" Iqbal asked. "There is much hatred in Pakistan between the Sunni and the Shia. Yet we who have a very different faith than they are respected. It is because the Aga Khan in his wisdom and benevolence has built hospitals. Many, many owe their lives to the Aga Khan. He is a great man."

Iqbal's office always smelled of sandalwood. Matthew had never seen him burn incense. He had a picture of the Aga Kahn next to his business license, and a small photo of his father and mother in Gujrat. His father was a poet, not the famous Iqbal, but a poet skilled in the art of the ghazal. They were standing on the mound of the city Nicaea, the city built by Alexander the Great on the field of his victory over Porus in the fourth century B.C.

"It is important to help people. That is why I became a bail bondsman. Did I ever tell you my story?"

Matthew had heard the story quite a few times, but since he knew that Iqbal had once again got him out of jail, thought he had better go along with the ritual. Maybe Iqbal was trying to tell him something.

"I knew that I had to make some money. Without money

you are powerless, you cannot help your people. You cannot further the good in the world. Men are able to do good in proportion to their power. So I was looking for a job. My brother, who had also come to America, was studying to be a lawyer. He will be a great help to the Aga Khan Development Network, which is helping us overcome the Texas laws which forbid our funeral customs. I went to the office of a bail bondsman when the boss was not around. I walked in and introduced myself to the man behind the counter. His office was small and dirty. I pulled out a hundred-dollar bill and I ripped it in two. I gave him half. 'You may have the other half if you show me the boss's office.' 'I cannot do that,' he said. 'Then you will not have this,' I said. So he showed the boss's office. It was big and clean and had a large-screen TV and an aquarium with neon fish. Tetras, I believe they are called. So I knew the boss made a great deal of money. I know that even though the business was located in a poor part of town, he spent his time away from the ugliness. He could deal with whom he wanted—that is why his office was far in the back of the building, protected by fine locks and dedicated men. So I discovered what I would need to do to be the boss."

Matthew thought, If I were to pick out a job, it would be by reading about it. That's my trouble. He had gotten scuffed up in the holding cell that night, when the police mentioned to the mainly black population that he was there for attacking a black man on the john in his own business. A big ugly man, whom Matthew saw as an ape, had threatened to sodomize him, and probably would have if a guard hadn't walked by. Matthew smelled bad, he had not been able to eat or sleep, and he was facing a charge of assault. He needed a lawyer, but what he really needed was a clue. Iqbal was still talking. "The Ismailis in Tajikistan are in much more dire straits than the Tibetans, but of course, since they're Muslim, they don't get the press. Or the food. Am I boring you, Matthew?"

"No, not at all. I am a little tired."

"Of course attacking one of our friends is no doubt a tiring endeavor. Soon a cab will come to take you home."

Matthew wanted to hit him. Matthew wanted to sleep. Matthew said, "Have you enjoyed being a bail bondsman?"

"Of course. It is very important in life to discover one's true condition. This is very hard. Some people do this by traveling and letting foreign cultures abduct them. Others by acting in the theater—trying on all of Shakespeare's masks will teach you very much. But if you cannot do these things, you must find a job that will allow you to see the fates and dramas of as many of your fellow men as possible. You may work in a hospital. Or in an airport. I work here. Everyone I see is cut open so that I may examine them in their direst needs. Have you ever read Mishima? He says that you should never judge a man or an apple until you have cut into them. This is a fair, but brutal-sounding, observation. I have seen many apples, truly they are the Fruit of the Tree of Good and Evil. Many apples have sat where you sit."

"And what sort of an apple am I?"

"You are a small apple, but not as yet a rotten one."

"How would you know if I am rotten?"

"You would lose your shape as you sat in the chair. You would talk too much about what had just happened to you in the cell. You are thinking of what you need to do. That is very hard."

"But you are mad that I attacked Stephen Kozalla."

"Yes. So what? That I am angry you have lost your reason and hurt a friend doesn't lessen my observation of you, nor my awareness of your virtues."

"So what do I need to do to become a big apple?"

"Stop reacting and start acting. The first time you were here, it was because of your wife's killer. But you didn't plan your killing, you just tried to kill the guy. You almost committed suicide by cop that night. You probably wanted to, on some level. This is natural. Loss of the beloved is the greatest of all losses, so it put you in a base state. Grief is the second basest state you can be in. Fear is of course the most base state for a human being. So you had tried to die, and you had the whiteness of a corpse. The second time you were here for theft. What was it that bothered you so greatly that you would leave the home you huddled in after Haidee's death? Were you stealing a rare potion that could restore health? Were you a beggar man stealing a loaf of bread? No, you were stealing a book because you thought the man that bought it wasn't worthy of it. You were righteous, which is the third most base state. Did you think after the auction as to what you were doing? No, you thought the rich man was stupid because he came from Dallas. There was no thought about what was right. And now, you were delusional in the thralls of fantasy like the schoolboy who fantasizes he will save his sweetheart from a black-clad robber who jumps from behind a bush. This is the fourth worst form of baseness. It is more noble than the rest because you are reacting to a product of your own mind, rather then the raw world like an animal. But if you refine your mind, then you will be reacting with products that are worthwhile. You must perform that alchemy so that your mind becomes worthwhile."

Every bit of this had passed in one ear and out the other. Matthew was thinking about his second arrest.

There had been an auction. It had been six months after Haidee's murder. He had attended it for the same reasons that he gave the party eighteen months later. It was going to galvanize him out of his depression, lightning to the thing on the slab.

There had been a few people. Mainly high-powered book dealers and some collectors that he knew. It was a sort of secret thing. No signs, no notices. You had to know someone to get in. It was held in a hotel room in a downtown hotel. He remembered looking at the pink granite capitol dome just before he walked into the hotel, past its chlorine-scented indoor fountain, and into the room.

There had been a man from Dallas. Stanley Jordan, a slightly fat white guy with thinning hair that looked like copper wires dragged across his shiny pate. He was ill at ease. His wife had brought him. She was the sister of one of the collectors. Matthew had felt sorry for the guy. He so clearly didn't want to be there. It was a Sunday, he was missing a Cowboys game. He said something to Matthew about Troy Aikman, and Matthew thought he was one of the collectors he didn't know by name. Matthew nodded, and then learned that the Cowboys spring camp had been in Austin at the charming St. Edwards University in the south of the city. They are a Big Deal for Austin, like bringing MTV on the women's rugby fields. Matthew nodded some more, wishing that he had stayed home.

Then the guy asked Matthew about the books for sale.

Matthew had a lot to say. Normally he wouldn't talk this freely before an auction. You don't want to show your hand. But Matthew hadn't talked much in six months and the slightest social pinprick caused the words to flow like water from a balloon. In addition to the respectable Texana and more widely acceptable collectible books, there was a selection of late-nineteenth- and early-twentieth-century fantastic books, Harry Stephen Keeler, Cassutto, Heinz Evers, Guy Endore, but what Matthew wanted was *The Mystery of Choice* by Robert W. Chambers. Chambers was an ex-pat portrait painter in decadent Paris (try saying that three times fast). He did some minor espionage that did set up the conflict we call World War I. He wrote a lot of slightly weird very lightweight romance and three pretty spooky books. The best known is *The King in Yellow*, a series of stories about the effect a certain horrible play called *The King in Yellow* has on people.

Very small sections of the play are quoted, with ominous references to a sigil or glyph whose power of producing certain revelations is so strong it makes men mad, and even affects the structure of reality around the glyph. The glyph is called the Yellow Sign. *The King in Yellow* had a few queer remanifestations. When Howard Phillips Lovecraft encountered it, he changed his own fictional book the dread *Necronomicon* to resemble Chambers's work. Raymond Chandler wrote a strange homage to the book called "The King in Yellow" about a corpse of a jazz magician clothed in the fateful color. But even stranger, a woman named Mary Jones chose the name for her daughter, Cassilda, who wound up marrying and divorcing John. Cassilda was the weirdest woman Matthew had ever met, and he always thought that her weird came from her name. Matthew pattered on about *The King in Yellow*, how Lovecraft's copy came to belong to a man named Forrest Ackerman, who in turn . . .

Finally Stanley interrupted him and asked what this had to do with *The Mystery of Choice*, which was up for auction. Matthew explained that Lovecraft had written an essay about horror books, and that he had said great things about *The King in Yellow*, *The Slayer of Souls*, and *The Mystery of Choice*. The first was easy to get, the others had not been reprinted. So they were valued.

"You ever read it?" asked Stanley.

"No," admitted Matthew.

"You mean nobody knows what's in it?" asked Stanley.

Matthew tried to explain that many people had of course read the book, but that he hadn't and had always wanted to.

"You think it would make you crazy?"

"All books make us a little crazy."

Then Stanley had asked Matthew's advice on building up a collection. Matthew gave a sound basic strategy illustrating what books he would buy out of the existing sale.

The auction started.

Stanley bought every book that Matthew had suggested. Where Matthew had suggested a price, that was Stanley's bid. If the price got too high, Stanley passed. It was going to be a great collection, but you could collect well if you started with deep pockets. Matthew was planning on how to get this prize fish to the store when *The Mystery of Choice* came up.

It should have gone for eighty or ninety bucks.

Stanley began the bidding at one hundred twenty.

Matthew went to one thirty. Surely this guy that he had helped out so much wasn't going to steal this book from him.

One fifty.

One seventy-five.

Then Stanley said, "Two hundred twenty-five."

Matthew had the money to bid higher, but it was already ridiculous.

He bought some minor items toward the end of the auction.

He got up to leave. It was late.

Stanley walked over to him and said, "Son, I taught you a lesson today. Don't give away information for free. Information is your most precious commodity. To show you what a nice guy I am, the missus and me will buy you dinner."

What Matthew wanted to do was to smash the guy's face. What Matthew decided to do was to go along to dinner—listen to the fatherly lecture, and then (a) get the guy in his bookstore, where he would sell him some overpriced crap and (b) get him to lend the book to Matthew so that he could now have the experience of reading *The Mystery of Choice*, which seemed likely to hold the answers to all of life's problems.

They ate in the hotel restaurant.

The wife was ashamed of her husband's loudness. He had made his pile selling fertilizer. This is why you can't write satire. She thought it must be wonderful to work in a bookstore. Oh, to *own* a bookstore. They bought art. Art is good.

The man was expansive. Maybe he would get into the book trade. It seemed a matter of knowing what you needed and getting there with the cash first. He could use a guy like Matthew. He was imagining a whole used-book–store empire, spreading the acid tang of old books into the houses of the newly well-to-do. See, Matthew knew how to spot the books, but he just didn't have any business sense. But Stanley had business sense. He could sell culture. How different could it be from fertilizer?

Matthew agreed that he had a point.

Spread culture around, it's what the world needs.

Matthew was thinking about going home and lying on the bed with his clothes on, which is what he did two or three nights a week. Stanley asked him about other culture in town.

Well, Matthew thought, there was that new experimental jazz ensemble at the Isis Room. Yeah, Stanley and the missus should hate that.

"There's a hot new band at the Isis Room on Sixth Street."

"Are you going?" asked the missus.

"No, ma'am. You know us working stiffs, early to bed and early to rise, but it's very cultural."

Stanley wrote his room number on the check, and they rose to leave.

Some change and his room key slithered out of the right leg of Stanley's trousers as he and the missus walked to the door. Matthew picked it up and started after them. Then he looked at the room number on the check that gave a rather meager tip to the waitress. He pocketed the key and he went to the hotel lobby. He saw a powder blue Lincoln roll out of the hotel parking garage taking Stanley cultureward.

He decided that he would simply go upstairs and pick up *The Mystery of Choice*. He was sure that Stanley would never miss it. Afterward he could drop the key in the key drop-off and drive on home. He could even be a magpie and leave one of the books he had bought in its place.

He got a Cabell from his station wagon and went up to the fourth floor.

He went into Stanley's room.

It was a total mess. The beds had been stripped, and the bedding was all over the floor, as were towels and food wrappers, and someone had taken a shit on one of the sheets in front of the TV. The books were in a neat stack next to two suitcases. There was a clean area and a filthy area.

You can do anything, if you can pay for it.

Matthew walked over and picked up the book. He couldn't believe that anybody could live like this. Was the man's home like this, or was it something he did only when he was living as a paying guest?

"If you're looking for trouble, son, you found it."

Stanley and the missus were back. It was obvious that Stanley was one of many Texans who took advantage of the concealed-weapons bill. The gun was no longer concealed and was pointed in Matthew's direction.

Stanley held him at bay while the wife called the desk, who called the cops.

Matthew had said that as he was about to drive home, he thought that Stanley might enjoy the copy of *Jurgen* that he had bought. He carried it up to the room, where he found the door ajar with the key in it. He had just stepped in when the Jordans, having had a fight on some matter of aesthetics, returned suddenly. Matthew thought perhaps he had scared the thief away.

Matthew's lawyer got the whole thing dismissed by getting a statement from the policeman who had picked up Matthew concerning the state of the room. He let it be known that if the case was ever aired then the question of Mr. Jordan's (or who knows, Mrs. Jordan's) shit on the sheets would be a public item. You wouldn't think that a fertilizer seller would be afraid of a little shit, but there you are.

Matthew's lawyer took him aside after that and told him that he would never, ever have anything to do with a nut like Matthew.

As the cab took him home, he was wondering where he would get another lawyer, and how much of his life's history he could hide from him.

11 Kriegspielhaus: Both Kin and Kind

In the mailbox was the usual junk, and a small cream envelope bearing the return address Kriegspielhaus. Matthew slowly made out the name: "War-Game-House."

It was a wedding announcement.

"John L. Reynman and M. Camilla Galen proudly announce the Solemnization of their vows of Love in a wedding ceremony to be held in the Austin Rose Garden (in Zilker Park) on 1:00 Saturday April 5 with a reception to be held at the Cassetto House immediately thereafter. R.S.V.P."

Matthew recalled that April 5 was Booker T. Washington's birthday. He had gone through a real black history phase in an attempt to show his seriousness to Haidee. He had even written a poem about Booker T. Washington:

The Great Booker T. Washington

The great Booker T. Washington
    once said
    that plowing a field has
    as much dignity as writing a poem.
I respect Mr. T. Washington,
    but I suspect that

he gave poets
way too much dignity.
Their appropriate level of shame
For creating the Spell,
the rhyme, the jingle,
the patriotic song
that makes others do their magic . . .

Their appropriate level of Shame
Should be quite high.
Very high indeed.

Let us make war against them.

Even love hadn't redeemed it. There was a phone number on the card, and Matthew decided that he would call it. He needed help outside his circle of his friends, someone that he didn't think had anything to do with Haidee's ashes. John might know a decent lawyer that could get him out of trouble.

"Kriegspielhaus, may I help you?"

It was a woman's voice.

"Hello, yes, is this Camilla Galen?"

"No, Matthew this is Cassilda Jones. How the hell are you?"

"I, uh, I thought you and John were divorced."

"We are. I was never cut out for the wife thing. I'm a scarlet woman through and through. I guess you got our wedding announcement?"

"You mean for John and *Camilla?*"

"Yes, they make a lovely couple. I do hope you'll come. I'm sorry that the announcements went out so late, everyone getting them today will think it's an April Fool joke, but the printer screwed up John's business name, which by the way I think sucks because I think that everyone will think he is designing Nazi war games or something. But John wanted the name to be perfect, so everything is screwy. I just heard from your mother that she's coming up with her boyfriend."

"Mom has a boyfriend?"

"Oh, you have been out of the loop. I had heard from John that you had pretty much vanished after what happened to Haidee. I was splitsville from John then, I didn't even know about it till John came up to Amarillo last year during his little adventure, I figured it was too late to send a card, as if a card, a mere set of words, would have any value for a human life. I've been meaning to paint her for you. A portrait if you would like. I don't know why but she has been in my dreams a great deal lately. I see her under moonlight—that would be her proper element, don't you think? Oh, I know you would like her during one of your fireworks shows running back and forth to load the cannons while you touched them off—her face lit by the different colors of lights burning in the sky—but I think that's too much, that would be like a mask rather than Haidee. What do you think?"

"I think a portrait would be nice. Is John there?"

"No, he's off at the Perry Castaneda Library researching for this game he's going to do. You know how he is, he has to overresearch everything. He got into game design because it lets him work his butt off in libraries. Paul and Saul are the same way about the law. I wonder sometimes if something happened to Elaine, if she was scared by a giant bottle of ink. I mean we know some weird things did happen to Herman."

"What weird things?"

"Well, I had better let John tell you. It's his story and I know how you Reynmen are—all those arguments between you and John and Elaine about who would get to tell a story. Jesus."

"I wanted to call John because I need help."

"Good. He's at a time in his development where he says he needs to help somebody. He said that he was expecting someone to show up with Need. I'm glad it's you. I always liked you a lot, and I want to do this painting for you of Haidee in the moonlight. You know the Roman goddess Diana would often look into windows. She was the goddess of moonlight, and persons looking out at her would dream that they could caress moonlight, holding her gazelle-like beauty that moves swift as a shadow, so they would run outside to hold her but their arms would find nothing. It would be better to see her looking out of a window, so that if you went inside you could hold her since she couldn't flee. Maybe I'll paint Haidee inside a window frame, or paint her on glass. Oh, I do so want to do this, I hope you can help me and that John can help you."

"Yeah, I think that sounds good. What I really wanted to ask John about was if he knew a good lawyer."

"Oh, that's easy. Camilla is a lawyer. She's at Dewey, Bricklayer, Crow, and Galen."

"Can she handle criminal stuff?"

"Oh, sure, she took care of John when he found that corpse in his house."

"John found a corpse in his house?"

"Yes, but I think on the whole it was a life-enhancing experience for him. It got us back together."

"I thought he was with Camilla."

"He's going to marry Camilla, they'll have a nice little marriage with a white picket fence, I mean that metaphorically, I think when he sells the house he's looking for a place with a rock wall, he told me that your home in Amarillo had a rock wall and that was his favorite thing to play on, he liked to climb up it and peer over at the Hahns' house, and pretend he was in some ancient castle watching for the enemy troop. I should do a painting of that for him. Half of it would be the rock wall and half an attack army of skeletons in tarnished armor. No, I would actually make the bottom half of the painting be the rock wall and the top half the army of the damned."

"I thought you did writing."

"Well, I taught writing. I've had a few things published and so forth, but your mom took this course in painting, and she turned me on to it, and I'm not half bad. Well actually I had a show here in Austin just before South by Southwest. I started to come to your thing, your reading with Hull. I've always wanted to do book covers, but I don't know how, and I thought I would come and ask Hull, but I thought that would be using you, and I didn't want to start our new relationship off with using you. I am at a stage in my development that is 'one hand washes another.' You don't know how to do book-cover art, do you?"

"Well, you mean how the publisher picks the artist and so forth, not really. No. I can tell you a lot about certain artists, particularly mystery and SF covers."

"If I dropped by the New Atlantis could you show me some of your favorite covers? Maybe they could give me some ideas."

"Sure. I—"

"Oh, I'm sorry. You're in trouble and I'm trying to get you to show me book covers. Have you done something weird again?"

"Well, yes."

"It's that Reynman blood, I tell you. You guys can't help it. I heard about your troubles from John last fall."

"John has kept track of me?"

Somehow this notion filled him with an instant wash of relief. In the midst of his weariness it seemed that he had a secret witness. Somehow that was very important, even if the witness couldn't help him very much.

"Well, of course. He's been Elaine's spy on you through the years. She wants to know everything going on, she needs to know about every layer of action as it is laid down."

"So Mom cares, too."

"Blood always cares. It may not love, although that's the best thing in the world, but it always cares. It has the capacity to know the real you. That's why I'm dreaming of Haidee."

"But Haidee isn't a blood relative of yours."

"She loved you, you are John's brother, I was his wife and now I'm his mistress, of course there's a blood bond. Don't get lost in DNA trails. That's important, but it's important for other reasons."

"When did you start dreaming of Haidee—I mean, if you know?"

"I know exactly. I keep a dream diary. I used to keep it to help out with writing. I would make these weird short stories where I would take the plot line of a classic story like James Joyce's 'The Dead' and the story of whatever was going on in my life—like my affair with Mason—and one of my dreams and then I would mix them together. In retrospect they all sucked. But using the images from my dreams for my art has worked really well."

"Yes, you were going to tell me when you started dreaming of Haidee."

"I've had too much coffee this afternoon. It's piñon coffee, coffee with piñon nuts. It's the best. It was the night of the Hull thing. I guess it was because I saw that poster announcing his reading and I was thinking of you and her, and then I had this dream about her."

"What was the dream?"

"I dreamt that she was wandering through that part of the city near downtown. Say over on Eleventh and Nueces—where all the old homes have been made into lawyers' offices. I could see her illuminated by a moonlight tower. Someone was after her somehow. I couldn't tell who, some man I think. He was going to pour something on her. She kept running, till she fell into a rabbit hole. Then a fire burned there."

"You said you've been dreaming. What were the other dreams like?"

"The other dreams were similar if not the same. In some she seems really scared, in others she is totally amused by this fellow's attempt to chase her. It's not every night or anything."

"That's very interesting. Do you put much stock in dreams?"

"I don't except as raw material, you know for the paintings, but John does sometimes. He says that 'dreams are preparations for travel.' He thinks we dream so that we get stirred enough to take trips. He thinks that if mankind lacked the power to dream we would all still be in Olduvai Gorge."

"So his theory would be that you are fixing to travel somewhere that Haidee is, I mean that somehow the dream portends you're going somewhere?"

"Not like that. The dream will open certain associations in me that will become a need to travel somewhere. But that's John's theory. He also thinks that war-gaming would save the world."

"So did H. G. Wells."

"Yes, I know, I've heard the theory enough. Wells also thought that if we fucked more often, that would save the planet."

"I thought you would sort of go for that, what with being a scarlet woman and so forth."

"Look, sweetie, sex is great, but it doesn't save anything. We might all have bigger smiles all the time if we fucked more often, but people would still fight. It's because they are people. To get the most out of being human you have to accept the negative and the positive. In fact, coming up with the right blend of both may save yourself, in my not so humble opinion."

"Did John pick the name of his company because he wanted to save the world?"

"No, John went through this Crowley phase. Magick with a *K* because *K* is the eleventh letter of both the modern English and the Hebrew alphabets. It is supposed to denote magic generally. He has all these theories about *S* sounds, *Z* sounds, *K* sounds, *R* sounds, and *L* sounds. Oh, it's also the beginning of the word *kestis*. The Greek word for 'pussy'. Please don't ask him about it in front of me. I will pull my red-dyed hair out by its black roots if I have to hear it again."

"I notice he's involved with two women whose names start with *K* sounds."

"Look, don't start that shit with me. I remember those word games that you and Haidee used to play that none of us understood, or wanted to know about. I don't even like Scrabble. It's another nutty thing in the Reynman line, like your dad and crosswords."

"OK—oops, there's another *K*. I mean, tell John I called."

"Well, hey, are you going to the wedding?"

"I don't have a gift for them. What do they need?"

"They need a decent can opener. They've got this electric number that drops the can halfway through opening which throws the soup on the counter, so they use a crappy little handheld device that is carpal tunnel in the making if you want my opinion."

"I can get them a can opener. I'll be at the wedding. But don't tell Mom. I think I'm over my issues with her enough to be there, but if I become a coward in the next four days, I don't want her disappointed."

"OK, I won't tell her. I think it would be good for her to see you, and I think it would be good for you to see her if you're about to be in some sort of trouble. Seeing your past walking around can help you get through all sorts of issues."

"Like what?"

"Well, the first thing is that it reminds you of how much

you have already got through. Secondly, it reminds you how weird life is—all the strange twists and turns you had to go through to get where you are now. This is very important because it can make you open your eyes to the strange twists and turns that you're about to go through. It is sometimes very good to be very awake before you have to act. Of course at the moment of action, as Nietzsche says, you have to forget in order to be able to Do, because the action must displace the thought."

"You quote Nietzsche now?"

"Well, you know what they say, what does not kill us makes us quote Nietzsche."

"That would be a great bumper sticker."

"Actually John went through this Nietzsche phase, every few minutes another damn aphorism. I mean some of them were very wise, but you can only listen to so many aphorisms till you get aphorism fever, what with the sniffing and nose blowing and the maxims and so forth."

"Then the apothegms."

"And then the adages and the farting."

"The farting?"

"You can't make wisdom without breaking wind."

"On that note, let us part."

"Hey, Matthew, it's been good to hear from you. I hope everything works out for you."

"You too."

"Bye."

"Good-bye."

He put the phone down. He should go in to work. If John could fix him up with this lawyer, things would be great. Of course John might think too highly of her since she would be his wife in four days, yet it might take a family lawyer to be able to put up with the weirdness.

The phone rang, and he assumed that it was Cassilda calling back with more gay banter. He remembered that John had said she was bisexual.

"Hello, Matthew?"

It was Rodger Falconer.

"Yes, Rodger?"

"Did you do anything that would piss off gay people of color?"

"Maybe, why?"

"They're picketing your store."

"I see. What kind of picketing?"

" 'Whyte literature denies dark lavender. This store is friendly to attacking dark gay men. Mental instability runs rampant here.' It looks like about four men and a woman. Or maybe it's five men. They're walking around in front of the store."

"Could you tell me if they're saying anything?"

"Nope."

"How close did you drive by?"

"I didn't drive by, Heidi spotted it on TV. There seems to be some kind of white men's alliance that has taken up your side in this thing. White Men Against Pornography."

"Oh God. I hate those guys. They got ticked off by a bookstore having Doug Rice's *Blood of a Mugwump* last year and they marched for days. If they're on my side, I've just lost half my friends in the book trade. I had better get down there and scare them off somehow."

"Probably no need to hurry. Night will come soon enough, and maybe you can put up some signs of your own in the morning."

"Yeah, I can get a good night's sleep."

He hung up the phone.

It rang instantly.

The *Austin American Statesman* wanted to talk to him

about his views on gay men of color and the question of literary censorship.

He hung up the phone.

It rang again.

He unplugged it, grabbed some clothes, and left for a motel.

It was not a nice night.

12 Lamed in the Notebook

"Thanks for being here," said Matthew.

"What's a brother for?" asked John. "Do you have to keep the store open?'

"Well, I do need to work over the books in the warehouse pretty bad, but I want to make a stand."

"I'm surprised they are still at it," said John.

"It's only been a few days," said Matthew. "But it seems longer."

Outside of the New Atlantis they could hear the picketers across the street. The police had told them they couldn't block the doorway to the store, so they marched in front of the bank where Selma worked—carefully not blocking its entrance either. Back and forth. Back and forth. They would yell at potential customers that the store wasn't gay-friendly or black-friendly, or friendly to people of color. This kept most customers out. Selma had come, and Rodger Falconer, and Anthony O'Callaghan, and Norman. There were others that had come as well. People who really weren't black-friendly, or gay-friendly, or friendly to people of color. They were disappointed at the lack of writing that fit their need for constant reinforcement of views the world wisely denies as the millennium hastens.

John had smiled at one of the men, a bearded bear of a man, and the guy had a look of recognition and zipped out of the store.

"What's the deal there?" asked Matthew.

"Some years ago that guy was in People Against Pornography," said John.

"Yeah," said Matthew. "I remember PAP."

"They were picketing that little gay bookstore on Lamar, not too far from here. I drove by and saw their 'Honk if you hate Homos' signs and then pulled my pickup into the parking lot. I went up to the fellow that just left and said in the most shocked tones I could muster, 'You mean there's a gay bookstore here?' 'Yes,' he told me. 'Great,' I said, 'I've been looking all over town for one.' Then I went in and I bought maybe a postcard or something but I asked for them to wrap it up like I had bought something really big, so I could walk out of the store looking like I had dropped a fortune. I told them what I had said and they were getting on the phone to call some of their friends to pull a similar stunt. On the way out I winked at the big man and pulled off. It was the last PAP antibook attack I ever saw in town. I don't know if I got them, but I love to take the damn credit."

"That's a great story."

"Life's the process of acquiring great stories, tales of your travels that you share with other travelers."

"Yeah? Well how would you tell the story out there?"

"Well, first off, I'm not out there. I'm in here taking the day off to help out my brother. So I could tell the story as a family saga, the thing we dreamed we would have to tell if we hadn't wound up with different lives—you and I here and Saul and Paul in Washington. But that's not that great of a story. It's too

Disney Channel. But I would try for something light. What's going on there is a petrification, your friendship for Mr. What-is-his-name?"

"Kozalla."

"Kozalla is petrifying because of your paranoia. Not an uncommon result of negative magic, so I would fight it with a story full of 'weightless intelligence.' Perseus is your hero. He avoided the petrification of the Medusa's stare by traveling on sandals of lightness, lighter than air and cloud."

"Calvino."

"The guy's name is Calvino? I thought you said it was Kozalla."

"No, your quote about Perseus, it comes from Calvino."

"Really? I heard it on the 'Dillo the other day when I had to go to jury duty. The guy didn't attribute it so I thought it would be safe to steal. If you can't trust your fellow jurors-to-be, who can you trust?"

The shadow of someone came to the door, the abusive yelling came from across the street, and the shadow moved on.

"If I could only apologize to Steve," said Matthew.

"Have you tried?" asked John.

"I can't get him by phone."

"Well, take out an ad. Explain what you thought you were doing."

"But I don't want to do that. I don't want people to know that I am looking for my wife's ashes."

"You afraid of how crazy that sounds? At this point you can give up worrying about sounding crazy. You might make that into a selling point later. You could rename the store Crazy Eddy's Used Books."

"Why not Crazy Matthew's?"

"Doesn't have the same ring," said John.

Matthew said, "I don't want people to know I'm looking for Haidee's ashes so I can surprise the guy who took them. I have to hunt them down."

"You do know that they're only ashes, don't you? That it's not the same thing as her? It's just some calcined salts."

"It's not the ashes at all that I need, it is the promise. When we shot our last fireworks show in Doublesign, I promised that we would both be made into ashes, then ground down, and fired off together. It was a beautiful idea. Ideas are worth fighting for even if no one else understands why you fight."

"I'll buy that. If we don't infuse ideas into us so that we have meaning, then all of our journeys are useless; we might as well just stay home. What's your plan for tracking the guy down?"

"Well, I don't have much of a plan so far. I keep thinking that one of the people will betray themselves by attitude."

"And then what? Do you think that you will suddenly sense the guilt and then say something like, 'I know you have my wife's ashes, haul them over here!' and they'll say, 'It's a fair cop, but society is to blame'?"

"All right, I see a tiny flaw in my thinking. I had actually been picturing one of the scenes out of those Charlie Chan movies—I would get everybody in a room and sort of pace around and then with a subtle piece of misdirection and cutting off the light, get a confession."

The light went off in the store.

"What the fuck was that?" yelled Matthew.

"Well, either you have failed to pay your bill, one of the protesters turned off your power, or one of us is about to confess. Since I didn't do it and I don't want to find that some hitherto unknown multiple personality of yours did, I suggest we call it a day and drive home."

Matthew locked up the shop.

People across the way cheered. Matthew walked behind the shop and flipped the power back on, refitting the flimsy lock that someone had cut through.

At least no one seemed to be picketing Matthew at his house.

But someone had driven his car up across the yard.

The front door was open.

Someone had taken a shit on the front floor. For a moment Matthew wondered if Stanley had shown up to wreak vengeance. Why not all the people in his life? The college roommate that hated him, the guy who used to rent the store next door, his cousin Kevin? They could all appear—only hope and denial has been holding them back all these years.

John darted past him into the house, and suddenly he realized that he might not be looking at a tableau like before, but in fact there could be somebody waiting here. He ran in as well. John had pulled out a handgun—like many Texans he had a concealed-weapons permit.

The jack-o'-lantern candy jar was shattered.

His phone had been pulled out by the wires.

He ran into the kitchen, where bowls were busted on the yellowing linoleum.

The whole house was trashed.

There was a note on his desk, next to the monitor of the Mac where he kept his inventory.

"I am not going to wait. Waiting is silly."

It was signed, "William."

There was a notebook on the desk. A purple spiral notebook with half the pages torn out. It did not belong to Matthew. He noted it and ran on.

A voice from outside told them to stop what they were doing and come out with their hands up. John holstered the gun and they walked to the door. A police car was outside. One of Matthew's neighbors, the woman with the cats, was yelling at the police that it was OK, that these two men had just arrived. The guy who had made all the noise was gone. He had driven off.

The police were running up asking for IDs and explanations and so was Matthew and the neighbor lady was talking about first she thought that someone had had an accident with china, then she thought she heard a shot, and the police were wanting to know who John was and why they were home in the middle of the day and was anything missing, and they would get a team here to do fingerprints, and more people started coming and they took the note and pieces of glass and porcelain and Matthew swept up and John was calling his women and they came with falling of night.

Cassilda brought tacos. Egg and cheese, beef, bean and cheese, cheese and potato, and lots of mild sauce.

John kept pacing around.

Looking at the front door and the back door, he said, "You know, he had to have a key to your house."

"How do you know?"

"Well, I can't tell anything has been forced open, or tampered with. Pity Mrs. Moynihan didn't see him enter," said John.

"Or catch the license plate number of the car. What's wrong with people, they not watch television?" asked Cassilda.

Matthew went into his office and looked at the shot computer monitor.

"He killed my computer."

Then he picked up the notebook. Half of it was gone. Torn out, but a sentence on the first page of the remaining text caught his eye. *I am continually distracted from the Great Work by my desire to tell Matthew Reynman of my plans.*

Above the first sentence was a big letter, Hebrew, Matthew thought. He showed it to John.

"It's a lamed. The first letter in Levi or Leviathan."

Matthew looked through the book. There were eleven sections remaining, each topped with a letter of the Hebrew alphabet. The first four sections were in English; the last seven were written in an outlandish script that suggested snakes and hooks and almost seemed to crawl off the page. He showed it to John, who shrugged; Cassilda and Camilla had no clue.

"Should I give it to the police?" asked Matthew.

"Well, after you read it," said John.

"After you photocopy it," said Cassilda. "Those glyphs are neat. I bet they were painted first, not done in cheap ballpoint pen like there."

"I have a photocopy machine at my office," said Camilla.

ל

I am continually distracted from the Great Work by my desire to tell Matthew Reynman of my plans. I realize that this small voice of ego, no doubt born of countless Saturday matinees where Fu Manchu tells Wayland Smith his plans.

I have been a minor thief for years, stealing other men's crumbs, but now I know that I have completely stepped into the Abyss, there is no going back now. I get a huge hard-on because of the sheer excitement. Every time that I realize that I am Doing my Dream, that this is it, that it is here and now, I get such a huge rush. (Pardon the Madison Avenue cliché.)

My money situation is pretty grim. Everything I've saved up over the years is being spent like water. I know that you have to use gold to get gold, but the fact that I'm not doing the day-to-day grind anymore makes me a little scared.

I feel like I did when I stole Playboys *from the newspaper store in Binghamton. I was so scared that Dad would find out. Now God is Dad, if I believed in God—by the time this is done, I will be God.*

Lamed. Lamed. Lovely Life, Lovely Lust. Leopards and Litmus. I will test her acids, they will make me pure. When I first studied the Art, I thought that acidic taste that some women give off just before they come was the alkahest. If I could just eat women enough, I would surely be immortal, refined to pure gold. It made my first wife happy, but then she became a lesbian. Lovely Lesbians Lovingly Licking Luscious Lips. Lamed. Lamed. Lilith. That's what I want, an equal not an Eve. But Eve is a tad more interesting, since she was made from living flesh, her name is "Hawwah" = Living, from the verb "Haya" "to live." I could call her "Eve," but that Worked out badly for JHWH, even a thief like me knows better than to steal what does not work. Lakes of Life, Locks and Love, Lissome Lusts of Devildom! I Long to Unlock thee!

LLLLLLLLLL!

I am continually distracted from the Great Work by my desire to tell Matthew Reynman of my plans. I realize that this small voice of ego, no doubt born of countless Saturday matinees where the big-brained villain gloats over the hero, and explains the nature of his nefarious scheme to destroy the earth and its hapless inhabitants in great detail. Of course I am not the villain, in fact I have done nothing to the real Matthew Reynman, although I doubt that he would agree. I do, however, value his intelligence, and my chief fault in the world is the desire for people to think me clever. I could have real riches and power in the world if it were not for that, and after all I entered into this path to have women and gold. Well, women and gold and knowledge. It's that last element that fucks me up.

I will write my fantasy down in order to exorcise myself of it. I see it as happening in one of two ways. It is sad that I have so little control of my thoughts even at this late stage of my Initiation. I find myself thinking about this as much as four or five times a day. Anyway, method number one would be to write him a letter (or even give him parts of this notebook HA), so that when I had moved from Austin to the final state for the GW I would be safe from any last-minute thoughts of derring-do. I have long ago ceased to worry about the involvement of the police in this matter. They wouldn't believe a man who says his wife's ashes are gone, for Christ's sake. I could write him a letter. Best to deliver it in some very mysterioso way—perhaps have it concealed in the doorway of that pathetic little bookstore he has given his life to, so that one day when he slams the door, bang! down it will fall on his head. The other method, which becomes a true daydream and therefore an actual impediment to the Work, would be to capture him and take him to some rural location and tell him what I am going to do with his wife's ashes. Perhaps he would even see the great good that would come from such an action and become my assistant. I will really need an assistant for the final part. I've come to accept that now. I had thought of trying to do it all alone, but I am going to have to have somebody to run down to the convenience store and buy bread and lunch meat and so forth, while I sit with the athanor. I saw what happened when Algis didn't have an assistant. That shouldn't have happened to my worst enemy. Well, maybe my worst.

I would kidnap him at night. It's staying light longer now, and the wildflowers are beginning to bloom, but I notice that Matthew's habit is to stay down at the store till 9:00 every night. I could stand in the alley where he parks, tap him with a sap, load him into my car. No, I guess into his station wagon, my car isn't really up to carrying bodies. Yet another sign that I am not a criminal mastermind. I'd need to cuff him, and off we would go to some moonlit location that was sufficiently dramatic. There, when he came to sitting in a chair that I would provide for the occasion, I would tell him about the Work, and explain it till I get his blessing. Of course since this is fantasy he always agrees in the end.

In reality, I don't think he would be as receptive. He could never let go of her. In fact, his mind holds her too tightly now, he has made her perfect in her death. All of her flaws, all of her weaknesses, all those little things that used to bug the hell out of him, have been released. This is what I'm counting on. As long as he does have a perfect picture of her I can do my Work. I can bring the picture alive. It will be the greatest alchemy done in modern times.

I not only have something better than mud to work with, as JHWH had for Adam, or Flesh, as for Eve, but I have dreams (and a few ounces of essential saltes).

I have not yet found the perfect site and time for her resurrection. A variety of places suggest themselves to me, many far out of the reach of my deflating pocketbook. I know that not only will I have to buy the site, I will have to buy some protection. There might be sights or smells or sounds that would attract the curious neighbor.

A completely rural site has certain advantages. I thought of the Bastrop area with its Lost Pines, take one of those little roads near the medical research park. God knows no one would question an odd smell or flash of light there. But I am a little leery that whatever the hell it is they are doing might not mix well with what I am doing, and I don't know if I want that to be the first sight that greets her eyes.

Obtaining the tinctures and the vessel have proven a bit harder than I had expected. This is due to my laziness—I wish I could use the self-comforting idea that the "forces of the universe" are against me, which is the idea that keeps magicians in their slough of laziness. I had spotted the perfect vessel at a charity store months ago. Since I couldn't imagine anyone buying something of that size and shape, I did not obtain it. Of course back then performing this Work was only a theoretical idea, in case the opportunity ever presented itself. And it could have taken other forms of more Frankenstein-like nature.

The tinctures are another matter. I have tried some experiments with homeopathic waters of various flavors, or perhaps I should say various lacks-of-flavor, with rather pallid results. I am therefore going to have to brew my own extracts from the local wildflowers. Now such things as bluebonnets and Indian paintbrushes are not in the old manuals, but I believe it is what the flower Symbolizes rather than its chemical properties that matter. This is not a matter of Science but of Art.

I wonder if there is any way for me to find out what her favorite flowers were. Maybe I could manipulate him to plant a memorial garden for her and then he could tell me what flowers she loved. It will be very important to capture her attention early on. I have to have the correct Door for her to walk through.

I am bothered by her preference for white boyfriends—I

wonder if Matthew knew that he was not the first?—of a certain imaginative/educated type; it might signal a weakness in self-image. She might have wanted to collect a certain power that way. Of course her re-creation in Matthew's mind will probably end any weaknesses of that sort, but I must always remember that they came from very different backgrounds, and despite their obvious love for one another they may very well have never truly communicated. I must consider whether this is a good or bad thing, and if I need to exert certain controls over the finished product. I will rack my brains to see if I can come up with certain practical experiments that I can do ahead of time. If I could find the right social stage I might be able to manipulate certain people into performing the pageant that would give me the answers, but that sort of social/magical work takes time and I believe I had better work on the matter at hand while so many things appear favorable. Otherwise I will be snared by the Velcro of life, getting a new dishwasher, renewing my driver's license, all the little pieces of mundania that trap us and keep us from being magicians. Those tiny matters are always at hand, and in the end they win by making old men of us all.

It is only our magic that we use to hold old age at bay, the true moments when we don't act as men but as gods. But if I don't conquer my problem with fantasy, I will miss the great moment that might just be ahead.

13 Mom at the Wedding

The slight fog in the morning air carried the smells of roses and bluebonnets, Haidee's favorite flowers, to Matthew. She had loved the rose garden at Zilker Park in the spring, and she would have loved to be at John's wedding, even if she would have found the circumstances a trifle bizarre.

Cassilda Jones wore a black leather miniskirt and matching top, and busied herself kissing John and Camilla, who was wearing a rather conservative white wedding gown edged in lavender. John was in a tux. Most of his gamer buds were in semigrungy gear. Mom, Elaine Reynman, was in a purple polyester pantsuit that probably had not been in fashion (even in Amarillo) when Dad died. Mom's *boyfriend* Henry or Harry or something was in a lemon yellow leisure suit and panama hat. The minister wore a gray opalescent robe that looked like a *Star Trek* reject, and this intense bald-headed photographer was in all black. Mom walked over to Matthew. He had been dreading this.

"So I see you came to your brother's wedding. He didn't think you would come."

"I have no trouble with John."

"So you're still mad at me."

"Yeah, I guess I am still mad at you."

"That's been sixteen years. That was me right when Herman died."

"You've had a lot of time to apologize."

"Everyone has lots of time to apologize, everyone else has lots of time to listen to apologies that never come. Nobody has time to just get on living."

"What's that, *Reader's Digest* philosophy?"

"I didn't come over to exchange barbs with you. I came over to thank you for coming, so I could see you."

"You're welcome."

"John says you're in trouble."

"John is probably right."

"If there's anything I can do, let me know. I'm not interested in apologies, but I am interested in seeing my kids live and be happy."

A sort of spacy flute music began to fill the air. Matthew couldn't spot the source.

The minister, she was some kind of Univers—no damn John had said, some off-brand religion—struck a chime bar and then began to speak:

"Let us open our eyes, our ears, and our hearts, for we are come to witness a special act of Creation and magic, the like of which has never been seen before nor will be seen hence, for it comes from the hearts of those before me. It will transform them and make them as living jewels bonded by veins of pulsing gold. We cannot add to the sacredness of this moment, but we can see that it is witnessed and marveled at across the expanses of space and time.

"At this moment our eyes become the eyes of Love, Herself, and her essence pours through us into the sweet-smelling air of this garden and we are lifted up, empowered and prepared to hear your holy vows.

"The mysteries of love, of desire, of fear, and of will are seen within you. Call them forth that you may make the bond between you stronger than stone, lighter than air, more changing than the ocean, hotter than the flames men may kindle.

"Do you Camilla Galen say to all who may hear that this is your choice of man, cast in the form of your dreams, for you to cherish and teach and be taught by as you roam the vast earth?"

"I so say," said Camilla.

"Do you John B. Reynman say to all who may hear that this is your choice of woman, cast in the form of your dreams, for you to cherish and teach and be taught by as you roam the vast earth?"

"I so say," said John.

"There is another here who holds these in bonds of love, who desires not such a ceremony of bonding. Does she say that she will hold dear what she has seen here, and will work through her heart to make this more perfect?"

"I so say," said Cassilda.

"As every living thing desires completion you have found one another, and give then these rings one to the other, that you send a sign of your love and commitment to work on your love and your selves to all the world, that they may marvel at what you have found."

John and Camilla exchanged rings, kissed, and then embraced Cassilda and kissed her as well.

"We have seen the tying of the threefold knot—Sacred, Beautiful, and Joyful. Our hearts now drink in this moment that we will remember it always and remembering it feel the pang of love at our center. Go into the world, for now you are living jewels, the Crown of your own love."

Everybody applauded and as the happy threesome made their way to their car threw birdseed.

The reception was at the Cassetto House, an elegant Victorian building downtown. Matthew doubted that John could afford to rent it; probably Mom had done so.

There was cake, and a little buffet spread, and punch. The photographer brought silvered almonds, Matthew's favorite. He was talking to one of John's fellow game writers; the guy was working on an article on the new *Dark Shadows* game cards. Matthew was having a hard time grasping the idea of the card games, and this guy was telling him that if he sold *Magic: The Gathering* at his store it would double his income. John was trying to share running home from school to watch *Dark Shadows* as a kid, when Mom walked up.

"Granny always said you wanted to be Barnabas."

"I guess I can now. Allen here was telling me about this game," said John.

"No, it's not a role-playing game, it's a card game," said Allen. "You don't become a character, you have a card with certain properties like a chess piece."

"Like *Magic?*" asked Elaine. "Henry's grandkids play that. They beat the poogies out of me one afternoon."

"See?" said Allen. "If you carried it, bang, double income. So why did you want to become Barnabas?"

"I don't remember," said Matthew.

"For the women," said Elaine. "Were you old enough to watch the show?"

"No," said Allen.

"Well, Barnabas could just call these women. He would hold his cane"—Elaine illustrated with gesture—"and call these women. John liked the idea so much he carried around his grandmother's measuring ruler. You know, one of those old-fashioned yardsticks. It made Granny mad. She was a seamstress and used the yardstick hemming up the dresses of well-to-do church women. She would tell them, 'My grandson must have it playing vampire again.' They probably thought it was the stake."

"The nice thing about mothers," said Matthew, "is that they can embarrass you even decades after the fact."

"It's our job," said Elaine. "We go to a special school for it."

"Your grandmother seems pretty tolerant to me," said Allen.

"That's a grandmother's job," said Matthew.

"One that I've never had, despite four sons," said Elaine. "You'd think with him"—she pointed toward John, who was being force-fed a piece of wedding cake by Cassilda—"what with two I'd have a great stake."

A young woman arrived at the front door. At the sight of her, all horseplay stopped. She made a beeline for Camilla. She handed Camilla a small gift wrapped in pink shiny paper. However, her eyes didn't have the shine of the other wedding guests', and her language was low and had a snarly sound.

Henry Crawford, the man in the lemon yellow suit, walked over and said (mainly to Elaine), "Carol Galen, Camilla's daughter, doesn't exactly approve of the life of sin here."

"Well hell's bells, I don't approve, but I learned the hard way to keep my mouth shut," said Elaine, and then she looked very embarrassed.

"She's sort of a grandchild," said Matthew.

Allen, sensing tension awkwardly, said, "Why are grandparents tolerant?"

Henry smiled. "It's a story thing. You get so many stories in you while you live. Everywhere you go, everything you do, you get stories, and stories demand to be told. You can't leave earth without telling your stories. So old people need young people—who have this big empty silence inside them—to drop off their stories."

"Then," said Allen, "you don't really need grandchildren. You could use other children."

"Or cats," said Elaine. "Do you still have your cat, Matthew?"

"Yes, ma'am," said Matthew.

"What I do is write my stories down. There's a seniors' literary group in Amarillo meets at noon the first and third Tuesdays of each month. I am going to write down my best stories," said Elaine.

"Mom, that would be great," said John walking up—clearly glad to have left his stepdaughter behind. "Which stories are you going to write about?"

"Well, mainly about the Depression and the war and Herman's brother, of course. Lullaby Reynman, he was the only famous person I know."

"I'm famous, Mom. I am a very well known game designer," said John.

"Except for my son John, a very well known game designer," said Elaine.

"It's true, ma'am," said Allen. "At Atlantis last year, everybody wanted to meet him."

"Atlantis?" asked Elaine.

"It's a local gaming convention," explained John.

"Well, Atlantis and New Atlantis, there's got to be a connection there," said Elaine, proving the hypothesis of some obscure familial algebra.

"I run the New Atlantis bookstore," explained Matthew to a puzzled-looking Allen.

"Oh, do you know Norman Papin?" asked Allen.

"Norman used to work for me," said Matthew.

"Do you know about his good luck?" asked Allen.

"No, what?"

"Well, he just sold a novel proposal to GASA for their Continuing Chaos series. It's a set of books that comes with a die inside that is special for the game. They sell really well because of the die, because you can't get it in a regular set, so it's a great item. The book is called *Lot of Fate*. You know Norman's been trying to sell something like that for years."

"Well, I'm surprised," said Matthew. "Please don't tell him I said this, but he worked on projects for years and never finished any of them."

Allen said, "He's had some kind of breakthrough. He told me that he had finally burned off some of the things that were holding him back."

"How did he do that?" said John.

"He wouldn't tell me. Just hinted it was some kind of secret process, very mysterious, and that if he got it right he would make not only a lot of money writing, but he could sell the secret in Anthony Robbins–like seminars," said Allen.

Matthew said, "Any idea when he had this breakthrough?"

Allen said, "Oh, sure. It was during South by Southwest a few weeks ago."

"How nice for him," said John. "He give you any hints about the 'secret process'?"

"He talked about an episode of *Unsolved Mysteries*. One day an out-of-work father took his sons fishing in a remote forest area where they discovered some stones in the river carved with a variety of arcane symbols. The father and his sons were deeply struck by the signs—What could they mean? Who could have carved them? They went home filled with a sense of mystery and awe. Within a short time business opportunities poured the father's way and the family was soon prosperous. They attributed their good fortune to the power of the stones. Experts from a nearby university determined that the signs were carved recently and were not Amerindian petroglyphs, although they appeared to be imitations of similar designs. The family had come by their turn of good fortune from the stones—but not because of the particular shapes or qualities of the signs themselves, but rather because of the sense of mysterious power which had struck the father and sons upon seeing the stones," said Allen.

"That's very interesting," said Matthew, "mysterious signs."

"And now he's broken into the lucrative field of game writing," said John.

"Hey," said Allen. "It's the midlist these days, that and mysteries by people no one's heard of. Soon all beginning novelists will be doing book four in the novelizations of *Buffy the Vampire Slayer*."

"That was how Joyce started," said Matthew. "Book three in the *Forge the Soul of My Race* series. Who can forget book one, *Tarzan Comes to Ireland?*"

"You laugh," said Allen, "but only because it's funny."

"Well, I'm surprised," said Matthew. "I never thought he would finish anything. I know he started to do several projects over the years."

"He said he had done something that made him feel lucky," said Allen.

"Like what?" asked Matthew.

"He just said it was something mysterious, but he wouldn't tell me. He told me that I couldn't guess in a hundred years," said Allen.

"Well," said John, "I'm glad for Normal—Norman. I met him once at one of Bill's parties," said John.

"The guy that ran Lone Star Gaming?" asked Allen.

"Yeah," said John.

"I did a demo of *Toon* there once," said Allen.

"Sounds like you have a pretty small community," said Henry.

"Books, games, books, and people trying to eke out a living in them," said Matthew. "Here in our little village of Austin we are a simple folk living on the margins of the great world economy, our lives are as precarious as a Fiddler on the Roof!"

"But what keeps us together? What keeps our little lives from falling apart tossed by the ocean of economic factors we cannot nor dare not explain? The answer is one word: Tradition."

Just as John was about to start singing, Carol Galen slapped her mother and ran from the room. It is amazing how the sound of one hand slapping can absorb all noise.

"I think," said Camilla, "that Carol might not be adjusting to our lifestyle too well." She was beginning to cry. John and Cassilda ran over to her.

"So," said Matthew. "Mom, how come you are taking John's lifestyle so well?"

"I have decided to keep my mouth shut. Because if I open it I will say things I mean, and I wasn't brought up to go against things I mean. So I say very little. It's part my fault anyway. When Cassilda moved back to Amarillo, I kept telling her that John was still in love with her. If it hadn't been for my scheming, I'm sure she would have forgotten him. Until his trouble he was pretty forgettable. Now he's got substance, like your father did when he died, but he got it a lot earlier."

"Well, that's very honest."

"It took me a long time to be honest with my kids. I was never honest with my parents. I was honest with Herman only a couple of months before he died. I have often thought that maybe my honesty killed him. That it was the shock of honesty that did him in, the last of a few shocks throughout his lifetime. Only now am I learning about balancing honesty and silence. I know some of my honesty has set things in motion that I don't approve of, or wholly approve of. Once an honest word is said, it can never be called back."

"Well, that is, eh, certainly true," said Allen. "I haven't tried any of the green-bean salad."

"It's great," said Elaine. "It's the kind they make with dried fried onion rings and clam chowder. I know the recipe if you like it."

Allen fled Elaine's symposium, leaving Matthew wondering what one says to one's mother and her boyfriend. *So y'all get it on much?* seemed inappropriate. Matthew saw that Henry was trying to think of something to say, and he liked him for that. There are certain bonds best forged in awkwardness.

Henry said, "You were a friend of John's first wife?"

"They were a couple and we were a couple, and when John's marriage went south, that kinda ended things," said Matthew.

"I know what you mean. When my wife died ten years ago all the people we knew were couples. It was murder getting to know people that didn't come in sets, because every couple was just a reminder. I'm sure you had the same problem."

"Well, a lot of our friends were through the store, and many of them were single for one reason or another."

"That seems to be more of a pattern for your generation. My daughter had a lot of single friends after her divorce."

They talked about weather, how wet it had been this spring in both Austin and Amarillo, and how pretty the bluebonnets were on the drive down to the wedding. Things grew relaxed, and Matthew was hoping that he could get to know this man.

The rent ran out on his coffee, so Matthew looked for the john.

He went in, relieved himself, and heard the door open behind him.

"Hello, Matthew, long time no see."

It was William Delaplace.

Matthew turned. William had a gun.

"Let's be very quiet," said William. "You can zip yourself up."

"Hello, William. So is this it?"

"Matthew, Matthew, would I end the happiness of a wedding? Now what a cad you think I am. I just wanted you to know how interested in you I am."

"Is that why you left me the notebook?"

"I left you the notebook because I have a new role in life, Matthew. I want to make people's dreams come true. I have decided to fight on the side of happiness. For example, how many times since your little wife died have you wanted to join her? Well, I'm here for you, homey. Just not yet."

"Who does the notebook belong to?"

"Oh, now if I went and told you that, you wouldn't have half the fun of figuring it out," said William.

"Well, I thank you for your concern in my life, but if that's all there is, I guess you can be going now," said Matthew.

"You're certainly a brave one. I understand you're very brave in bathrooms. But I don't want you too brave just now. Not with so many happy people. So I'm going to leave, and you'll just stay in the bathroom for a while. You might just set and do some hatha yoga. If you come out too soon I'll grant your wish early."

"How will I know when to come out?"

"Come out when you're bored. You told me once that someone who cultivates his life with books always has several minutes of fantasy he can rely on before boredom kicks in. Here's a great moment for you to try it out."

Matthew sat on the toilet. He was breathing very deliberately, so that he didn't panic. There was a room full of people out there. William was just going to leave. That was all.

William left.

Matthew tried to think of something to fantasize about.

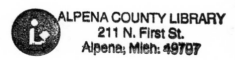

All he could think of was a commercial for his shop many years ago, when he discovered that radio doesn't exactly pull them into the store. *If you're the kind of person that reads only one book a year, New Atlantis isn't for you.*

There was a shot outside, in the salon.

Matthew jumped up and ran.

John was leaning over Elaine. There was blood on his right hand and Elaine's face.

מ

Edgar Allan Poe, perhaps the finest alchemist in America, was one of the first to investigate—at first on a purely fictive level—the art of remanifestation. His heroines needed little to return to this world, a specially atmospheric room, a set of teeth, or (in his best tale) someone reading a story aloud to a man in a certain heightened nervous state. It is not generally realized that storytelling is a form of ritual. It is after all the presenting of a set of images in a certain sequence to produce a change in the subjective state of the reader/listener. People would be surprised how much magic they could unleash in their own lives if they simply read ghost stories to each other on moonlit nights. Poe's own wife had died young, and his first experiments at remanifestation were the common sort that most people try in the serial monogamy that is the late–twentieth-century culture pattern in America. He simply tried to re-create her in each new woman he met. He later did try an alchemical experiment involving electricity and mirrors. The success of this device was not known, but it did pass ultimately into the collection of Dr. Alfred Pointers, the Memphis spiritualist. In Poe's later life he put his theories of remanifestation into a treatise called Eureka *wherein he decided that remanifestation was an atomic property. In the fullness of time, every atom that was in your body right now would someday be in exactly the same pattern. Eternal reoccurrence was inevitable for mechanistic reasons; now this provides a great deal of joy for someone who has had his great happiness in early life. After aeons he may rest assured that this happiness will be his again for the taking—his soul somehow being an emergent property of the assembled atoms.*

The problem with whole-body theories such as Poe's or the Christian idea of resurrection is that such an assemblage would have exactly the qualities that the person had in life. There is no need to re-create a person with all of his or her warts. That would merely be bringing more imperfection into the universe, which is no doubt a cosmic crime. Certainly the Bogomils had that idea down—which is why they avoided vaginal intercourse and mirrors. There may be some more hope in the current cyber-immortality approach wherein one hopes to have one's brain downloaded into some convenient mainframe. Such a mass of programs could be edited, debugged, optimized in various ways, so that a low-grade alchemy—not unlike the transformation that one goes through during college—could be obtained. The drawback here is that so much of the person is his or her body, that such a pale facsimile could only appeal to those wretches who live only in their heads and have therefore missed both the Purpose and Possibilities of life. I think that I am the only theorist on the North American continent that has a true picture of what might be obtained and knows the vistas this opens up for human evolution. However, my egotism is as much a stumbling block as Mr. Poe's materialism. Poe could not imagine a true demon in the shape of a raven, no Hugin and Munin for him; instead, it had to be a trained bird with its one word of doom, and a neurotic whose only hope of meaning in his life was to participate in his doom. Freedom for Mr. Poe was to actively be part of that horror that was meant for you. It made him a great American writer, but didn't give him enough hope to carry out the Great Work.

14 None but the Hopeless and the Bored

"Of course I don't believe it," said Matthew. "I mean I believe that someone believes it. But even then I don't think they really believe it. I mean I can't imagine that imagination at work in the world as we know it."

"Well," said Yunus, "that's the point. You gave all this stuff to the police, and what did they tell you—that it was a joke that William Delaplace was pulling on you. They don't believe in imagination either. If you don't think that someone is messing with your wife's ashes in order to bring some facsimile of her back to life, then you'll never be able to figure out who it is and get her ashes back."

Matthew said, "No real person tries alchemy. Magic is the pastime for the hopeless and the bored. I see them in the shop year after year."

"If boredom is their enemy, then their ally would be imagination. For most the ally can't win, but what if someone not only won against the enemy, but against the root causes of boredom—the laws of space and time?"

"This is the real world. This isn't a bad movie," said Matthew.

They were talking in the ICU waiting room at Seton Hospital. Matthew was holding the Xerox of the notebook that had been left in his home.

"This is 1999, as we are continually reminded by that song on the radio by the Artist formerly known as the Artist Formerly Known As Prince back when he was Prince Cougar Mellencamp or whatever. This is—or at least it should be—the year of the imagination. You told me that growing up you felt that 2001 would be the year something happened, because of the movie. Imagination is the one part of human life that separates us from animals, makes us do things beyond the seeking of pleasure and the avoidance of pain. Whoever wrote that notebook is a greater artist than all the books yellowing down in your picketed store."

There were others in the waiting room, looking as lively as the people whose news they waited on, minute by minute. Time flowed to nothing here, a good hour was a great hour and days last many months. Even walking down to the Coke machine was a quest; the kingdom might fall whilst you dealt with dragons.

Matthew knew that Yunus was talking too much to keep him from thinking about his mom and his brother, and loved him for the useless effort.

Matthew said, "What makes him a greater artist?"

"He lives by imagination. He no longer plays at imagination being his god, imagination is his god."

The doctor came out and asked to speak with Matthew.

There was a little room.

His mother was in stable condition. It was very serious. The bullet had not pierced her brain, it had gone just under the brainpan. She had only been conscious once since she was brought in. She might die. Seventy-seven is a bit old to take a shot to the head. She might die. Matthew should call his brothers in Washington. No, he didn't know about John, that was another doctor. Yes, the police wanted to talk to him. They had already talked to the doctor. What had Matthew been doing when his mother was shot? She might die. She might die. She might die. She might die. Then there were some medical terms that he didn't understand, and then the doctor was shaking his hand, and he decided that he hated the doctor and the doctor was lying and that Mommy was fine, and then he was in early middle age again, except that he had a man waiting outside with an alchemist's journal. He weighed twenty tons when he got up. The world is either nightmare or number. When it is nightmare, everything is happening all at once, everything is significant, anything can turn into any other thing. When it is number it is empty, composed of the three great realities, Zero, Number, and Successor. Matthew needed number very badly; he hadn't had it since he woke up the night of the SXSW party.

Henry Crawford was chatting with Yunus. Henry was old enough to know about ICU reality, so his smile wasn't a fake one. It was the smile of life against death. The archaic smile.

"How bad?" Henry asked.

"She might die," said Matthew. Or he tried to say it—there was something that went wrong with his throat while uttering the subjunctive auxiliary.

"Don't think this is a platitude," said Henry, "but that is pretty much a reality that we all face every day, and when you are Elaine's and my age, it is not a deniable reality. Are you going to call your brothers?"

"Yeah."

"Elaine told me that you weren't on speaking terms with the twins. Do you need me to call?"

"Do you know them?"

"Elaine and I went to Washington in ninety-seven for the cherry blossoms. So I've met them."

"No. If she dies we'll have to talk. I can't start this without an action of good faith," said Matthew. "I'm going to wait for a few hours, until I know a little more. I also want to find out about John's hand."

"He's on the next floor. The girls are with him."

"Do you know John?"

"Last fall I met him and helped him track down the source of his problems," said Henry. "But that's a story that you need to hear from John."

"So you know everyone in the family but me," said Matthew.

"I told Elaine that we needed to come see you this year, it wouldn't do for her to die with bad feelings between her and her boys. You were on the list."

"And now she has come and seen me and got shot."

"Well, she's been shot before."

"My mother's never been shot."

"Yes, twice before. Once when she helped Lullaby Reynman fighting some Nazi spies, and once by accident on the farm in Amarillo when she was fourteen."

"That's nuts," said Matthew.

"I told Elaine it was past time to tell her stories, but she was afraid that if she ever told you boys how weird and dangerous life could be, it would release you to a weird and dangerous life. When stuff started happening with John, she realized that she had been protecting you in the wrong ways. Weird shit just happens to your family."

Matthew looked at Yunus. Yunus was reading the notebook.

Yunus looked up and said, "Did you see that the third chapter is a recipe for chocolate cake?"

"Yeah," said Matthew. "I saw. I think I'll go check on John."

Weird shit.

ב

D.B. Bowen Eblis Cake with Moneymaker Frosting

½ cup unsweetened chocolate, finely grated
¼ cup extra strong French roast coffee (freshly brewed)
¼ cup milk
1 cup light brown sugar
1 egg yolk
1 nondairy creamer stolen from restaurant

Combine together while heating over low flame, until mixture is smooth. Let it cool down to the temperature of an excited woman's thighs while combining other ingredients.

1 cup light brown sugar
½ cup butter or margarine
3 egg whites (stiffly beaten)
2 egg yolks
¼ cup milk
¼ cup extra strong French roast coffee
2 ½ cups flour
¼ teaspoon baking powder
Pinch sea salt
1 teaspoon REAL Mexican vanilla
1 teaspoon baking soda

Cream butter and sugar together. Beat in yolks. Mix milk and coffee. Sift flour with baking powder, salt, and soda. Alternately add coffee-and-milk mixture and sifted flour, then stir in cooled chocolate mixture and vanilla. Gently fold in beaten whites. Pour into 2 greased and floured 8-inch round cake pans. Bake at 350°F for 35 minutes or until done.

Moneymaker Frosting

2 squares unsweetened chocolate
2 sticks butter
1 ⅓ pound confectioners sugar
2 eggs
2 teaspoons REAL Mexican vanilla

2 teaspoons cider vinegar
20 pecan halves

Melt chocolate in microwave. Melt butter on stove and cool. Beat egg. Add cooled butter, melted chocolate, and confectioners' sugar to beaten egg. Stir in vanilla and vinegar. Beat until smooth. Frost 2 8-inch layer cakes. Put pecan halves on cake in money-drawing sigils, such as the rune fehu.

If this cake is made while the moon is waxing, it will confer powers of imagination upon the persons who eat it as well as causing them to make great amounts of money from the product of that imagination. This recipe is said to have belonged to Stephen King's mother-in-law, who passed it on to him when he was working at a Laundromat for $660.00 a week and was unable to find a teaching position. She had come across the recipe in a classified file drawer when she had worked for Margaret Mills Scientific Kitchens. As Mr. King's wife, Tabitha, was at that time working at Bangor Dunkin' Donuts, it was some months before Mr. King tried the recipe. The results are well known.

If, however, the cake is written during a waning moon, it has the power of removing the faculty of imagination from the souls of those who eat it. They will interest themselves in practical moneymaking schemes.

John's right hand was bandaged so thickly it looked like he had a big ball at the end of his arm. Camilla was on the right of the bed, Cassilda on the left. There was a drip IV on the right, and above John's head was a monitor that displayed John's heart rate and blood pressure. Matthew hadn't seen this kind of equipment up close in years, not since his father died in 1983. John smiled at him when he walked in. "You know, brother, I have never been shot, and I think it is an experience to be avoided. My lovely wife was shot once just for knowing me."

"I don't know how to tell you how sorry I am," said Matthew.

"Hey, bud, it wasn't you that did the shooting as I recall, so I wouldn't worry about it," said John. "How's Mom?"

"Pretty bad," said Matthew.

"The bullet passed through my right hand and into her face just beneath her left eye. It exited into the Sheetrock. I hope I don't have to pay for that," said John.

Camilla said, "Although you were renting the facility, I don't think a claim could be made of negligence against you. You did not engage in any behavior that was apt to cause the shot. It might be wise to prepare a countersuit against the house alleging their negligence in providing access through the rear window."

"You rented the Cassetto House?" asked Matthew.

"Yes," said John.

"You're doing better than you used to."

"Well, I do own my own gaming company now, and my latest card game, Crossing the Seven Deserts, is doing great. It's a bubble, of course, but make money when you can."

"My congratulations. A lot of men I know don't sleep with two beautiful women and make a great deal of money."

"Not to mention," Camilla said, "getting free legal advice."

"And someone that designs his cards for him for free either," said Cassilda.

"Well, that pretty much blows my sympathy for the day," said Matthew.

"Have you called the twins?" asked John.

"No. So far I've been avoiding it."

"Better do it soon, if Mom is really in a bad way. You know when Dad was dying Mom didn't tell them the truth, she told them that everything was OK and they never had a chance to come see him."

"What should I tell them?"

"That Mom's dangerously ill, that she was shot at my wedding. We sent them cards. They'll know about the wedding. They might have some difficulty understanding that the man that shot Mom was the man who shot your wife two years ago."

Matthew went to the pay phones in the lobby. Having not traveled in three years, he did not know how to use his phone card. Clearing that hurdle, he hoped his little-black-book phone numbers for Paul and Saul were correct after—jeez—four years? Five? They still worked for the Bureau of Indian Affairs, but the chances the phone numbers were good were minimal. The first failed entirely, but the second did get the legal floor, and a woman who knew Saul, thought the world of him apparently, and was able to forward the call.

"Saul Reynman."

"Hello, Saul, this is Matthew."

"Matthew? Oh, hi how are you doing?"

"Well, I've got bad news.

"Bad—about Mom?"

"Yeah, how did you know?"

"Well, it's not the old days when you would call me from the shop because you found *Life as I Have Known It Has Been Finger-Lickin' Good* by Colonel Harlan Sanders. So it's got to be Mom."

"She's here in Austin. She's been shot."

"Shot. Mom's been shot. Is she alive?"

"Yeah, but not doing good. She's here at Seton. Let me give you the number . . ."

The call went on long enough for bare details, Saul said something about getting a plane to Austin, picking up Paul and heading out, and something about knowing Mom shouldn't be hanging around Matthew and John at this time in her life.

Matthew felt dirty, and tired, and he felt that Saul was right. He knew why William Delaplace had shot his mother, although he was sure the damage to John's hand was coincidental. One night William had come into the New Atlantis late, just as he was closing. William said he had something to celebrate. Pay raise, new job, something. He told Matthew to call Haidee and say that he would be late, he was going to take Matthew out for a little men's entertainment. They went to a titty bar, and William paid for a table dance, so a little brunette could shake her snatch in their faces while he kept buying setups for his bourbon. After William had dropped thirty or so bucks, and the girl realized that there wasn't any big money to be had, she went on exercising her trade with more likely candidates. Matthew drove over to William's and they sat in his tiny apartment, killing the fifth. It had been a long time since Matthew had been really drunk, maybe since college days, and he had been working hard and by God he deserved it. William had gotten real spooky about midnight, talking about murder, about wanting to kill people. He kept asking Matthew if he could kill anybody, who would he kill? Matthew had been dwelling on his anger toward Mom that week—some little something had triggered his thoughts of her—probably buying a collection of *Family Circus* cartoon books, Elaine's favorite. So he said he would kill Elaine for her remarks about Haidee. He didn't really mean it then, but it fit the mood of the evening. William had said he wanted to kill some dancer at the titty bar for promising him things that she never delivered on. They talked a lot about the worthlessness of women. For Matthew it had been a game. He didn't really feel that way but it was funny to be sitting in this tiny apartment and doing the "dames is poison" routine. He wanted to break out the cigars. He drank a lot. They drank all of the fifth, and Matthew managed to drive home somehow. Well, he guessed he did. He and his car did wind up at his house later. He went into the front bathroom and puked his guts out. The next day, he claimed to have the flu, you know really badly, and told Haidee to stay away from him. She sure didn't want to catch this. He had never told anyone about the drinking and the weird tone that William had had in his voice, because he couldn't bear anyone's saying, "Why did you keep hanging around with the guy?" He had thought it was just talk. William had no doubt marked his mom for a murder attempt then—my God, did he speak the doom of anyone else? Maybe he had killed off an entire town. He had told William that he hated Paris. Maybe Paris was the next on the hit list, or his postman, or some asshole that cut him off in traffic that day, or some customer trying to sell him a copy of Murphy's *Speller*.

He walked past the big mirror in the lobby. There he was, with his brown hair beginning to have a little gray, his little potbelly. He smelled like a used-book store with a little bit of stale cat piss thrown in. He would be there now, sipping acidic South American coffee from the shop next door from his chipped mug with a picture of Lieutenant Worf, talking to somebody about the desirability of spending another four dollars on a novel that he should read, or talking about his summer hobby of being on a professional fireworks crew as though it were already some kind of nostalgia, yet another obsoleted bohemia sinking beneath him like the treads of an escalator. He thought of not going upstairs, not waiting to hear of Mom's dying, not waiting for William Delaplace to track him down and shoot him, not questing after some serious nutcase with Haidee's ashes and a penchant for letters in Hebrew. Fuck all that. He had let himself be dealt out of the game long ago. He brought death to those who knew him and a slow rot to himself.

But the train of thought didn't stop him. It was as though his body had already become a zombie, moving to the will of the zombie master, while the brain moved in another direction. He pushed the UP button on the elevator but prayed to a god that he didn't believe in that the elevator would crash.

He got off on the ICU ward. Yunus was studying the notebook. Henry was not to be seen.

"He's in with your mother," said Yunus. "It was the time they let people in and you were gone so he went in."

Most of the waiting room was gone.

The phone rang. A stressed-out fat woman with dull brown hair picked it up.

"Is there any of Elaine Reynman's family here?" she asked.

"I'm Elaine's family," said Matthew.

He took up the phone.

It was William Delaplace.

"That you, Matthew? I didn't know if I could get you. I heard the ambulance dispatch take her to Seton. So how's she doing?"

"She's dying." Matthew had thought of saying that she was fine, but maybe then he would come and finish the job.

"Well, that's good to hear. This is an example of being careful what you ask for, you might get it. Do you remember how often you said that to me? As though some evil god were lurking to pick up a half-formed wish and stick you with it. But now you have an evil god in your life, don't you, Matthew?"

"Yes. You're an evil god all right. If I worship you, will you turn all your attention to me?"

Matthew looked over at Yunus to be sure he wasn't paying any attention.

"A god has to do many things, my boy. You were a god to me. Remember how busy you were?"

"Yes, too regrettably busy to have paid you the attention you deserve."

"But I could be a merciful god, Matthew, I could grant you a benison. What do you want?"

"I want you to kill me."

"Really?" William sounded overjoyed. "Really? So soon? I

thought I would have to terrorize you for days just to get you to ask. You really are a nice man. Of course I'll kill you. Now this isn't a trick, is it? I hate tricks. It isn't good to play tricks on a god."

"It isn't a trick."

"I'll be delighted to kill you, and I tell you what, since you were nice enough to ask, I'll do it painlessly."

"OK, where do I need to go?"

"Well, that's a bit of a problem. I have a prior commitment. I have to go out of town at least until late mid-May. So that would be six weeks. Can we get together say May eighteenth or so? Will that be a problem?"

"Sure. I'm pretty sure I'm free on May eighteenth."

"Excellent. Excellent. You don't know what this means to me. I was afraid that I would go away and you would start loving life again and I'd have to start from scratch. Oh, this is so fine."

"Where should we meet?"

"Oh, that's tough. If I tell you, you might pull a trick on me."

"I told you, no tricks."

"Oh, I believe you, Matthew, really I do, but in the next six weeks you might change your mind and the police are only a phone call away. You just go to many of your favorite haunts on the eighteenth and I'll catch up with you at one of them."

"Well, I'll try my best."

"That's all any of us can do, Matthew. You told me that many times."

Then William hung up.

Henry was walking back into the room; his face said that things weren't good.

He said, "Was that the twins?"

"No," said Matthew. "I called them in the lobby. They'll be here tomorrow."

"That may be too late," said Henry.

"I don't want this to be happening. I want to wake up."

Henry sort of hugged him and then they sat down. After an hour Yunus pursed his lips and sighed that he had to go.

Stephen Kozalla got off the elevator as Yunus got on.

Stephen walked over to Matthew.

"Man, I heard about your mom, and I want to let you know I'm calling off any bad stuff that may be going on between us. There won't be any more picketing at your store. You've had enough hurting."

Matthew thanked him and he left, and it was time for Matthew to go as well. Henry was staying the night.

It was only nine o'clock when Matthew drove into his driveway, only nine hours since the reception. Matthew had been relieved that Stephen had called off the picketing, but as he put his key in the door, he began to wonder how Stephen could have found out so fast.

15 Seeking a Sacred Space

From April 5, when he got the call from William Delaplace, to April 21, the birthday of Charlotte Brontë (Matthew had put a little display in the window of New Atlantis), Matthew Reynman's life alternated between Night and Day. Not "night" and "day," those natural divisions that help keep mankind asleep, but dreadful Night, which was sitting in the ICU waiting room while Paul and Saul—their hair grown as white as Herman's since Matthew had seen them—speculated subtly on the deleterious effect of having Matthew as a brother, and bounteous Day, where the simple knowledge that he was going to die on the eighteenth of May had given him great freedom and made life into a species of Play.

The latter did not in any way mean that Matthew Reynman was a quitter. One does not make a go of it as a small businessman for nine years as a quitter, nor survive the death of one's love. But the independent businessman longs for something that most of us lack—some external structure. Now not much—it was seeking a satanic freedom that has led these souls into their bossless lives. But some structure is needed by the human mind when it falls back from its godlike flights. And knowing when the game is up is the ultimate structure. It gave Matthew a touchstone for every decision that he made, and his strange new confidence gave a certain macabre freedom to his friends.

The deadline removed all the nagging concerns of daily life. A customer comes in with her sack full of college textbooks—well you know that crap isn't going to sell, but it's a steady customer so you want to give her enough credit so that she keeps patronizing you. Always a tiny anxious moment for the used-book seller. Not anymore. Give her ten bucks, twenty bucks. Pay that insurance bill? Not if it can be made to come due in June. Restock the shelves—heck, just toss them in the garbage.

It wouldn't affect the value of the business too much. He had a will drawn up giving everything equally to his brothers. He had it stipulated that his ashes were going to John. He had a weird feeling that if Haidee's remains were ever found, John would find them. John could mix the ashes together and give the result to the Fire Ants, or at least to Rodger Falconer, who was a Fire Ant from way back, and they would still have their pyrotechnic funeral.

The only concern he had was trying to figure out which one of his "friends" had stolen the ashes. But it had become more of a game. Knowing that he was going to die, he felt that he would get more points from knowing the perpetrator's name.

He told no one about the phone call from William.

They would interfere and maybe wind up like Mom or even John—out of the hospital now and obsessed with the notebook. No one need know.

The notebook, which he had planned to keep a secret, had become known to his friends and was having a weirdly corrosive effect. It gave them each reason to examine the other for secret practices that would indicate the flaws of character. So each found in each a horrible moment in some past remark that caused the retrograde movement of truth. "I always knew (s)he was scum." Each would share his or her suspicions with Matthew in sudden phone calls made seconds after he or she had solved the caper. Now when they would meet each other in the store they looked with evil eye and furtive glance.

There were three exceptions to this. The first was Norman Papin, whom nobody seemed to be able to get hold of these days, he was so successfully selling and writing books. The second was Rodger Falconer, who had been out of town—up in Fort Worth settling his mother's estate. Third were Doug and Janet Falconer, who living in Fort Worth seemed to be too removed from the action of the notebook, and of course they were also helping Rodger.

John had decided early on that Yunus must be the culprit. He had found that Ismailis were historically associated with alchemy. They had a tradition of free philosophic inquiry, and many great Islamic alchemists were certainly influenced by them (even if not of the sect), like Jabir (the reuniter after whom algebra is named), Razi (the builder of the great hospital at Baghdad), and Ibn Khallikan (the creator of literary biography).

Matthew's prime suspect, Stephen Kozalla, had been able to clear himself. He told Matthew that he had simply got a phone call from Selma Sacks.

Selma on the other hand said the knowledge of Matthew's mother had simply come from a "man" that had called her. The "man" had told her to contact Yunus and Stephen.

Selma had her own theory. Nicholas Askel Denning-Roy had to be the author of the notebook. It was too full of literary references to be anyone else. Who else could mention Poe, Pound, and Maugham with such ease except a guy that has spent most of his Social Security disability on books the last ten years? The whole weird chocolate-cake thing, now that had to be written by somebody desperate for literary success. The ashes were just another impractical scheme, like when he lost all the money his mother had left years ago trying to start a church that handled horned toads instead of snakes.

Yunus provided the name of Greg Madonia. Yunus was also obsessed with the chocolate cake, and the idea of writerly success. Greg had after all printed two chapbooks of his poetry over the years, *Breaking the Stillness of the Wind* and the well-titled *Throw Away This Book*. At any given time, Matthew had on his shelves at least two copies of each, which he would toss away, and then buy two more from Greg, so that he could enjoy the illusion that his poetry was being read by some elect audience. The ashes had been stolen—according to Yunus—in an act of revenge. Greg had one day, no doubt, noticed the copies of his chapbook in the Dumpster behind New Atlantis and decided to take something as precious from Matthew as Matthew had taken from him.

Of course Greg came to the shop the next day after Yunus had been there, and conversation showed that he at least knew of the notebook, had heard about it from Stephen, who had heard about it from Selma and so forth. He told Matthew that he was going to write a poem about it, in fact a series of poems about it for a chapbook contest some local press was having to remove ten-dollar bills from the overly inspired and undertalented.

The day after that Nicholas Askel Denning-Roy in his writerly charcoal gray beret stopped in. He had, you see, heard of this notebook from Greg, who had been asking technical questions about non-Western poetic forms, since Greg believed that Western poetry had exhausted itself. Nonsense, Nicholas had told him, the muse is as active now as she ever was, but on second thought that might be wrong, as one might guess from the number of movies made from TV shows that filled these last years before the millennium, and in any event perhaps some great shock could get the writerly juices flowing again and perhaps Matthew could, eh, lend him the notebook for literary analysis and possible juice-flowing shock?

Matthew had declined, claiming the notebook was in John's hands. John had by this time made his own copy, resolved to break the code of the last seven chapters, as well as tracking down the esoterica contained throughout. Matthew, who was beginning to see the notebook as a sort of game that could keep him busy till the eighteenth of May, was in a small way sad that John had grown so obsessed. He wished that he could let John in on the big secret so that John could enjoy the game aspect. John, after designing games for so many years, was the perfect person for that revelation. He had always wanted to share something with John. Something very secret and magical. This was in part a younger brother's fantasy; that some piece of hidden knowledge will obscure the inequality of age, and on another level it was some sort of jealousy toward Saul and Paul. Matthew had always wanted to be a twin and in subtle ways resented John for being born three years rather than three minutes before him. But this was such a strange and childish notion that he had never mentioned it to John.

Matthew's other growing regret was that he knew that the scene of action with the alchemist was going to take place somewhere other than Austin. Perhaps the alchemist had already left, which might explain Norman's absence. In any event the last chapter not written in code was fairly explicit on this idea. The last chapter, being so full of clues and possibilities for figuring things out, had been read again and again by Matthew for inspiration. He was reading it on April 21, when Rodger Falconer came by and talked about his mother's ashes.

ס

I am dutifully filling out the entries in my little Oliver Haddo journal. <g>. I am anxious to proceed to the next phase of the work which will require the correct choice of assistant and location, as well as three trial experiments. I have obtained good results with the rose ash, restoring it to full bloom inside of a retort, but the moment I broke the glass the forces of entropy intervened and returned it to ashes, which were not suitable for reconstitution. . . . This has caused me great despair: if I cannot move something up the ladder from minerality to vegetable status, how can I move up it through animal, human, and angelic? Nevertheless, I have obtained ashes of a diamondback rattlesnake, a dog, and a human being. I will try my hand at each before I will proceed to the Great Work.

The choice of sacred site is a tough one. Despite what many modern magical manuals would say, a place of power is not determined by its terrain. The reason our ancestors' ancestors chose hilltops and clearings and so forth was because of the effect that such places had on their imagination. Magic springs from and returns to the mind; it does not belong to the order of things named by the mind. I have been considering the method of Mr. Ezra Pound, the chief of American alchemists in exile this century. He used what he called the ideogramic method—of fusing together many known qualities to produce a synthesis both known and yet going beyond knowledge because it informed those things—those previous objects of knowledge—in a transforming way. Pound held some (slightly incorrect) views about the nature of Chinese ideograms that he felt made them the perfect vehicle for poetry. According to Pound, the Chinese abstracted meaning by choosing a constellation of known qualities that (given Pound's assertion that the natural object was always the best symbol) could not help but be poetic. For example, if (according to Pound) your Chinaman wanted to write RED, he composed a figure that partook of four existing ideograms:

ROSE *CHERRY*
IRON RUST *FLAMINGO*

Pound praises the juxtaposition of concrete things as a means to pick out an abstract idea, In fact the Chinese word for red ch'ih[4] is composed of man + fire = flushing from anger, but no matter, what is important here is the method of combining known things to create something that changes what it was made out of. This breakthrough marks Pound as perhaps the greatest spokesperson for alchemy. He considered the building up of super ideograms a form of directo voluntatis, *the Dantean notion of acting upon ideas directly.*

Pound's method, so often used against us by the wizards of Madison Avenue, is a help in finding a sacred space. I must look for a space where, as I do the Work, I am surrounded by those things the Work itself should not only be nourished by, but transform, that is to say:

DARKNESS	*OPTIMISM*
CHEMISTRY	*BEAUTY*

Now at first these may seem not to be concrete objects, but this can be seen to be so. Darkness is essential for the Work because it is a work of the unmanifest. If I awaken one day with gold in my pocket or love in my life that was not there the day before, it has come out of the unmanifest. The unmanifest is the region that the profane call the future. I will need a spot drenched in darkness, haunted and ill-omened. Perhaps a community based on oil wells, that draws its existence, as well as that of Western civilization, from a dark hidden region every day.

Optimism is essential for the Work because it is surely the only force that mankind uses to combat the knowledge of death. I think that it is a small-town commodity. There are certain miracles that could never happen in the city. It is perhaps the fact that I did the working on the rose's ashes on an Ozone Alert day that I failed.

Chemistry is essential to the Work not only for obvious reasons, but also for my long-term financial goal. After I raise one person from the dead via alchemy, chemists and doctors can study the process and I can license it out, thus making huge fortunes and having control over life and death.

Beauty is essential for the Work because it alone sustains the mind.

If I can find a place with these four qualities (as well as the mundane needs of quiet and security) then I will have an adequate supply of inspiration to do the work.

I must learn to read the Book of the Earth to find the spot where nature and the hand of man have placed these four elements. But I long ago swore to know the nature of every herb and stone and to know of the worm as it turns. My time is growing short. I know I must have learned the Art soon.

Tomorrow, which is ruled by the numbers for Wine and Night, I should learn a new piece of the puzzle. I am impatient; my life has too long been without beauty, without optimism, without chemistry, without darkness. Only now do the Doors open.

Matthew had heard the bell indicating that someone had entered the shop, but only looked up as Rodger Falconer was slouching toward the SF section.

"Hey," Matthew said.

"Hey," Rodger said. "Well, it looks like Mom did have a little money saved up. I just got back from Cow Town."

"So how are Doug and Janet?"

"Janet has decided to take up lance work. You remember that American-flag display you lit the first year at Doublesign? That's lance work."

"Sounds time-consuming."

"Well, she is the epitome of thoroughness. Doug is the same way. It's not easy being the black sheep."

"Tell me about it."

"Well, when I left there were people picketing the store. I see that's cleared up."

"A lot has happened since then."

"Your tone says maybe too much."

"Well, more than I want to talk about. So was taking care of your mom's estate hard?"

"Well, all Mom had was cash, and none of that was in anything more complicated than a CD, so that part was easy. We divided up her books and the furniture she still had out at the home. Dividing up the photo albums was hard."

"Why did you take so many months to do the division?"

"Well, probate takes time even in a simple estate."

At least that was something that Matthew wouldn't have to do.

"You know," said Rodger, "something kind of weird happened with Mom's ashes. Doug and I went out to the grave, and there was Dad's plaque, but no plaque for Mom. So we went to the office and they said that they don't put up the plaque until the ashes are inurned. We said that Mom had been dead for six months, and they checked their computer and said they had no record of the ashes being delivered. We drove across town to the crematorium, and sure enough the first thing they said was 'We don't deliver.' They went in the back and brought a little plastic box, 'Gwynn Falconer.' Janet meantime is wondering where the hell we are, and gets a call from the graveyard saying that they had probed the grave and our dad's ashes are there but not Mom's, so by the time we drop off Mom and go home, she's pretty spooked, a little Texas thunderstorm has come up and the power is out. It was the beginning of a ghost story."

"That is strange. Does Doug know where we'll shoot this year?"

"We went out and talked to the people at Titan, and they're going to give us Doublesign again. Doug's not real happy. He was hoping for a bigger show, something that's electric, but I love it. I think fireworks should be set off by hand like God intended."

"Well, I'll be there," said Matthew, followed by the first pang of regret that he had since William had told him that he was going to die on May 18. He wouldn't be there. He would be dead for six weeks and change when Doug was shooting fireworks over the lake at Doublesign. "I'll be there," he said again, sad and sick sounding.

"Well, I sure hope so," said Rodger. "I always picture you that night when you and Haidee first shot with us in Schertz. Your hands were covered in the black oily grease that forms on the inside of the cannons, and Haidee reached over and painted that mustache on you, and you fell down laughing. Oh God, remember how hard the ground was? God, we spent all day burying the cannons. You were such a genius when you asked the people at Doublesign to dig the trench for us. Oh Lord."

"You got to learn some things as time goes on."

"Till you get as old as me and then you start forgetting. You know what they say, there are two signs of old age, the first is memory loss and the second is . . . the second is . . . the second—." He walked up the stairs to the SF loft still playing out the old joke.

Matthew thought of his father's death. He was nineteen that summer and he had not got a job because of his father being in the hospital. He was home from Austin, and pining for Haidee (they were married that August). Herman had died of an ailment that he had picked up in Brazil. He was six weeks in the hospital dying. But every week after the first he was getting better and better. On July 3, he was able to eat ice cream. On July 4 he was able to get all the tubes taken out that had pierced his body. On July 4 Matthew had called Paul and Saul and told them how smart they were for not coming to see Dad, they could come and visit him in the fall when he felt better. It had been four years since the errant shell had broken the windows at Aunt Martha's.

That night was the first night that no one spent any time with Dad. Mom and John rested at home. Matthew called up an old high school buddy and went to see the fireworks show put on by the *Amarillo Globe News*. It was the best he had felt in weeks and weeks. He had always loved fireworks, but that had been his best firework moment until the night that Haidee and he shot their first professional show. The next morning, a weak point in Dad's aorta burst and Dad bled to death in a very few minutes. Mom and John and he were there. For weeks he thought that God was punishing him because of the fireworks.

It was nine years later that the chance to shoot fireworks with Rodger had opened up. After John's D&D game had stopped, Matthew tried to be a Dungeon Master for a while and Haidee had dutifully dragged three people home from work for the game, one of them being Rodger. Rodger was terrible at D&D but great at poker, so there were poker games over the years, and the occasional movie, and new restaurants. Both Haidee and Rodger liked weird new cuisines—so they dragged Matthew along to the Ethiopian place, the Indonesian place, the Macedonian place, and so forth. When Rodger called them one June 1 and told him that the regular members of Falconer Brothers Pyrotechnics couldn't make it, Haidee had volunteered in a flash.

It had been miserable hot digging in the hard Texas ground, but they dug while Haidee and Janet handed out sweetened iced tea; this was years before Matthew knew about his diabetes.

It had been so much fun to walk through the crowd with their red Titan Pyrotechnics gimme caps on, letting the people know that they were going to be the ones that would be firing the show. They hinted darkly of the danger involved, the lost limbs, the missing fingers, the man who had his head shot off.

("Did it kill him?" "No, but he can't wear hats anymore. We call him the headless fireworks guy," Haidee had answered.)

Then as dusk came and Matthew stood by the lance work in the shape of an American flag with a lit fusee burning orange in the gathering gloom, he had begun to worry about how safe it all was. Then "The Star-Spangled Banner" was over and he touched the fuse. The quick match had all two hundred lances burning in red, white, and blue in about twenty seconds and he was running down the hill in the dark to the line of cannons. Haidee stood in front of a yellow ice chest filled with three-inch shells. She would hand him the shells and he would take the caps off the fuses as he ran full tilt toward the line of cannons. He would swing the shell by the fuse into the cannon and drop it, leaving the fuse pointing out for Doug to light.

The first shell that had gone off—two cannons away (at least nine feet)—had such an explosive pop that he thought something had hit him in the chest. And then the sky above him was cherry red, flamingo red. Then he was running back for the next shell to load.

It was scarier on the second run; neither Doug nor Rodger had told him that the cannons smoke after the first shell has gone off. It takes a certain amount of guts to swing a small ball full of explosive powder into a metal tube that's smoking.

But he did it and ran for more.

On through the three-inch shells, the four-inch shells, the five-inch shells.

Doug and Rodger had let Haidee light one of the finale racks. Forty three-inch shells shooting into the sky at the same time. It was great—it was the only fireworks he had a chance to see go off. When you are lighting or loading you don't have the time to see the shells explode.

Then it was over. Twenty-five minutes of heavenly eternity.

The crowd hooted and hollered, and some great human being yelled, "Great show!"

It was magic. It was better than sex.

The cleanup was just as hard, and in the dark. But it was full of afterglow.

It hit then. He wanted to live.

Plain. Simple.

He wanted to live.

"Yeah," he said, "I will be there."

Rodger stuck his head out of the loft.

"I heard you, but I am glad you're so inspired."

16 O Night Our Mother

On the thirtieth of April Elaine Reynman was released from Seton Hospital. Matthew and John helped her get on a plane with Paul and Saul. They had used up all of their vacation time, and so they wanted to take her back to Washington, D.C. Henry Crawford had to drive back to Amarillo, Texas, for a few days and then was planning on joining Elaine in Washington.

On the way home from the airport, John drove for the first time since he had been shot. Matthew began the conversation with, "You know tomorrow is Joseph Heller's birthday. He's a year younger than Mom."

This simple beginning allowed Matthew to maneuver through the intricacies of *Catch-22*, and on to his own situation, his desire for life and his fear of the eighteenth of May.

John listened politely, then said, "I don't see what the problem is. Just don't be here on the eighteenth."

Matthew said, "That's a plan?"

"Sure it is. Look, this William guy has one obsession. He's looking for the Rules of Life. Do you remember when you were ten and I was thirteen, when you told me about coffee?"

"No, that sort of slips my mind right now."

"You had decided that coffee had the power of gnosis. It

informed the adults of things, and if you simply drank it you would know all the 'secret stuff' they knew. I was sort of a cruel little bugger, as all pre–junior high types are, and I agreed solemnly and encouraged you to make and drink a whole pot."

"Yeah, I do remember that I was awake all night and got in trouble for waking Mom and Dad up. Other than reminding me of your obnoxious self, what is the point?"

"Your friend William thinks at about a ten-year-old level. He thinks that people know things that he never got to learn. He thinks that he can puzzle out life for formulas of being happy or sad or getting money or whatever. He's the type of guy that makes selling 'Alleged Money Drawing' candles into an industry."

"OK, I'll buy that. And?"

"He expects that you'll play by the Rules. What you need to do is steal his rules, do something off-the-wall."

"Won't that make him mad?"

"The guy killed your wife, shot your mother and your nicest brother, and took a shit on the floor of your house—are you truly worried about his feelings?"

Matthew laughed.

John said, "Making him mad is probably a good idea. Shake him up and see if he'll do something stupid."

"Wouldn't it be better to just tell the police and have them guard me, and trap him?"

"Ask yourself this—have the police done a good job catching this guy so far? Telling the police, especially by letter, when you leave town is a good idea, but I wouldn't rely on them to protect you. This guy is smart."

"I thought you said he thinks like a ten-year-old."

"Ten-year-olds can be very smart. They just don't know how the world works. When I designed *Ulthar II*, it was a nine-year-old that cracked the cats code within a month of the thing being released."

"We should get a nine-year-old working on the notebook code."

"Actually Cassilda told me last night that she thinks she might know what it is. We'll drop by the store just before closing if she has cracked it."

"Do you think I'm a failure because I wanted to die?"

"Look, Matthew, what are we? We—you and I—are the low rungs of the intelligentsia ladder. All intelligentsia suffer from a guilt complex; it is at the center of their souls. It is the income tax we pay for wanting to make other people richer."

"You don't seem to have much trouble with guilt."

"I burned mine off and not even the ashes remain. I replaced it with curiosity; I want to see what the next stopping point in the road is. If I didn't have curiosity, think how fucking mad I'd be for you getting my hand shot."

"That was pretty callous," said Matthew.

"Brotherly criticism is callous," said John. "It's the alkahest our 'friend' is looking for."

"Well, with two women it's not like you need it for jacking off."

"Flippancy, that's the spirit that will carry you through this."

Just before closing time, John, Camilla, and Cassilda came into the shop.

"I've got good news and bad news," said Cassilda. "The letters are Enochian, a magical cipher created by Dr. John Dee and Edward Kelly. John Dee said it was the language of angels, and used it to track down certain transmissions in Kraków. It's got quite a rep in Western magical circles. Aleister Crowley used Enochiana to get his *Liber 418*. Four hundred eighteen is the number of the 'Great Work.' Crowley's magical records for that are here in Austin at the HRC. But to the point, I've tracked down the letters as the twenty-one letters of the Enochian alphabet."

"What's the bad news?"

"Well, whoever wrote it, and I think you will agree with me as to the culprit after you read the first section, was increasingly paranoid. The first section is transliterated English. The second is transliterated Latin, and the remaining sections are ciphered transliterated Latin—I think. I've got the first section worked out, and as soon as I can I'll do the others. But it won't be easy or, I'm afraid, very accurate."

"May I see the first section?"

ע

Hiring William Delaplace seems to be what the gods have told me to do. William is the criminal Matthew Reynman told me about the night of the reading. I picked up the Austin Chronicle *and there was a personal ad from Matthew Reynman to William. Since this was the day of Wine and Night I knew that William would be a good assistant. Now I don't think he will be a reliable or safe one, but I do think he will add the necessary spark of Chaos that the Work needs. When I saw the ad I dropped what I was doing and rushed down to Matthew's shop. I had no plan in mind, for on the day of Night and Wine, only improvisation will see you through. I walked in and began spinning a tale about some book I wanted to write, and while I was there, some useful fool called and asked for an SF book. Matthew ran upstairs, and right next to his phone he had left the information for calling the voice mail for his personal ad. I copied it down on the back flyleaf of a book of American black writing, and then to attune myself to the chaotic forces of the day stole the book just as Matthew's black fairy friend flounced in. I went to my car and tried the number. No messages yet. Tried on each quarter hour and got my William Delaplace in the hour. I deleted William's message, and then I called him. He was staying in some downtown hotel. I knew it would be dangerous to meet him, but it was a dangerous day so I arranged to take him to lunch. He is completely lunatic, just as Yage Tomas said his helper was. I suppose if I had met him under different circumstances*

I would have tried to help him out, but as Yage used to say, "A man's damnation is his own damn business." He was uninterested in the alchemic part of the work, except for the possibility of it truly hurting Matthew Reynman. I suspect that he is either a disbeliever, which should end shortly as I try my new experiments, or perhaps hopes to kill Haidee again in a perfection of the murderer's art. I am sure that murder goes by too quickly for it to be artistically satisfying. Bang! and it's over. Must be like those scenes where you quit your job and then two or three days later you realize what you should have told your boss. He told me that he plans to kill Matthew Reynman and that he really wants the guy to suffer first. Fine, I said, but it can't interfere with the work you do for me. "What kind of work would that be, sir?" I told him that I wanted him to guard my lab both here in Austin as well as the other place, which I have narrowed to three. He was to keep the law, neighbors, and above all Reynman from finding it. "How would Reynman find it, sir, if you don't tell him?" "He's still in love with the girl. That may give him certain powers as the experiment nears its conclusion." "Well, wouldn't it be better to kill him, sir?" I loved the way he kept calling me "sir." Turns out he had an abusive father that left him and his mother when he was seven. He both wants to find dear old dad to love him and to suffocate him. I've got to tread very carefully since he clearly sees me as his father. Of course I've got father-figure issues as well—anyone that gets into the occult does. You both love and want to unthrone God. Oedipal feelings are a bitch when you think of the universe as your mother. Infinite Stars Infinite Space, Isis I adore you. Anyway, I told him, "No, killing him too soon will keep his dreams from helping me in my work. I can't imagine her alone: to truly make her Galatea I will need that special imagining that can only come from the adoration we have for the dead." He didn't follow that, but he has no love for the dead, nor I would imagine for any of the living, including himself. I told him that I would pay him fifty dollars a day cash money and see to his room and board. Before he started to negotiate I pointed out that (1) he was on the lam and (2) I was a very powerful magician to have known that he was out there and invite him to this meeting. I hope he doesn't get wise and call that damn number again. Maybe my magic will keep Matthew away from the phone for a few days. One can only hope that I've learned something.

William Delaplace is a big man with dark brown hair and a general coarseness of features that reminds one of the great apes. However, his brutish demeanor is partially redeemed by his eyes of a gleaming sort seldom seen today save in asylums and the occasional pulpit. His fear of showing his true self—particularly fear of prison shrinks and their "psychoanaloosing"—comes not from having a secret to hide but from having a deep knowledge that there is no core self. He is in a uniquely bad position, as though he were a mask which, suddenly awakened, realized that it covered nothing. He both believes and fears that life is a masquerade and that at some point we all have to remove our masks, in his case the removal leaving nothing. He is of course deathly afraid of water and mirrors. Mirrors have terrible memories, and they know terrible things. They will trap him somehow and they will tell him these terrible things. In this he is the perfect incarnation of the movie vampire, fearful of mirrors (and of water) because it has the power to show the true self uncovered by persona—and this captive communion would destroy him. I have never met a man so fearful, yet so inherently frightening.

Of course I realize that seeing the weaknesses in this hulk I am also seeing myself. I too have avoided the mirror for many years, particularly after my success. In the middle of life I found myself in a forest dark. That was why I decided to try to create a perfect woman. It would appeal to my animal nature that I had let overcome me in the course of life, but having such an angel would likewise—must likewise—cause me to strive to be better. Only in the relationship with a good woman can a man find happiness. I note that in my writing I have never had any of my male heroes actually have wives, or any kind of relationship with a woman other then sexual James Bond stuff. Although sticking my face in my books, I can't face the true even in the mirror of ink.

After the meal William left, but he will see me tomorrow. Tomorrow I must discover the site for the final operations as well as beginning the experiment with the snake. The name of tomorrow is the Day of Foundation. William is clearly fearful that I would follow him, but I don't want to know where he lives; one shouldn't know too much about Chaos, or it stops being Chaos, and becomes just another pain in the ass.

Matthew paused in reading the ע section and looked up.

Cassilda had watched him like a hawk while he had read.

"So?" she said.

"So," said Matthew. "It is Rex Hull."

"I thought that was right from what you told me. I was really disappointed. I tried to write a short story in his style about Taylor Keziah Mason. I love his short stories, especially 'Mr. Samler's Surprise Package.' "

"So it's a simple matter," said Matthew. "We call up Detective Blick and tell him about Hull."

"Well," said John, "let's think about it. First you're going to claim that this notebook written in alchemical code from the time of Shakespeare reveals that the killer that's after you is working with a well-known mystery writer to remanifest your dead wife's ashes, and if you can crack the code further, you'll know where they're doing this. Based on an esoteric understanding of the poetics of Ezra Pound."

"I might put it a bit differently," said Matthew.

"The point that I think John is trying to make," said Camilla, "is not that Blick will scully you, although this will happen, but that it would give time to Messers. Hull and Delaplace."

"Well, as long as they are caught—what's the difference?"

"Well, number one," said Camilla, "is that you might be able to get Haidee's ashes back before he puts them into an alembic and mutters some dreadful Latin over them, but more important, vastly more important, is that you want to be sure that William is caught."

"Or killed," said Cassilda.

"Are you suggesting that I kill him?" asked Matthew.

"I don't think it's a bad idea. I don't think he's the sort of man that is going to reform, and I think you would live your life in a sort of panic of turning your head and starting at every noise for the rest of your years while he lived. Of course Hull is planning on killing him—I can see by your expression you didn't read that far. You would need to find the corpse in that case so you could rest easier."

"I don't think I could kill someone," said Matthew. "Not anymore."

John said, "Well, I certainly wouldn't recommend killing someone either, but if you let this guy slip past the police, you'll regret it forever. He needs to be caught and caught in a manner that makes sure he is locked up forever."

Matthew said, "Any suggestions for this miraculous capture?"

"Well," said John, "not yet, but brilliance takes time. You know, or since you suspect William is truthful, that he is out of town right now. You could do something that would help your case, like buy a camcorder, and other record-making devices."

"I think you should kill him," Cassilda said. "Haidee was a lovely lady, sweet and smart and all things good."

Something about her tone bothered Matthew. It was that same suggestive tone she used when describing her relationship with Camilla.

"I didn't know you knew Haidee that well," said Matthew.

"We knew each other very well," said Cassilda.

The image of a white woman and a black woman that had served to create such excitement twenty years ago was a shocking image now. It wasn't the eroticism, that was OK, or would have been OK. It was the shock that had been waiting in his mind since he had spoken to Stephen Kozalla on the day of his arrest. His latest arrest. The fact that Stephen and Haidee had gone to see blaxploitation movies together. He couldn't have done that with her, and he couldn't believe that she had snuck out of work to do so, particularly with Stephen. She used to lecture him on how Stephen never took his blackness seriously. Now what had been held in abeyance in Matthew's mind suddenly rushed in. He hadn't *known* Haidee, at least not as well as he thought he did. Part of what he had *known* was his imagination. Not sneak off from work? Yeah, that was his hang-up. He was, Jesus Christ, seeing Mom in her. He didn't feel too well. He didn't want to think about what Cassilda was hinting at. He didn't need that certainty right now.

John, apparently wanting to head off a tense moment, said, "Why don't we grab a bite at the Lost Weekend?"

"I love their Welsh rarebit," said Camilla. "Mr. Bildad is a great cook."

"No," said Matthew, "I need to finish reading this section that Camilla has translated and then do some setup for the shop. I've got to do my end-of-the-month bookkeeping."

"Well, in that case," said John, looking daggers at Cassilda, "we'll head off. Would you like us to come by later, with a box of rarebit and a bottle of stout?"

"Thanks," said Matthew, "but cheese is pretty hard on diabetics, and beer is a killer. I will probably have a veggie sandwich at the Hobbit Hole and, following the advice of Saint William, a glass of wine for my stomach's sake. I really, really want to thank you for doing the translation so far."

"The next section looks like it is in simple Latin, but I haven't done Latin since high school, so I don't know how long it will take me to do, but I'll get right on it," said Cassilda.

They were out the door almost at once, Cassilda laughing

on the way to Camilla's Mercedes. When he had heard them go, he closed up shop and went to the twenty-four-hour deli.

He decided that he would do something that he almost never did: he ordered a Khocolate martini, vodka and creme de cacao with a chocolate kiss in it. He drank the high-proof, high-sugar drink, ordered a second, and turned to Camilla's typescript where he had left off:

. . . one shouldn't know too much about Chaos, or it stops being Chaos and becomes just another pain in the ass.

I will need to get a ready supply of cash to pay my Igor, and I should load my .357 magnum that that fan gave me because she loved Little Gardens. *I am a terrible shot, but with that kind of firepower, accuracy is not important.*

Now that Delaplace has been out of my sight for an hour, I am suddenly struck with the dilemma of what to do with him once he is no longer needed. While he had been talking with me in the motel restaurant I assumed that once I had finished the stage of the Work that requires me to have such a crazed guard as him, I would turn him over to the police in some covert manner. I realize that this won't work at all, for a creature such as he could not possibly keep his mouth shut. I suppose the wise thing to do would be to kill him, perhaps with one of the poisons that are needed for various phases of the work. I should by that time have another servant raised up anyway, a person more deserving of life than Mr. Delaplace, but I am not without a certain feeling for my fellow men, although years of casually killing off a character that doesn't fit my aesthetic agenda has made me somewhat looser about these things than I should be.

Poisoning would be the easiest. My cryptonymy must grow strong at this point—a fellow as cunning as William might open this door a bit too quickly. I must pay greater homage to the sign of Ink, in which all secrets are Hidden.

Matthew had two more drinks, making this the most he had drunk since his diagnosis four years ago. He decided not to eat, but to go back to the store. He wasn't going to think about Haidee and Cassilda, that was all there was to it. He wasn't going to think about Haidee and Stephen in the movies, maybe they were smoking crack together laughing at him, he was too uptight to get the jokes, he was maybe a nice enough fellow, but not somebody that you would share your secrets with. He wasn't going to think about that at all. It was a warm and pleasant twilight, it would be night, and night, Haidee used to say, forgave all things.

"But," Matthew said to the passing car, "even the night has an end." It was a lyric from an Electric Luddite song. He was taking the back alleys, as he always did, and he decided he would stop and rest for a minute on a stoop. It was sort of wobbly. No, he was sort of wobbly, but leaning his back against the steel of the door felt good, yes, that was what he needed.

When he awoke, it was dark. He was still drunk, but not too drunk to notice that he had let go of the typewritten sheets and that they were scattered down the alley. The smell of garbage and old restaurant grease was strong, and was about to—

He stood up, threw up, and felt better, even a little less drunk. There was no point in picking up the scattered sheets now; besides, it had been clearly turned out on a computer. He would get another copy from Cassilda on May Day.

He felt that he wasn't alone in the alley. He couldn't see anyone, but there was somebody nearby.

"Hello?" he said. "Hello?"

The idea that it was William suddenly struck him. What if William had just been playing with him, not waiting till the eighteenth?

He tried to see where every spot for stealth might be. Behind the Dumpsters, in the shadow of the doorway. People could be anywhere.

He decided that he would walk back to the store whistling a jaunty tune.

He took three steps and broke into a run. About that time the wind decided to pick up and slapped some of the sheets against his legs. He panicked at their touch and ran out of the alley and on to the street, where a horn blared at him and a BMW missed hitting him by so few inches that he could feel the force of the car's slipstream.

He turned and looked back at the alley, which seemed empty.

He trotted to the other side of the street. He would walk calmly back to the shop. He did have end-of-the-month stuff to do, that wasn't a lie.

When he turned on Lavaca Street and saw his shop, he froze.

The lights were on.

He was sure, well as sure as he could be in his semidrunken state, that he had turned the lights off.

I'm the responsible one. I turn lights off when I'm finished with a room. I don't sneak off to movies.

He walked to the far side of the street and began approaching his shop. He couldn't see anyone inside through the narrow windows. He walked on to his station wagon, unlocked it, and took his gun out.

He would try the front door. He *knew* that he had locked the door. That was such a deep impulse since the robbery his first year in business that he could do it in his sleep.

He tried the door.

It was unlocked.

He opened it, setting the bell to jangling.

Someone vaulted over the SF loft and hit the light switch, and then was running.

Matthew yelled, "Stop!"

He heard the intruder going out the back door.

He trotted behind, stuck his head out there to be sure no one was lurking in the alley, then locked up the door.

He turned on the lights, and then locked the front door as well.

He walked upstairs to the SF loft. There were a few books on the shag carpeting, and two twenty-sided dice.

There was also a blank pocket notebook, with green covers.

17 Perhaps Rex Knows Something

It was a dark and stormy night.

Matthew had sweated Cassilda's translation of the notebook for too long. It had not been simple Latin, it had only looked like Latin, so she had to consult certain texts on cryptography. *Trithemius's Steganographia, Giambattisa Potra's De Furtivis Literarum Noti*, Falconer's *Cyrptomenysis*. The days went by. It was the evening of May 15. He was going to leave by night, everything was packed. He had his letter to the police written, saying that he feared that William Delaplace would make an attempt on his life on May 18. He had snuck things out to his station wagon for a week. Just tiny things, a shirt, some socks, leaving a bag of groceries in the back after going shopping. He felt as if he were watched all the time, that his slightest action might give the all-seeing William a clue. In his growing paranoia, he felt as though William would not only decipher *him*, but actually read signs of Matthew's future that Matthew himself did not know—and thus Matthew's life, like sheep entrails, would tell the final fates.

It was a dark and stormy night.

Lightning had begun flashing in the purple sky.

Haidee loved nights like this, she loved to be in them, they made her horny and excited and given to making up songs all at once.

But he was still puzzled about how well he knew Haidee. How well are you supposed to know someone that you have been married to for fourteen years?

The lights went out in Hyde Park.

He was scared. He had taken to keeping the lights on in the last week as though whatever message that William would send him could be kept at bay, by light. He had internalized Rex's idea that the dark = the new.

It was a dark and stormy night.

There was a knock at the door.

Swallowing hard he answered it, gun in hand.

It was Cassilda. She saw the gun before he had a chance to put it away. She said nothing, but there was fear in her face to increase the embarrassment in his.

"I've got it. Well sort of," she said. "Each chapter is written in a different code. He used the Enochian letters throughout except in the last two chapters, where he occasionally lapses into the Roman alphabet. He seems to have been pretty scared of William. The code isn't perfect. There are words I couldn't get."

"Have you finished the translation yet?"

"No, all I have are two more chapters, but the first will tell you where to go, and maybe even what to do," she said.

"How long until you finish the book?"

"I don't know. As his fear goes up, or maybe his excitement at getting near the end of his experiment, the handwriting gets worse, words are left out, and I haven't even figured what codes he is using for most of it yet. Look, I'm not a professional cryptographer, I'm a tarot card reader that likes mysteries."

"Yeah. I'm sorry. I'm pretty overeager here," said Matthew.

They went in, and he lit candles, thinking that he had never lit candles in his house except for Haidee or her memory.

"Did John find out about Rex Hull?" asked Matthew.

"Yeah. It was as we figured. John tried to get hold of him, and eventually tracked down his agent with the lure that John wanted to get gaming rights to *Dad's Last Pitch.* The agent told him that Hull had been incommunicado since the day the notebook was left at your house. He had told her that he was going off for the summer to write a mainstream novel about perfect love."

"Oh God."

"Camilla tried to break into his house—she likes petty larceny, it's the lawyer in her—but no luck. She and John are trying to hatch some scheme that will let them break in with police help. John has majorly good karma with a detective downtown, but their scheming little minds have drawn a blank so far. You have any flashes on the bookstore break-in?"

"No. I'm sure it's connected, but when paranoia sets in you think everything is connected. It's like reading a book, everything must belong somehow."

"We know the lab he was using was somewhere near his house, from the stuff I've deciphered so far, so we're looking for that. It's all in the stuff I've just printed out for you. We'll keep looking while you're gone. We're going to send an anonymous call to animal control people about the snake in Memorial Garden Park, which almost has to be the park mentioned."

"Snake?" asked Matthew.

"Just read it. Do you have the letter for the police?" asked Cassilda.

"Here," he said.

"And the keys to your shop?"

"Look, I don't know if having you and John run the shop is a good idea," he said.

"One, it will distract William. Two, we have experience dealing with murderers. Three, I've helped run bookstores before."

"Yeah, it's thinking like that that kept John off the debate team in high school."

"Read the book, give me the keys. You've got to go."

פ

This was a day and night of great good news and bad news. I know that the alternating strains are part of the inner work of the alchemist, but there's a big difference between knowing and Knowing. Even at this stage in my Initiation I forget that humans forget the growth stages as they are happening.

At eight this morning I released the snake from the closed vial. It was a big beautiful rattler. It was a western diamondback, whose ashes I had obtained from a dealer in strange herbs and drugs in Tucumcari. It was a full six feet long, with nine buttons showing that it had almost lived a decade. It had been compressed in the vial, and when I shattered it, it expanded like an adolescent penis. I was fearful that it was bloating, which many ancient authors warned against. Its light brown skin was dull and torn, showing a need for a fresh skin, which I took as a good sign.

I had purchased a hundred-gallon aquarium earlier, as well as a heat rock for the snake. It did not rattle at first, but did strike at me, leaving fang marks in my boots. Getting it into the aquarium was easy. During my excitement I had almost forgotten that William was in the room. I glanced over at him after I had the snake in place.

He was pale and sick. I had thought the foul smell of breaking open the vial had sickened him, but I saw almost at once that he was fearful and disgusted by the operation. This may lead to worse consequences.

We left the lab, resolving to check on the snake after lunch. I had meant to keep him away, but once he had left the dreadful smell, his interest in the experiment began to kindle.

He asked many questions about how I had treated the essential saltes of the snake and the dangers involved. The great danger, I told him, was to call up something that you could not put down. You should never deal with a being more powerful than yourself, a remark he found funny. I decided not to tell him of the elixir or the chants in case I would find myself in a sorcerer's apprentice story.

After lunch we returned to the lab.

The snake seemed to be in agony. Then she surprised us by giving birth. I had assumed the snake was male and likewise I had forgotten that pit vipers are viviparous. She ate about half of her offspring.

This drama held us entranced until four in the afternoon, when I realized that I had to make some calls to assure that I got the site for the Great Work. William seemed to be part of the program at this point, so I left him to watch the snake. I told him that he would have to go to the pet store and buy some pinkie mice for the young snakes if he wished to keep them alive. He nodded, watching the aquarium fascinatedly.

My calls on the properties at Luling and outside of San Antonio were a bust. Luling would have been great because of the oil wells. The San Antonio property had a few nice mythic resonances (largely added by Whitley Strieber) as well as being close to some of my favorite restaurants.

I could not get through on the other two.

On the way back to the lab, I was beginning to think that William might have been the better choice of the two candidates. At least he was less likely to try and mess around with the magic.

Then the bad news.

William was gone and the aquarium was empty.

While I was trying to take that shock in, he returned.

It seems that he has a sort of mother fixation and was outraged that I had practiced my Art on an expecting snake. At first I thought he was joking, but from the veins bulging in his forehead and the way he trembled while he talked, I knew he was dead serious. My gun was not on my person (I WILL NOT MAKE

THAT MISTAKE AGAIN), so I began to reassure him that I had no idea that the snake was a pregnant snake, that in fact I thought it was a male snake.

I tried to act as shocked and apologetic as I could.

He doubted that I knew very much, since I couldn't sex a snake.

"That's hard to do with ashes," I said.

I asked him what he had done with the snake and he told me that he had let it go in a nearby park. I mentioned that maybe that wasn't a good idea, first since a local elementary school used the park for recess, and second because I really needed to see how long the snake would live.

Even as those words were leaving my mouth I realized their stupidity. I had figured that a murderer would be fairly uninterested in life. I had seriously misjudged here. He seems to have some very big problems with experimentation. *He had been the object of some weird drug testing to affect his dyslexia as a child and it had produced hallucinations. No one had expected the problem, and all his folks did was whip him for his weird tales.*

I had no idea that this guy was so far around the bend. Probably his tenuous connection to reality has really helped my experiments, his presence removing certain constraints that normal people have in their minds.

I spoke as calmly as I could for at least an hour, and he seemed mollified. I, however, am terrified.

It was getting on to seven when I left the lab. I doubted that I was going to secure a site before sunset, and that the momentum of the Working was gone.

On the walk back to my house, I saw a very old-fashioned ring sprinkler watering a neighbor's yard. Two mockingbirds had come to play in the water and as I looked to the west I saw a rainbow form in the watery spray, and it hit me at that moment that the number of the day was 800 as much it was 80 and that stood for the Rainbow of Promise as much as for Foundation. Filled with hope I got home just as the phone was ringing.

It was Rostoker Realty in Doublesign, Texas. It had been low on my list; I had heard that they had a haunted house to rent or sell. They didn't advertise it that way, of course; I had heard it through the parapsychological grapevine. Mrs. Rostoker told me that they could rent the "old Hainey" place to me. I made a joke about Green Acres, *and then I heard her right, "the old Chainey" place. It had been the property of a somewhat controversial doctor, some sort of naturopath who had advocated gold therapy.*

Nothing could be better.

I arranged to take the place in a week, which should give me time to do work on at least one more set of ashes before the Great Work must commence.

I will tell William tomorrow, and work ways of keeping in contact with William's replacement if things go south.

Matthew put the typescript down. Reading by candlelight had been fatiguing.

"So?" asked Cassilda.

"So. I'll leave for Doublesign tonight. You'll take the cat home?"

"Yeah," said Cassilda. "You know anything about the 'old Chainey place'? John told me that you spent some summers there with a crazy aunt."

"It doesn't ring any bells, but Aunt Martha pretty much stayed to herself. I knew her neighbors, the Simmses and the Reals. The Falconer Brothers have done firework shows there for five years, but that only helps me know where to stay. There's a little hotel, the Mirabeau B. Lamar, God knows how they keep in business. I'll be there."

"Aren't you worried about running into William?"

"If William has been off working with this man, I would like to meet him. Surprise him once."

Cassilda got the cat's schedule. Matthew got a sandwich and was on the road.

It was four hours to Fort Worth and another hour and a

half to Doublesign. On the way he thought about his first run-in with the police.

He had been thirteen. John had given him a string of Black Cats, small firecrackers. He was going to shoot them off behind the warehouse where Dad worked, which was OK because it was out of town, but he and another boy got bored. They had bought a roll of caps at the Toot-n-Tot'Um, and were setting them off using hunks of caliche in the alley behind Granny's house. They got to wondering if they put a Black Cat in the middle of a roll of cap, and exploded it, would it make all the caps explode? They were only going to do it until it worked. To make the whole matter scientific, Matthew went to get the magnifying glass his grandmother used to help her with her sewing. They would light the fuse of the Black Cat with the magnifying glass, and then run away.

The first few experiments had proved futile so they had had to pound each of the caps in a row to make them explode. Then Matthew looked up and saw a cop car passing the alley, with another kid motioning the cops on.

Matthew and his guilty friend put all the explosives underneath his grandmother's fence and ran around front. The cops were at the house of some known bad kids, and Matthew and his friend sat down on Granny's porch swing and tried to look real innocent.

The cops came up in a moment, asking them if they had heard any fireworks go off.

They said they had; they thought maybe someone was shooting them off in the park.

The cops asked if the boys knew anyone that might be involved in such an illegal activity.

Oh, no, they said.

The police mentioned the many years that one would serve in jail for shooting off fireworks, the years for lying to the police, and the years for even having fireworks in the city. Pretty much Matthew's life would be absorbed.

The cops left and Matthew and his friend ran back to the back of the house to get the fireworks and hide them. They were worried for months, for the whole summer every time they saw the cop car, and the cops made it a point to always wave at them. Matthew hadn't realized until years after not only did his friend and he look guilty as hell, they must have smelled of black powder.

For years Matthew had thought he could lie very well, because he had fooled the cops. Only college changed his mind.

He got into Doublesign around midnight. He had a heck of a time waking the manager of the Lamar Hotel to let him in. The old man didn't hear so well, but he knew Matthew from years of the fireworks show. He didn't like Matthew because of Haidee, but probably thought he did as good a job of concealing his true feelings from Matthew as Matthew thought he had from the cops. The old man pointed out a new restaurant a couple of blocks away. Matthew got his room key, thanked him for his advice, and crashed.

Matthew slept till ten the next day and had an early lunch at the Kuntry Kitchen.

He took a booth in a corner and decided on iced tea and chicken-fried steak.

"Matt! Matt Reynman. Well, I'll swan."

The waitress, a blue-eyed blond woman whose heavy makeup and slightly too large breasts brought the phrase "Truckstop Trixie" to mind, clearly knew him from somewhere. He was at a loss, and tried to get her to bring that little black name tag closer so that he could read it. He smiled, and she did move just close enough to read the name, "Orfamay." Oh God.

Orfamay. Orfamay. Orfa—

"Orfamay Simms," said Matthew. "I guess it's been twenty years. My God. How time does fly."

Orfamay was one of seven Simms children that had lived next to Aunt Martha's. The only girl—born right in the middle of the great litter, he recalled. She was two years younger than he, which would make her thirty-four.

She looked like a passable but sexy forty-five.

"Well, it's not Simms anymore, hon. It's Kennedy, but I'll change it back when I can afford to. Well, I declare you look just the same. Now what brings you to Doublesign?"

"My station wagon."

"You are a hoot. No, I mean why are you here?"

Matthew had understood the meaning. He was trying to think of a lie.

"I own a bookstore in Austin, and I am on a book-buying trip looking for old and rare books," said Matthew.

"Austin, Texas. Well I'll swan. You were from Austin, weren't you? No, you were from A-ma-rillo. That's right."

"So have you spent your whole life in Doublesign?"

"Not yet," she said, laughing at her own joke. "I moved away right after high school with my first husband, Billy Real. You remember Billy."

Matthew vaguely remembered that one of his tormentors had been named William, but he nodded as if she had mentioned a close friend.

"We lived in Dallas, then in Shreveport, then in Miami. And then I got married again."

"To Mr. Kennedy?"

"No, he was down the pike a little. Let me get your order, hon. You know if you have time I would love to talk about old times with you. I just can't believe you're here after all this time. You're just so cute." With this later, unexpected pronouncement, she pinched his cheeks.

A chicken-fried steak, green beans, mashed potatoes with brown gravy, and a roll with margarine later, Orfamay asked, "Now you saved room for dessert, didn't you?"

"I skip desserts."

"Well, we've got the best devil's food cake in the world here, I ain't lying. It would be a sin to miss it."

"What makes this devil's food cake so good?"

"Well, you ain't going to believe this, but a fellow gave the recipe to Mrs. Bupkin when he came to town, he said it was his gift to the community. It is de-lish. And"—she leaned close so he could see her heavy breasts—"it's supposed to make you lucky."

"Does it?" he asked.

"Well, I don't know, but we have some little lottery winners since he came to town, and a couple of people started new businesses. But best of all it's delicious. Sure you don't want some?"

"No," said Matthew. "I'm not sure what phase of the moon it is."

She looked puzzled.

"Forget it," he said. "I forgo desserts because I am a type II diabetic."

"I am sorry to hear that. My third husband was a diabetic. I can cook great sugar-free cookies."

"I bet you can."

"So what do you say, let's get together this afternoon for a talk and maybe a walk around the lake like we used to?"

"That would be great."

On the way back to his hotel room, Matthew tried to remember if he had ever walked around the lake with Orfamay. He could sort of remember doing it once, but the two-year age difference had been the Great Wall of China in those days.

At two o'clock he was at the little gazebo where the mayor

always made his Fourth of July speech. Orfamay had washed the excess makeup off and was wearing blue jean shorts and a pink halter top.

"Hey," she said.

They started on the walk around the concrete sidewalk that ringed the shallow pond that was called Doublesign Lake.

"You know," she began, "after your aunt's place burned down they never built anything there. You want to go by where it used to be?"

"Sure." He had been several times for the fireworks show, but it was fun to walk on a bright May day with a good-looking and probably available woman. He hadn't looked at a woman that way for two years.

It was just a grassy spot with some overgrown bushes. The old well had been covered with some new aluminum.

"So no kids will fall in."

About that time the deputy's car drove by, and Orfamay stepped behind Matthew. The deputy had a big bloated face, too red, reminding Matthew of a new potato.

"You not like him?" asked Matthew.

"He gives me the creeps. He just started a few weeks ago. There's something not right about him."

"Is he the new fellow that gave out the magic cake recipe?"

"Him? No, the new guy is called Stephen Ashe. He's some kind of scientist. Everybody likes him. He gave some money to beef up the town library, he paid to have some public hazards fixed—like the well here. He's a nice guy."

"Where does he live?"

"I don't know. Why?"

"Well, if he has bought one of the old homes there might be some books in it."

This led to a trip next door, to the Simms homestead, where Mrs. Simms showed Matthew her *McGuffey's Reader* and her *Webster's Speller*, which he gravely agreed were no doubt quite rare.

"Mama?" asked Orfamay. "Where is Mr. Ashe staying?"

"It's at that old clinic, where they treated people for cancer until the feds shut them down," said Mrs. Simms. "Your aunt used to work there a jillion years ago."

"The old Chainey place?"

"Well, that wasn't its name. It was, let me see, the New Jerusalem Cancer Clinic, but that was the doctor all right, Dr. Chainey. He was a good doctor. He cured my mother of cancer after the real doctors in Fort Worth gave up on her. He knew some things."

18 Tzuris of Orfamay

On the morning of May 17, after a dream in which Haidee asked him, "How is a crypt like a cryptogram?" Matthew read the other chapter that Cassilda had prepared for him while he waited for Orfamay to get off work. He felt an afternoon visit to the old clinic might be just the tonic he needed.

צ

Today was the day of water, and I began soaking the ashes that Moon-named woman had given me in order to pay for her therapy. To give Life to that which once had Life is a threefold affair. It is not, as the profane believe, a simple matter of the right chemicals added to the Saltes at a given time, although such actions are needed. It is a matter of reconstituting the Five Elements in the right mix. Earth is already there, it is the Saltes, most people on this overburdened planet will be not but a handful of dust when all is said and done anyway. Water must be added not for the chemical properties of oxygen dihydroxide, which are pretty staggeringly weird, but for the link it gives life to Change. Water freezes, melts, becomes vapor, it is moved by the Moon, it seeks its own level, it dissolves all Saltes—that is to say anything of Earth. All of these properties are Needed by Life. They make us our worst and our best, and ensure that we will always spend some time in each mode regardless of good or bad intentions. Fire that burns as Anger or Love or Art makes sure that the Life moves around. In our modern age since Mary Shelley wrote her great spell, electricity may be used for Fire. Air lets us speak to one another, to send words and dreams across the frightening abyss that exists between each human. Aethyr lets us Remember what we want to become, it too allows for communication between beings, but of a subtle sort. Each of these must be added one by one in this Order. The first four can only be added by one skilled in chemical arts, but the last is an art known to all—it is known by the grandfather who gives his railroad watch to a particular grandson. We know when we see death that we have to concentrate our experience of Life so that we can give the Gift that speaks volumes, even when we are silent. We must prepare the items that we leave behind. This simple action is the magical deed that everyone does, we illustrate the action by enchanting a sword or a mirror, but the real moment is when that watch, that figurine, that whatever was left to the living will also speak to them. This is a part of the magical art that is available to all. This gift that bridges death shines like starlight, and is the one thing that mankind has to keep it from going mad in a world of fools. As I soaked the Saltes today, I realized more and more that William is bringing too much Chaos to the Work. He beat up a teenage boy last night. The young lad had approached him in the rest room of a park known for its homosexual encounters, and offered to let William blow him for twenty-five dollars. William began beating the boy, the assembled population began beating William, and he came to my door at three in the morning demanding pain pills and covered in blood. I read today in the Statesman *that a boy was found murdered there, his head busted on a urinal. I gave him the morning off, with as many pain pills as I have left from last year's abscessed tooth, and this afternoon I am keeping busy picking up supplies at local chemical houses. (There are ten more sentences after this, but he switched ciphers on me again. I tried feeding it to the Trithemius home page, but no dice. It looks like he was writing pretty fast, and may have just been fucking up. At the very end he switches to simple English transliteration again): I don't know if he has done this, but if so I would have to kill the specimens.*

The last lines brought Matthew fully awake. He thought that "specimens" must mean Haidee and the snake and so forth. He didn't really realize that he believed that the alchemist might be successful till that moment. But now he feared that there had been success and then murder. He hoped Hull was in Doublesign so he could kill him.

He was amused that Cassilda had been using some cryptography program she found on the Web. He had been believing that she had some vast esoteric skill at deciphering things. Cassilda had told him the letters that Hull used were from an artificial language called Enochian, not from the prophet of that name, but from the Hebrew word *enoch*, meaning "to initiate." Initiation, Matthew supposed, was a process of deciphering the world. Of finding the hidden truths that lie behind the seeming truths. It had been a seeming truth that Hull had wanted to hear about Haidee because he was a nice guy. In reality he was looking for a dead woman's essential saltes to try some eldritch rite on. If you could read the secret texts, you could be really effective in the world. You would still have to struggle, of course, but you might gain the godlike skill of knowing what the effect of your actions would be.

Orfamay knocked at the door.

"I'm ready."

She was wearing a red-and-white halter top and blue jeans cutoffs, embodying some great American dream. The money she had spent on breast augmentation had been wisely invested, thought Matthew. The "old Chainey" place was just outside of town, on a quiet tree-covered farm road. The gate was a big wrought-iron affair with the words "New Jerusalem Clinic" written across the top. A chain and padlock held it closed. The fence on either side was painted white pickets about four feet tall. There were three buildings that could be seen from the road. The largest was a slate gray one-story ranch house with white trim and big picture windows. The other two buildings were covered in white stucco with dark gray trim. One was evidently a garage since the gravel driveway ran from the gate to it; the other was a smaller two-and-a-half-story affair that had a very steep roof that had openings to the air. The yard was mowed, but there were no flowers in the overgrown beds and the hedges and small trees needed pruning.

"Doesn't look like anyone's home," said Orfamay.

"All the better for a surprise visit," said Matthew, and they both smiled the conspirator's smile, a gesture so ancient that it brings on some very pleasurable primate chemistry. Matthew had a rug in the back of the station wagon that he used when he needed to keep books off of dirty floors. He laid it across the pickets and helped Orfamay cross the barrier, enjoying the feel of her firm warm butt on his hand. He then tried to sort of vault across, discovered that he wasn't in his twenties anymore, and then pulled himself over.

They left the rug in place in case they had to leave quickly. It was risky—the station wagon and the rug—but there was nowhere to hide them. Few people come down such roads, and Texans by nature tend to leave other people's business alone.

They looked in the big picture window. It's hard to see into a darkened room, but they could tell that this was some kind of living room made into a reception area. There was a big desk with an old-style phone and huge typewriter on it, next to two brown filing cabinets. There were chairs and a big fireplace. The front door was locked, and Matthew and Orfamay decided to check other doors and windows before breaking in.

The windows on the rest of the big house were covered in blinds and drapes and, judging from the filth and dead flies they had behind them, hadn't been opened in many a year. The back door was locked as well.

The garage had a new blue Lexus in it. It was Rex Hull's car; Matthew had seen him park in front of his store many times. One bumper sticker read KILL YOUR INNER ELVIS; the other showed an eye-in-the-pyramid design and read JOIN THE CONSPIRACY.

"That's Mr. Ashe's car," said Orfamay.

The car was unlocked. It smelled of cloves and allspice like granny's kitchen at Christmas. There was nothing odd in the glove compartment, some receipts from the Kuntry Kitchen in front of the passenger's seat, and a .357 magnum in the compartment between the bucket seats. Matthew picked it up, and the box of ammunition as well. It was both a bigger and a more expensive gun than he had ever held in his life.

"Are you going to keep that?" asked Orfamay.

"I am going to keep it safe, which means I am going to keep it for now," said Matthew.

She smiled a lot at this remark, and other primate chemistries began in both of them.

The small building with the steep roof was also unlocked. Inside was a small pentahedral chamber that tapered to a black dome with slits in it. A large cranking mechanism allowed you to turn the dome so that the slits in the dome would be lined up with the slits in the roof—alternately filling the room with light or darkness. Matthew played with the mechanism for a while until he got the room as light as he could get it.

Along one wall were two industrial-sized zinc sinks that you might find in a laboratory. They smelled of rotting meat, and a test of their faucets showed that water was still on at the clinic. Against the second wall was a curious sort of stove which had many small jets that could direct fire of different heights. The third wall had some sort of electrical device, not unlike the machine used to start the heart at a hospital. The fourth wall had a large glass case set lengthwise against it. Its general size suggested a coffin. It was heavily stained with some foul-smelling greenish goo. The last wall, of course, had the door by which they had entered.

"What kind of place is this?" asked Orfamay.

"Not," said Matthew, "a very nice one."

They decided to try and break into the main house. They would get a tire iron from the station wagon and smash the glass. They stepped outside, and were not pleased by what they heard.

"So what do we have here? Clinic's closed. Been closed for thirty-five years. I reckon you can't get cured for what ails you."

It was the deputy, and his appearance scared Matthew. The man looked like John, could have been his double, with about eighty pounds added. His face, his hands, his arms, his legs, his gut were stuffed with fat and bloated. He was so soft and overfilled, Matthew expected the skin to burst right away and a tidal wave of pus and ichor to wash over them. He couldn't fully credit that this was a human being. If the deputy was human, humanity was more inclusive than Matthew thought it *should* be.

Matthew smiled what he hoped was a winning smile and began his spiel. "Hello, I am Matthew Reynman. I know the clinic is closed, but I was hoping to speak with the current owner. You see, I deal in rare books and I thought there might be some medical texts here, particularly dealing with alternative therapies. Some books of that type can be very valuable."

"I know who you are, but you don't know shit. You see, Mr. Reynman, nobody here knows you. Nobody knows you're out here—looking for some kind of secret books—nobody gives a shit. That's what my job is, giving a shit. I give a shit for little shits like you."

"I appreciate your concern, Mr.—"

"My name," began the deputy, and then he paused for a moment as if to remember it, "is Aldones. Mason Aldones, everyone knows my name because my name is the thin line that keeps chaos at bay and lawlessness outside of our fair community."

"We're outside of Doublesign now," said Orfamay.

"Yes, young lady, we are. We are on the side of lawlessness here, in the region of chaos. Look how easily you both succumbed to the crime of trespassing."

The deputy had begun to rest his right hand on his service revolver.

"We called out," said Matthew. "I was about to leave a note for Mr. Ashe."

"Mr. Ashe don't need no note from you. You know why? Because he knows everything—he's not a little know-nothing shit like you. He don't have to find no books, because he knows everything. How could he do what he has done, without knowing everything? He knows if you are sleeping, he knows when you're awake, he knows if you've been bad or good for goodness sake."

He then drew his gun like lightning. It was a fast *liquid* move that made Matthew sick to see it.

"You see?" said the deputy. "I could have killed you right now and dumped your bones in the well, because we're out in the lawless part of the world. That's why we shouldn't come out here. I don't like coming out here, and little know-nothing shits should never come out here. You can appreciate the danger."

"Yes, sir. That's quite a lesson," said Matthew. "I'm glad someone as important as Mr. Ashe has someone like you to watch out for him."

"I don't watch out for Mr. Ashe. I don't need to see him or talk to him, because he knows everything. I doubt that I will ever see him again, and why should I? Did he not make the people of Doublesign rich with his magic cake? He told me on my first day at the job that this may not be the best of all possible worlds, but that he would tend his little garden. I just help. I am a helper in the garden. A little do-bee. I pull out weeds, the weeds of chaos. You're not going to be weeds if I let you drive back to Doublesign, are you?"

"No, my book-buying trip is almost over," said Matthew. "I'll be a good little cabbage."

"A good little cabbage, that's great, a good little cabbage. I like that. I like coleslaw in the summertime," said the deputy.

The deputy lifted the gun from pointing at them and shot it into the air.

"I guess we had better go now," said Matthew.

"Oh, no need to hurry. I think I'll escort you back to town. You don't know what kind of dangers there are out here," said the deputy.

"Thank you," said Matthew.

"Whereabouts in town do you need to go?" asked the deputy.

"I have to go to work at the Kitchen," said Orfamay.

"I'll just go back to the Mirabeau B. Lamar," said Matthew.

"Well, Kitchen it is then," said the deputy. "I am glad to see that you've taken such an interest in books, Ms. Kennedy. I am very interested in books myself. We'll have many long talks about books after your friend goes back to Austin. I can hardly wait."

"Neither can I," said Orfamay.

They drove back into town at thirty-five miles an hour with the deputy following one car length behind, his flashers going. Matthew pulled into the Kuntry Kitchen parking lot.

"I'll sneak over to your room tonight," said Orfamay.

"Be careful, real careful," said Matthew, who didn't know what else to say and was eaten with guilt that the mere knowing of him was going to cause so much grief to an innocent being.

The deputy followed Matthew to the inn. He got out with Matthew.

"Is there any money in comic books?" he asked.

"Well," said Matthew, "some comic books are worth a great deal, but it's not a market I know. Do you have some old comic books?"

"Yeah, a kid that was drifting through town had a knapsack full of them he was going to sell at a convention in Dallas. I picked him up for vagrancy. He sort of fell down and hurt himself. So now I've got these comics books to get rid of. You might want to come by and look at them. I'd cut you a real good deal since you came to Doublesign looking for books—I think people should be rewarded for coming to a little Podunk doing their business and getting the hell out. Don't you?"

"Well, I certainly think there should always be reward for effort," said Matthew, "but I wouldn't be able to tell you much about comic books, so I'll pass, but thanks for the offer."

"Oh," said the deputy, "I am sure you'll see them sometime. You'll be by. I've been reading them every night. I just love the Heap."

Matthew went into his room, threw himself on his bed, and lay still for hours.

He smelled very bad. He got up at dusk and got a snack at the 7-Eleven and took his Glybudiride. He showered, and changed into his other clothes, which were less smelly.

She knocked very gently at nine, and he sprang out of bed, pulled her into his darkened room as quickly as he could, and then put the chain on the door—as though such a tiny piece of metal could stop such a big man who had the law on his side.

"Sugar, you're too tense. He's hateful, but he ain't any worse than my second husband," said Orfamay.

"You mean you lived with someone like that? You couldn't live with someone like that, it's impossible!" As he said these words, Matthew realized what an absolutely lucky, wonderful life he had had, and he suddenly loved this waitress in the dark of his room for letting him in on the secret of his life.

"Oh of course you can live with someone like that, you can live with anyone, you just don't notice they're like that when you marry them. Or you can be really stupid like I was with husbands two and three and think you can change the bastards. Bastards can't be changed, it is not in their blood."

"Were you lucky with husband number four?"

"I've never been lucky in my life, Matthew Reynman. Husband number four let on as he had a lot of money and a weak heart and that maybe some night he would die in the middle of a blow job. I sucked that little root as anxious as a nun to please Jesus. His money turned out to be smaller than his dick, and all I got out of that marriage was a damn near permanent pain in the neck from so much sucking. Not that I don't need to work out that tension by making the same motions once in a while."

The next hour was a series of horror stories about her five marriages that made Matthew aware of what life can be like. His books had never prepared the way for such revelations. He didn't know that a man could slap a woman around every night for years, and she still want to cook and clean and make a house for him—he didn't know that a man could lie about his money, his business, his health, his past to a woman that he lived with. Oh sure, he had lied to women he'd slept with, years ago before meeting Haidee. But he hadn't known it could be like this. To hear this woman tell him all of this as though it was a joke, a sad story about how humans never learn, was much more chilling to him than the thought that in a few hours a psycho would be looking for him in Austin. Nothing should be like this. That cruelty like this existed in the world, was a good reason to blow up the world.

Yet her stories continued. How she had been abandoned in a bus station, "big pregnant in New York City" just before Christmas, and she got cold and hungry looking for shelter, and that made the baby come soon, it came on Christmas—and the little preemie Christ was given up for adoption. She wouldn't tell them her real name because she didn't want her son tracking her down and asking how the hell you could give birth in an unheated bus station bathroom. She had felt so stupid and afraid and guilty, and when she tracked the father down, he was in Atlantic City with a cheap hooker that made fun of her shaky looks.

Story after story after story, and soon it was after midnight, and Matthew, who had realized that he was the luckiest man alive, had been petting her and telling her that things could be different, found himself with a hard-on.

He tried to hide it, he said he didn't want her to think that he might offer her a better life, he was going to be long gone as soon as he had a chance to check out the clinic.

She said that she didn't look for chances anymore. You can't run away by looking for someone running faster than you.

A fuck, she said, was a fuck.

So for the first time since Haidee was killed, Matthew found himself eating pussy. Orfamay had trimmed her hair in the shape of a heart, carefully trimming it away from her cunt lips for easy access. As she pulled her cunt lips apart and he began tonguing her large and gristly clit, Matthew felt a moment of salvation, as though the salty juices held something that he needed to come alive. He ate at the Fruit of Life like a wretch lost in the desert would drink at a well.

When he fucked her later, he came very quickly the first

time, and it took a long while for him to get it up again. That had never happened, so he knew that in the time since Haidee's death age had visited him. But he fucked long and well, until he got tired and let Orfamay ride him like a bucking bronc. He only wished she had a cowboy hat and boots on. That had always been one of his fantasies, but he had never told Haidee, because it was the only one of his fantasies that involved a white woman.

He had flashes of her while they fucked, he could remember her now, her young body, her shy smile, all that had been taken away by the five husbands and the endless number of fools.

After they finished, he listened to her snore.

He knew that tomorrow he would see her as she really was. He knew that his love and concern would melt in the light of their differences, that her hard life and his good one would be too big an abyss. He wondered if he was the worst bastard that had ever come through her life, and if he had been unfaithful to Haidee by finally sleeping with another woman.

The really sad thing in the world, he decided, is that there aren't any magic cakes that you eat and they make you rich.

He fell asleep about three in the morning.

Once or twice he almost woke up, and hearing her snoring thought that Haidee was in the room. That was odd, he hadn't remembered her snoring. He remembered her being perfect—and he felt that memory flowing away from him—like a blossom on a stream. It circled and bobbed and was gone. He wasn't any less for it, since real memories remained, but he knew something was gone. He was in a garden and God had taken away his rib. That's what it was.

19 Queer Deaths and Odd Closures

There was a sharp rapid knocking on the door. Matthew saw that it was nine, and Orfamay drew the sheet up over her unnaturally firm titties.

It could be William.

It could be Mason Aldones.

But in any case it had to be death.

Matthew leapt up, grabbed the gun from his jeans, and flung open the door.

It was Yunus Iqbal. He was holding a folder in one hand, and staring firstly at Orfamay Kennedy with shock and the .357 with fear. "Good morning, Matthew," he said. "Can I come in, or is it a bad time?"

Matthew could see the deputy's car some blocks away, but he couldn't tell if the deputy was in it.

"Come in."

Yunus walked in, looking a little sheepish.

"Perhaps, Matthew, you should put the gun down and some pants on. You may wish to introduce me to your friend."

Matthew put the gun on the nightstand and began putting his pants on.

"Yunus, this is Orfamay. Orfamay, Yunus," said Matthew.

Orfamay drew the sheets entirely over her head as though this would make her disappear.

"I am glad to be making your acquaintance," said Yunus. "Ms. Cassilda Jones contacted me to deliver this document to you, as she thought it might help. She has found the codes harder and harder to break, but she wanted me to give this to you while you were still in Doublesign because she thought it says something that indicates that Hull's plans may have gone awry. She called me last night and asked if I knew where you might be. You had told me about this bed-and-breakfast after you had stayed here with your wife, you know your dead wife Haidee."

"Yes, I remember Haidee quite well," said Matthew.

"Well, I told her I would bring the documents," said Yunus.

"Why didn't you just fax them?"

"I wanted to rejoice in that you were still alive. I wanted to see that you were not dead, because you are a dear friend, so I got up at three and started driving."

"Thanks. I am glad to see you and I am really glad to be alive," said Matthew.

"I can tell you are glad to be alive," said Yunus.

At this moment, Orfamay began to wail beneath the sheets.

"Hon," said Matthew, "could you be a bit more quiet? Mr. Iqbal is an old friend, he has bailed me out of jail many times."

Oddly enough, this didn't reassure Orfamay, who began to wail louder.

"Hon, really, be quiet, the deputy is out there," said Matthew.

Orfamay stopped.

"Yunus, have you had breakfast yet? There's a great little restaurant down the street. Let's all have breakfast and I will look this over."

Over two eggs sunny side up, toast, grits, and coffee Matthew read.

ק

I am calmer today, well somewhat calmer. I have resigned myself to the idea that as long as I have William around I will have chest pains from stress. Today on the day of Vases and Vessels, I will pour the mixture and begin to heat it. When I found William taking a piss in the mixture yesterday, I thought to kill him, but then I reasoned that if he is supposed to represent Chaos, I had better let him be chaotic. The bigger fear I have is controlling the population of Doublesign. I think that the clinic is far enough away to discourage tourists and strays, but I will need to buy into the local law enforcement. I have begun a good-will tour of the area. The old sheriff is a little too nosy, but he has been the town sheriff for thirty years, and is not big on the get up and go. Maybe I can find him some young assistant that will be under my spell. It is imperative that the work not stop once certain processes have begun. I'm risking a great deal to move the man up there, but I think he will be a botched experiment anyway. I need to know how he reacts to the bromines and if my method of heating will produce enough results on so large a body mass. Otherwise I don't much care how he comes out. The clinic was run by a Dr. Chainey, who had in turned studied with Dr. Tomas. It has a unique star chamber which enabled him to channel the light of certain stars on the bodies of his patients. He had some theory about the healing effects of Aldebaran's light in particular, which may help in the quickening process. The older locals swear by his cancer cures; perhaps I will discover that secret as I look through his books and so forth. I don't know where he is buried, but if I discover this, I will raise him up and find out his secrets. I had never thought of myself as a benefactor to mankind, but discovering a cure for cancer ought to do the trick. And of course the money benefits there are much greater than what I might make raising the dead. I was amused by the lack of imagination of previous alchemists in this regard. Curwin in his Chymical Wisdom Booke *suggests that the alchemists might raise funds by digging up old graves and thus old family secrets. It is distressing to think that the dean of American alchemists made a living by blackmailing the ignorant folk of New England. I guess it adds a special meaning to the saying "He knows where all the skeletons are buried." My sources inside the police department tell me that a dragnet is being spread for William. Matthew Reynman is out of jail for assaulting that black man. He apparently went crazy the day I got the* Chronicle *ad info from his shop. I sort of remember his little faggot friend mincing in as I left. I wonder if there is some cosmic connection. William is real excited by the negative press that the bookstore is getting and I'm real glad that we're out of here in three days. I will have finished my twenty-two daily meditations, and then I'll burn this book as part of the fire that warms the Great Work. I am excited and fearful; my old dull life of being a mystery writer seems far away now. I think I'll arrange for my other cat's paw to watch the New Atlantis store—all of the strangeness going on there makes me think that there may be some link with the Work, which could be a problem. I have decided to name her ALCHIMIA, after the secret name of Virgin Lucifrea, the Rosicrucian Virgin, given in* The Chymical Marriage of Christian Rosenkreutz *in 1616. "My name contains six and fifty, yet has only eight letters. The third is a third part of the fifth, which added to the sixth will produce a number, the root whereof shall exceed the third by the first precisely, and it is half of the fourth. The fifth and seventh are equal: so are the last and the first. These make the seventh as much as the sixth has, and this contains four more than the third tripled." {Matthew, this rigmarole takes the number value of English letters A=1, B=2, and so forth so that C the third is worth 3, and tripled is 9 or equal to 11, the fifth letter in the name, ALCHIMIA—I worked all the ratios, and it works out fine—such as adding them all together and getting 56. This is some sort of English Cabala. Hull had played around with similar things in the baseball card clues in* Dad's Last Pitch*—I think it shows what happens if you spend too long at your keyboard.}*

Matthew returned to the world. Orfamay was discussing her trip to New Orleans with Yunus.

"So I told Sheila that she had better send that Dick Clark thing. I always send in mine," said Orfamay.

Yunus said, "You read it?"

"I read it," said Matthew.

"Apparently he meant to destroy the book for some reason. I think we can guess that he wasn't in much control by the time that the book was finished. John and I figured out that the last entry was written the day William put the book in your house."

"Does Cassilda have any clues as to what the next three meditations read?"

"No, it's really tough—at least the next two—which is what she has been working on."

"So are you headed back to town?"

"I could stay a day or two."

"I might need someone to take me on a little trip."

"Hey," said Orfamay. "I was going to take you."

"Hon," said Matthew, "I can't let you do that. You and I have to put on a little show of having a fight so that the deputy is off your tail."

"But—," said Orfamay.

"No 'buts'—you've got to live here; I'll be gone tonight," said Matthew.

"But you can't go back to Austin, the police haven't caught William yet," said Yunus.

Matthew said, "I can't stay here. I've got a psycho killer deputy after me here."

"Matthew, my friend, you do not live your life well. I have never had more than one psycho killer after me at any given time," said Yunus.

"As always, my friend, you are full of sage advice."

"Yes," said Yunus. "I have often heard you say to Selma that I am full of it."

Matthew paid for the breakfast, and the three of them

walked into the parking lot. Sure enough, Deputy Mason Aldones waited in his car. Matthew said in a low voice, "Remember hon, just for show."

"Just for show nothing," said Orfamay, and slapped the hell out of him and marched back into the Kuntry Kitchen.

Matthew and Yunus walked to the inn. He could hear the deputy laughing as they passed.

The theory was that Yunus would drive by the New Jerusalem Clinic, and Matthew would hop out and go over the wall. Exactly an hour later Yunus would drive back. Matthew had a tire iron and the gun from Hull's Lexus.

Over the fence was easy, as scared as Matthew was.

He looked around, saw no one, heard nothing, and advanced on the picture window, which he smashed thoroughly with the tire iron. It is amazing how loud breaking glass is. The first impression was the stench that billowed out; Matthew came close to losing the two eggs sunny side up, toast, and grits. In the reception area, a photo on the mantel caught Matthew's eye. New Jerusalem Clinic 1963. There were three men in lab coats and three women dressed as nurses. Two of the women he recognized; one was his aunt Martha Scott, the other her maid Sophie. He put the picture in his pants pocket. Martha looked exactly as she did when she was to die twenty-three years later.

Out of the reception area was a hall that led to examining rooms and a library-office. On the desk were a collection of Rex Hull's books, magazines that he had written for, interviews of him, and other impedimenta necessary for an ego trip, including a hand mirror which had certain signs written around its rim. Matthew guessed the guy would stare into the mirror and fancy himself a great magician. Matthew had been assuming that Hull was not here, but tried a yell at this point: "Rex Hull, I've come for my wife, you Satanic bastard!"

The lack of response made him feel silly.

The first two examination rooms he checked were empty and unused; however, as he was progressing toward the back of the building, the stench grew worse. He decided to try the room at the end of the hall first.

It was an alchemist's chamber all right, with strange charts, alembics and athanors, vials of strange liquids, crystals that smoked, a star map on the ceiling showing the constellations of another world—but it was the decaying corpse of Rex Hull that attracted most of Matthew's attention. The corpse was somewhat pallid and puffy except for the gouts of congealed blood that ran from the chest wound. Someone had stuck a sharpened broom handle into the middle of his chest, and the resulting blood had stained the blue wizard's robe, obliterating some of the purple and silver symbols that were worked into the velvet. After the pained expression of Mr. Hull's face, and of course the wound, the next thing to grab Matthew's attention was the chain around Rex's foot. It ran to the sink and Bunsen stand that held all of the chemical vials. Rex could have gone anywhere in the room with the chain but would have been hard-pressed to leave the room. At this point Matthew noticed there was a cot in the corner, with a filled bedpan underneath it. Matthew pulled himself together. He would have to examine the scene and leave. This was not something he wanted to be reporting to Deputy Aldones. He might should tell the sheriff, but that was a decision to make when he was out of Doublesign. Look over the room systematically.

The room had one entrance: in the middle of its south wall was the door from the hall. The two windows in the north wall were covered by drapes, as he had seen yesterday. Beneath the two windows was the cot and bedpan. On either side of this were elephant-feet umbrella stands full of scrolls. Matthew crossed to these. They were parchment written in the same characters and handwriting as the notebook had been. Along the east wall, to his right was a standard sink and Bunsen burner stand as might be seen in any high school chemistry lab. One of the pipes had the heavy chain attached to it. On the eastern wall were charts from *Gray's Anatomy* and what appeared to be drawings of the human body showing some sort of network of lines and stars whose meaning eluded Matthew. In the center of the room were two dissimilar tables. One was a somewhat ratty card table that had a paper plate on it, and a can of Dr Pepper. A black furry bit of mold on the paper plate might have been a sandwich. A small hexagonal table of inlaid wood stood nearby. An hourglass and a purple stone egg lay upon the small table. On the western wall hung a framed print of Botticelli's *Venus*—there were a myriad of threads that connected the print to small pieces of paper bearing strange sigils that were stuck with thumbtacks of varying colors. The ceiling had a large star chart with unknown constellations between two fluorescent lights—the only feature that reminded Matthew that this had been a mid-Texas clinic rather than some strange sorcerer's lair.

Matthew went to the body. There were bruises on the dead novelist's face. It seemed likely that Hull had been unconscious when the broom handle had been driven into his chest. Maggots writhed in the chest wound, and seeing this, Matthew did lose the two eggs sunny side up, the toast, grits, and coffee—managing by a great jerk not to profane the dead man. Matthew vomited under the table in spasm after spasm. When it was over he heard the deputy's voice: "You killed him. You killed God!"

Matthew was more or less on all fours; standing in the doorway was Mason Aldones with a drawn weapon.

Matthew looked up, his face slimy with vomit. "You idiot, does this look like I did this? That this is recent? This man has been dead for days."

"Then William must have killed Him, but that couldn't happen. Mr. Ashe knew too much for William to kill Him. He told me, He told me that only you could interfere. He said William had no will, that He could control him. It had to be you. It had to be."

"Why, because you were supposed to protect Mr. Hull?"

"My job was to see no one would come out here; now I have no job. Mr. Ashe was the only reason I had for anything, He was God. Nobody knew as much as Mr. Ashe, there is nothing I know that I didn't get from Mr. Ashe. He told me how to act, He told me how to act. Why are you here?"

"I'm here because Mr. Hull stole my wife."

"Mr. Ashe didn't steal no one's wife. He was all good things. In the Bible He showed me about the Tree of Life and the Tree of Knowledge of Good and Evil. He made those fruits. That's the key to magic cake, it's made from the Tree of Knowledge of Good and Evil. He commanded me to never eat of it, because He said He didn't want me knowing of good and evil. He said I was the man of earth. He knew everything."

"Evidently he didn't know how to keep William Delaplace from chaining him up."

"Oh my God!"

The deputy reholstered his gun.

The deputy said, "Look what he did to Him. He must have hit and hurt Him."

"While you were driving around the village picking up drifters to kill for their comic books."

"I should kill you for even seeing this. No one should see God dead and live."

"All I want is my wife back."

"You're not getting anything. Don't you understand, God is dead, God is dead, nobody is getting anything back, nobody is getting anything, the sun must stop in the sky."

"I don't think Hull's death is going to affect the sun."

"Oh my God, my God." The deputy began to pound the linoleum next to Hull's corpse. "What if you are right? What if the world goes on with God dead? What if we get up every morning knowing this and yet we still have to go to work, to drive?" On the word "drive" the deputy began to let out an awful keening wail. "How can we drive anywhere, ever again? We can't even move. I'm staying right here forever."

Matthew began to stand.

The deputy said, "I can't let you go. You'll go tell everyone, you'll tell everyone that God is dead. Doublesign is over, the winds will blow us away. Ashes to ashes. Dust to dust."

"You can't kill me—it wasn't your purpose. Your purpose was to keep people from coming out here. You have failed."

"But it wasn't my failure that killed God. It wasn't. It wasn't. It wasn't." Then the deputy embraced the corpse, knocking the broomstick out of the chest cavity. "Forgive me, forgive me!"

"Rex Hull wasn't God."

"I should kill you. Perhaps your lack of faith killed God."

"Look around you—what need would God have of these charts?"

"That's the Tree of Life," said the deputy, pointing out the east wall, "and that is the Tree of Knowledge of Good and Evil."

Matthew stared at each. There *was* something about the silly, outrageous print and yarn combination. It made something in his brain realize something, but that didn't mean it was a *good* thing. He looked back at the blubbering fat man, who had hit his hands against the floor so much they had started to bleed.

"Think, did God ever have a woman here, a black woman?"

"God would have no truck with blackness, and He had no need of a woman, He could give birth. This I know, because Mr. Ashe tells me so."

Matthew asked, "Don't you need to call the sheriff?"

"What can the sheriff do? I don't know that it is illegal to kill God. That might be legal. There are too many things in the world that are legal."

Matthew was trying for a very calm voice. "I think reporting a death is a *good* thing."

"Reporting the death of God? There will be panic in the streets, no one will stop at the stoplights anymore, the world will be full of drifters."

"Well, at least you could get their comic books."

"This is not a joke. You are so stupid, but I guess everyone would be stupid after God had died. Mr. Ashe was the sum total of all wisdom."

"Yeah, er, it must be tough. Well, I need to go mourn."

"Mourn?" asked the deputy.

"Yes," said Matthew, "I need to mourn the death of God."

"You're not just leaving to tell?"

"No, you're right, there would be panic in the streets." Matthew checked his watch—Yunus would be driving by soon. Matthew asked, "How did you know I was here?"

"I figured you would be back, and if I followed you you would spot me, so I just checked every half hour."

Gang aft agley.

"Should I send anyone after you to help you somehow?" asked Matthew.

"No, of course not, I am a grown man, I will cope, that's what grown men do, isn't it? Cope."

"You're very brave."

"I was made brave."

"I'll be going now."

Matthew walked very slowly out of the room, through the hall, and out the now opened front door. He crossed at a somewhat more rapid pace to the road.

It seemed like forever till Yunus showed up. Forever was six and a half minutes by Matthew's watch. Matthew stood by the deputy's car.

Matthew told Yunus to drive fast—after all, there wasn't anyone to give them a ticket. God's death had resulted in a period of lawlessness.

Yunus asked him, "Find anything?"

"A dead alchemist and a crazy cop."

"Any sign of Haidee's ashes?"

"They could have been anywhere, floating in some vial, stoppered in some bottle. I have let that go forever. I have seen what happens to people who hold on too tightly. I renounce the quest of looking for her ashes."

"It is a serious thing to renounce a quest."

"I am not doing it out of cowardice. I put my life on the line. I have seen misdirected love today, and I want to keep that with me forever."

"So what now?"

"I'll go back to the Lamar and pick up my things and go back to Austin."

"Are you nuts? It's still the eighteenth. You drive in now you could be there by dusk. Don't do it."

Matthew said, "You're right. I'll stay at the Falconers' in Fort Worth tonight, and then hit Austin tomorrow. I wouldn't be worth much. I hope the police nab him."

"Well, John has got his friend Blick watching the store and your house, and he and the girls are doing all sorts of business to make it look like you are there."

"Well, maybe that will catch him, but I don't think that William Delaplace is taken by illusion when he doesn't want to be. He clearly saw through the master illusionist back there. But he seemed to take his disillusionment hard."

"What are you going to do about Orfamay?"

"Nothing. Like she said, 'A fuck is a fuck.' I know that I am far from the worst thing in her life, but I know enough about myself to know that if I tried to stay I would be."

"You think she'll have more trouble from the deputy?"

"No. The deputy has to face the death of God. I think he'll spend the rest of his days in the New Jerusalem Clinic, nobody there to heal him. You know my aunt used to work there?"

Matthew pulled the framed photo from his pocket. Yunus glanced at it at one of the two stoplights in Doublesign.

20 Revelations of Norman Papin

Janet and Doug Falconer were in all ways the salt of the earth. They kept a clean beautiful home in Fort Worth, they were active in their church, built houses for the poor, furthered the cause of education and reason, and had a damn fine swimming pool. They were likewise good solid hosts, who took you down to a good barbecue place in a nearby strip mall. Everyone should know someone like the Falconers. Matthew Reynman sat in their den watching BBC comedy and looking through back issues of the *American Fireworks News*. HE WHO HATH ONCE SMELT THE SMOKE IS NE'ER AGIN FREE. And reading the books *Glitter, Chemistry and Technique Dictionary* and *Manual of Fireworks, Bonfires & Illuminations* and *The Complete Art of Firework Making*. Occasionally he and Doug would walk out to the little house by the pool where they kept the soda and he would have a Fresca or a Stewart's Diet Root Beer. He couldn't believe he was two hours away from Rex Hull's corpse, or four hours away from Rex's killer.

He would drive to Austin tomorrow. If he waited, even a day, it would be too long and he would never drive there and Fear would win.

"Hey" said Doug. "I've got a video on *The Dreaded Dud*."

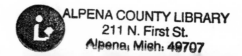

"You remember that night in Schertz, when we couldn't find that dud, and we looked for hours, and then you found it and started carrying it back with a lit fusee?" asked Janet. "Oh Lord, I remember the hell Haidee gave you."

It was a great night. When it came time for bed, Matthew went into their guest room, where Doug stored all of the horror and thriller paperbacks of his Irving youth. Matthew read a little of *Zacherly's Vulture Stew* before dropping into a dreamless sleep.

The Falconers rose early for work, and Matthew made it out by nine, locking up the house when he left. Everyone should know someone like the Falconers.

It was about two-thirty when he pulled by the New Atlantis Bookstore. Cassilda was inside.

"I was glad to hear last night that you were alive. The police watched this place and your house all day and night, and last night they caught someone trying to break in here. The police wouldn't tell us anything, not even John and Yunus—who sort of have ins—but Detective Blick wanted you to come to the station when you got to town."

"Wow, maybe there is a connection between what I saw there and what happened here."

"Yunus told us you found Rex's carcass."

"Staked like a vampire. I'll tell you all later tonight. If they caught William breaking in last night, I want to know about it. I want this to be over."

Matthew ran by the rest room and started to say good-bye to Cassilda.

Cassilda said, "I translated the next two parts of Hull's notebook. I guess you won't find it as interesting now. The last part still eludes me. Anyway, here are the next two parts."

Matthew said, "I can't tell you how much I owe you and John and Camilla and Yunus and everybody. I realized recently how very rich my life is to have such friends. I have awakened to my happiness."

"We only awakened to ours last year, when John saw life and death. We are duty-bound to awaken others in our travels."

"Well, I'll try to do my part."

Matthew found that he couldn't park near the police station, so he wound up parking in front of the homeless shelter called the GuestHaus. When he got in, Blick was out; he was told to wait, so he read.

ר

I am amazed at how quickly the man in the jar is growing. He may even be born on our first day in Doublesign. Surely this speaks well for William Delaplace's position in the Work. I am growing more relaxed about him, since I had a long talk about what we would need to do in Doublesign and he gave me his word that he would help me out there. The miraculous thing he sees in the jar probably has convinced him. We live so much of our lives without seeing a true miracle that when one comes along, most people either miss it or disbelieve it. The people that do believe are often of the worst sort. My ancestor George Hull, who constructed the Cardiff Giant, perhaps the greatest American hoax, certainly spent enough of his time dealing with the easily impressed who wanted to see in the stone man a miracle proving that the Garden of Eden was in New York, and that there were "giants in the Earth in those days." I suppose my making of life from the Earth is the same as his, but I shall show this Art only to the few who can see it for what it is, rather than set up my tent and let the hoi polloi in at $0.50 to see, $1.00 to Touch. This familial remanifestation of making miracles out of earth sort of makes me into the son of Frankenstein, and why not? His was always the best model. When I was a child Monster Horror Theater *was on Sunday mornings. Some Sundays I would go to church like other little Hulls, other Sundays I would* *stay home and watch* The Mummy *or* Dracula Meets the Wolfman. *That was my pact with Mom, alternate Sundays with Jesus and Frankenstein. Now I too can say, "It's alive! It's alive! I know what it feels like to be a god!" Great-grandfather's creation was said to have got a woman with child, which was no doubt a convenient miracle, much like the comely daughters of ancient Greece who could attribute an out-of-wedlock pregnancy on the randy Zeus. I shall most definitely have a child by Alchimia. Imagine what a line might lead to. She perfected from mortal shortcomings, and I, one of a line of magicians that bring life to the Earth. His Adam will be greater than my Adam, his Eve greater than my Eve. They will be a race of atomic supermen to rule the world. It was my destiny when George Hull dreamed of going beyond the family business of cigar making to wonder making right after the Civil War, or as my next-door neighbor says, the War of Northern Aggression. I had not in my four previous marriages ever felt comfortable enough to have a child. I realize that a biracial child has certain troubles to face, but with my money that should not be a great matter. I will do my parental part and watch Oprah, Ricki Lake, and so forth on the matter so that I have the issue of my time well in hand. I shall of course school him at home. He could get an essential education from me, and not be fed the nonsense and junk that leads men like William Delaplace to becoming what they are. Public schooling has much to answer for. My excitement grows hourly. I consulted the Chaldean Oracle as to whether I could trust William Delaplace to be by my side in Doublesign and received an emphatic "Yes!" My fear of abandonment, which has always been my downfall, can now be laid to rest.*

"Mr. Reynman? Detective Blick can see you now."

Matthew walked into Blick's office. Blick was not smiling.

"I wish I could tell you that we had caught William Delaplace," began Blick. "But alas we caught someone a good deal closer to you."

Matthew sat in the chair in front of the desk.

"He acts like a kid. I keep thinking he's seventeen, when he's twenty-nine. He is Norman Papin."

"Norman?"

"We caught him breaking into your store last night. We were so sure we had Delaplace, we even called off the surveillance of your home. He had a key to the store from when he worked there. He claims to know nothing about any of your troubles, said that he didn't even know that you were out of town. After a while he realized that he should shut up and get a lawyer. He's been trying to get hold of Camilla Reynman—I think it was the only lawyer he knew of. She isn't very interested in talking to him for obvious conflict-of-interest reasons. He has expressed an extreme interest in talking to you. If you're willing, I would really like you to talk to him. He doesn't seem to be a bad sort of guy, and I'm much more interested in what he might tell you."

"Well," said Matthew, "before I become more involved in police business I guess I had better report a murder."

It took Matthew two hours to tell about what he had found in Doublesign to an FBI man that Blick called. Then he went in to see Norman.

"Hello, Mr. Reynman, I want to tell you I didn't take anything from your store. I love that store—think how many hundreds of dollars I spent there."

"I don't think you would do anything bad, Norman, but I really want to know what you did or were about to do and why. If I don't press charges I doubt if the police can do anything to you, but I am in grave danger and I need help."

"I had heard from Allen that Delaplace had been to your brother's wedding. I played *Cosmic Encounter* with your brother once a long time ago. Anyway, I know you're in deep shit."

"So why did you break into my store?"

"It's a secret. I'll tell you, but it's a secret that can make you big money. But if everybody knew it, there wouldn't be big money to be had."

"I'm listening, but you're not getting any guarantees from me."

"OK, that's fair, you always encouraged me. You know I've tried to write books for years. I've done a far amount of media fanac, I did some *Star Trek–Prisoner* crossover stories. But I couldn't plot. I would just throw the characters together, have them crack their standard lines, and then blow up the bad guy. You remember?"

"Only too well," Matthew said.

"Well, I tried to sell some of that, and I got laughed at. Do you remember the night of the South by Southwest party?"

"Pretty well."

"Well, Mr. Hull had parked his car at the store so I had to give him and Mr. Iqbal a ride back to the store. I dropped Mr. Iqbal at the bond place and took Mr. Hull on to the store. I started telling him about my plotting problem. He said that there was a trick to plotting, but that it was kept secret so that only published authors would know. I laughed, but he said he was serious, so I asked what the trick was. He said he would tell me, but that I had to do a couple of things for him. He was suddenly so intense, like finding a snake in your backyard, his eyes lit up, and I just knew he was telling me the truth. So I asked what the things were. Number one, I had to blow him. Well I'd never done that, but it didn't seem like much of a sacrifice. Number two, I had to watch your store."

"My store?"

"Because of the secret. There are no plots left. They all ran out in 1850. The only thing that's left is rearranging them. The muses are a pair of dice. You find certain books, and by randomly picking together the plots of four or five books you have a best-seller. He said that's how he wrote all of his books.

He suggested that I go up to the science fiction loft and try it that night. So we went together. I went home and got some old D&D dice and we had no trouble putting a plot together. I went home, typed like mad, and sent it out. I got an agent and I've been putting books out like a madman since. So far it's all work for hire: ten, twenty thousand a pop, but I'll be doing stand-alone books by the end of the year."

"That's the secret? Dice?"

"You can see why the published world doesn't want it leaked out. Some have tried to make it public, Tristan Tzara, William Burroughs, Harry Stephen Keller. But they were silenced."

"Burroughs lived to a ripe old age and got a lot of literary attention."

"Yeah, if you think having a Nike commercial is literary attention."

"This is the craziest thing I ever heard."

"You want to see the canceled checks?"

"So how does that add up as a need to watch my store?"

"As soon as I made my first sale, I knew I had better listen to everything that Mr. Hull had to say, so I asked him the same question."

"Did you have to blow him for that answer?"

"Do you really have a thing against gay men like they say?"

"Look, this is a little odd, what was the answer?"

"He told me that there was a lot of mythic energy in your bookstore, not just in the Bacon name of New Atlantis, but in your being named Matthew, after the tax collector. He said that used-book–store owners collected a tax on literacy, and that gave them a special mystic connection to the world of writing. So if I got my books there I would have a better chance at the big money."

"It was you on the night of the thirtieth, wasn't it?"

"Walpurgisnacht. I thought there would be a lot of manna

in that night and I was right. My sequel to *Lot of Fate, The Runes of Choice*, was conceived that night. I sorta named it after that book you stole, *The Mystery of Choice*. GASA snapped it right up. For twice the fee as the first. I meant to share some of the wealth with you."

"How long does it take you to write a book?"

"About five days. You know when Moorcock moved to Texas, I heard him talk about writing a book in three days, so when I heard the Secret, I knew I could do as well."

"Were you supposed to report to Mr. Hull?"

"He said if I saw anything odd, I was supposed to let him know. He said he wanted to do something nice for you after hearing about Haidee. He is a good man, isn't he?"

"He's a dead man who sold you a bill of goods."

"You might not believe in the Secret, but it works. I have proof of it."

"All you have proof of is that if you develop confidence, you can do anything. You blew the wizard and he gave you plotting. Did you notice the guys ahead of you in line that got brains and hearts and courage?"

"You don't know. I've seen it work. I was a nothing, a nobody. Now I am on best-seller lists."

"Look, Norman, half of the Austin Writers League shop in my store. I've known them for years. There is no secret."

"They're not going to tell you. It would be like giving away the secret handshake."

"Is that all you know about Hull?"

"What do you mean? I know a lot about him, I've read all his books and so forth. I didn't know he was dead. What did he die of?"

"I'm afraid that's an FBI matter."

"Knowing him, probably *The X-Files*."

"Those aren't real."

"I know the show isn't real, but there's a real-life equivalent, you can bet your life on it."

"When's the last time you reported to Mr. Hull?"

"The day before your brother's wedding. Since then he's been out of town or something. I am sorry to hear that he's dead. He made me into a something. I got a girlfriend, we're going to travel next year to all the cons, and we're going to all the art museums of note in North America because she's always wanted to go. I got a car. I'm looking at getting a house. All because of the Secret."

Matthew told Blick to let the boy go, that he was just confused.

"Are you going back to your routine tomorrow?" asked Blick.

"I've got to," said Matthew. "I can't live in fear for the rest of my life."

"Our profilers think that if you make Delaplace wait a few more days, he'll snap—maybe just give himself up."

"I can't keep hiding. Besides, I need to make some money. I was pretty well-heeled when this started—and I can't put the drain on John and his family forever."

"Could you stay away from your shop for just a couple of days?"

"I'll stay away tomorrow. I have been needing to clean out my warehouse space since early March."

Matthew drove home, fed the cat, took his medicine, and then headed to John's. He spent some hours telling them about the dead alchemist. It was late when he came home. He knew that Blick still had the place under surveillance, and with the exception of a few hours on the eighteenth, the place had always been under surveillance, so he felt fairly safe. He still checked every room twice. Turned on all the lights, and then turned them off, checked all his closets, and under the bed.

Then he showered, and lay down very tired in his unkempt bed, sliding his legs under sheets that would have shamed Haidee for their filth.

It always felt so good to come back to *your* bed. He was completely relaxed when there was a sudden quick movement under the covers.

Something bit him, hard, and then there was a bone-crushing pain where the bite had occurred.

He rolled over and up and threw the sheets off the bed.

In the dim light of the bedroom he saw the longest snake he ever had seen, and its noise proved it to be a rattler. It struck again this time at his knee. The bite hurt but it wasn't as painful as before.

He hopped/ran/stumbled to the light switch.

It was a diamondback rattler, whose red markings were fresh and shiny from having recently shed its skin. It was still attached to his right knee. It disengaged, and he jumped on its back with both feet. The back did not snap, and he fell as the snake's muscles rippled beneath him.

He saw that the bite in his right foreleg was already swelling.

The snake was rapidly heading under the bed.

He grabbed its tail and swung it against the wall.

It took five or six swings before the head broke off, splattering the dingy white paint with oh-so-red blood.

The leg hurt like hell. He had never seen any part of his body swell like this before except his penis. As he limped-ran to the phone he thought he was getting a hard-on for death, and he broke into such laughter that, combined with his breathless fright, it made the 911 operator hang up on him.

Wait.

The surveillance, that would be quicker.

He limped-ran to his front door, popped out naked, and as

loud as he could yelled, "I have been bitten by a rattlesnake. Call me an ambulance!"

This did not produce the immediate response he thought it would.

Oh great, they're down at Shirley's Bakery having doughnuts.

He yelled again about the snake.

From the rental house across the street, two guys emerged, running toward him.

"Is he there, Mr. Reynman? Is he there?" they were yelling.

"I've been bitten by a rattlesnake!" Matthew responded.

"What?"

"A rattlesnake! Get me an ambulance!"

"Get him an ambulance, then get us some backup."

"You don't need backup. I killed the goddamn snake and I'm dying. Look at my leg."

The leg was indeed twice the size it had been less than ten minutes before. One cop was running back to the house. The other said, "Let's get you inside."

They stepped in.

"Oh my God!" yelled the cop.

The leg, in addition to being twice the size it had been, was actually turning blue. There was a part of Matthew's body turning blue, and it hurt like hell. It burned and hurt with sensations that Matthew had never had before and could not therefore name. *The pain out of space.*

"You said you killed the snake. Where is it?" asked the cop.

"In the bedroom. Why, do you want to question it?"

"It might be helpful for the poison control."

"Let's go get it."

"You got a bathrobe or something?"

"Yeah, that's not a bad idea, let me."

"Sit down and tell me where it is, you're not getting around too well."

At the hospital Matthew was slipping in and out of consciousness. They were shooting him up with antivenin and telling him that very few people die of snakebite.

"Disfigurement is the main problem."

The doctor's voice echoed in the great canyon where this drama was now taking place. "You are being punished for letting your wife die, that is the major cause of snakebite, wife problems. The snake always gets on well with the wife, gives her fruit and things. There are twenty-eight species of rattlesnake, very few bites in Central Texas. How do you think it got in your bed?"

I've already been punished for letting my wife die.

"There may be some tissue necrosis, some dead tissue we'll have to trim off. Bites in the extremities are bad for diabetics. The snake has always had it in for you, you know. It was there waiting, teaching the alchemist his art and the woman how to put on makeup to fool you."

"It's a blood toxin. Your leg will turn all sorts of interesting colors. The disorientation is brief; you won't remember any of this tomorrow. There is truth and there is truth. You've got to learn to distinguish between them."

The vultures rode the thermals rising off the canyon walls, they began to talk about him. He wished John were here; he didn't like camping. He should've stayed home. Mom said to sing a happy song.

"It had shed its skin between the bed and the wall."

"She's a big one all right. The mother of all snakes."

"Wasn't this guy on the news a while back."

"Well, he'll be on the news tomorrow."

"Yeah, I heard 'em outside, vultures."

"Yeah, but they can't fly."

"I think he may lose the leg. I have never seen poisoning like this."

"He'll lose a chunk of it. I hope he doesn't like swimming, it ain't going to be a pretty scar."

"Is he OK?"

"Well, I wouldn't take bets; there's something weird going on here."

The vultures stopped circling and began power dives. One was singing a song about bringing home a baby bumblebee.

They began to peck out his eyes.

21 Sparkler 451

It was a week before he was up and around. The shop has just been plain closed. But he had got a gift of five thousand dollars from Norman. That helped a lot.

There was a chunk of his right leg missing, as if a couple of ice-cream scoops had scooped the flesh away. The doctors were puzzled at the strength of the venom. The leg had turned all sorts of odd colors from the denatured hemoglobin. He needed a cane, but that would pass. Matthew just wanted to get back to work.

There had been no sign of William Delaplace. The police marveled that he had taken advantage of the three or four hours after they called off the surveillance to sneak a snake into Matthew's house. Matthew's contention that it was the snake from Hull's experiment was dismissed as ludicrous.

Mom was all better. She flew home from Washington; Matthew and John kept the whole snake business from her.

The police were unhappy with Matthew's starting work again, but his belief in their uselessness didn't help them to persuade him against the idea.

Matthew decided he would spend a couple of days working the stock in the warehouse and then have a grand reopening on the first of June. He bought a big sign for the front of the store and the police decided that was when William would hit.

On the morning of May 28, Matthew drove to the Turkey Buzzard Self-Storage Facility. The owner and the security guard were gone. It was a large facility, six rows of little garages covered in baby-shit yellow stucco with brown trim. The galvanized metal garage doors were unpainted. Matthew's two units were in the southwestern corner of the lot, which is to say they were the farthest from the gate. Matthew had discovered early on that there was a man-sized hole in the chain-link fence behind his units, so that when he needed to slip out and use the john at the Diamond Shamrock (or buy a cup of coffee) he didn't need to walk all the way to the front of the facility.

He opened both units. He needed to sort, price, and cull duplicates. He put one bookshelf in front of him. He would stick books there until it was full, then unload the priced books into his station wagon, which was parked directly in front of the unit. He pulled some piles of books to him on the big sheets of cardboard that he kept them on. He plopped his butt in the lawn chair, got out his price guides and pencil, and went to work.

When he got little dibs and dabs of books at the store he priced them there, but when he bought up estates, postal auctions, or bought out small-time specialty dealers—that stock went out here to be priced, and perhaps be orchestrated into a sale. It was a pain to do all the pricing at once, and the temptation to go off and read something was a constant one—it was always the used-book seller's vice. He worked for two hours before he gave in.

He still hadn't read Cassilda's last translation. She was still working on the last section, but with Hull dead, it didn't hold his interest. He pulled the translation out of the car and began to read.

ש

"And from that one intake of fire / All creatures still warmly suspire." Robert Frost

The thing in the jar will be ready in two days. The heating method is perfect and has given it breath. Today William asked me if the thing would be afraid of fire. I thought he was thinking of Frankenstein *movies and laughed at him. But he was reasoning from the fact the gentleman had been ashes. I explained that the fellow had been cremated, and that I had obtained his ashes from his wife. Didn't she want to keep them? he asked. No, I explained. She was Hindu and the ashes of the dead are not sacred, but rather a form of pollution. I started to explain that there was a caste of Brahmans that symbolically ate the ashes, and took on the persona of the dead man for reasons of ritual purification, but he wasn't interested. It turns out that his big interest is in the anguish that he hopes Matthew Reynman will feel at our resurrecting his wife. I don't like his approach in this. I fear that he may torture Alchimia, so I must use what I know about him to be sure that he doesn't come near her. I am not pleased with his hunger for torturing the thing in the jar either. It won't make much of a Guard if it has a warped personality. Maybe I misread William's coming to me. Maybe he isn't chaos, just pure evil. There are people who are simply evil in that they despise the happiness of others. I remember discussing this with Gabriel Thorn, when we were on speaking terms. I had doubted that there was any real evil, just things that broke conventional laws. I offered the idea of Machen's that evil would be stones in your garden putting forth blossoms. But no, he told me there were forces that work for stupidity and unhappiness because they can never have anything other than that in their lives. I suspect he may be right, although it is certainly late to find out. I have one more day of meditation to gain enough substance of being to do the Work. The emotional roller coaster this has been has certainly surprised me. I would have expected that each day would simply be a slightly greater state of optimism than the day before, but it is not so. Some days I am ready to start my Galatea, I feel I have caught enough of*

Reynman's dreams plus my hopes to make Alchimia. Other days I fear that maybe I am catching his fears and repressions. What if he didn't love her like he told me he had? Yet the poetry that fell from his lips like honey the night of my reading, I don't think that could be faked. And as far as my own hopes, I don't know that what I have done is so good. I know one person has died, I know that a rattlesnake was loosed in a public park. I don't know. This isn't what I started to do. My original impulse seems far away, and I wonder if I keep it because of ego, which after all screwed up four marriages pretty goddamn bad, or maybe even fear of William. Why does reflexive consciousness come so late?

Matthew was disgusted by the entry. Stupid hateful bastard, how can anyone admit to trying to steal the dreams of another and still think of himself in moral terms? The bastard would have been better off if he had looked at the *Frankenstein* movies. He crumpled up the paper and tossed it into the darkness of the storage unit.

He didn't deserve what he got, of course, but what a fitting end—staked like a vampire. Matthew still couldn't decide about what he had done to Norman. After all, the guy was doing what he had wanted to do his whole fanboy life.

He glanced at his wristwatch. John would be here soon. John didn't want him to have to load the station wagon all by himself. Damn. He hadn't done half of what he had said he was going to do. He would call John and tell him not to come for a couple of hours.

He went behind the unit and through the fence.

He called and got Camilla. John had already left. He got coffee and decided to risk a Snickers bar. It wasn't that simple sugars are bad; one just has to be careful, as the diet Nazi used to say.

He walked back, already tired. The trauma had really taken it out of him.

As he walked around to the front of the unit, he saw a man carrying two big sacks sneaking around the bookcase and into the unit.

William Delaplace.

Matthew charged the bookcase, knocking it and William over. Something glass broke in the sacks and gasoline spread across the floor. Matthew lay atop the bookcase and pulled Rex Hull's .357 magnum from the shoulder harness he had kept it in ever since the day at New Jerusalem Clinic. He put the gun to William's head.

"If you try to get up I'll blow your fucking head off."

"Where were you? I watched you come back here this morning. There ain't no way out."

"I didn't ask for your questions. If you don't answer mine, you're a dead man. Unlike a previous encounter, I have made sure the gun is loaded."

"Well, OK then, ask a question."

"Oh, right. What's in the sacks?"

"Gasoline, rocket fuel, and two pairs of handcuffs."

"Get one pair of handcuffs. NOW!"

William fished it out of the sack while Matthew rode on the bookcase, which pinned William to the floor.

"Put them ON!"

William did so.

Matthew said, "I'm getting up now, but if you move at all I'll kill your ass."

Matthew got up and walked around the bookcase. He kicked at one of the sacks. It had a metal one-gallon gas can. The other had a couple of glass containers, an electric match, and another pair of restraints.

Matthew picked them up.

He went behind William and shoved the bookcase up toward William's head, so he could clip the restraints on William's legs.

"You got me, man," said William. "Checkmate."

"What were you going to do?"

"Burn you alive. The rocket fuel was hard to get, even with all the chemical houses I'm authorized to buy things at. It burns at four thousand degrees—that's so hot that water burns when it hits it. The gas is just gas. I was going to roast you alive. I figured that was as close as you could get to a pyrotechnic funeral. I can still do it if you let me go."

"I think I'll pass on that option. So how does this match work?"

Matthew switched the electric match on.

William screamed, "My God, man, don't do that—I'm lying in a pool of gasoline!"

"Oh, William, you disappoint me. I thought someone that could chain up Hull would appreciate the whole death-trap idea. You know it's just you and me here."

William whimpered.

"Of course," Matthew continued, "if you told some things, I might just let the police have you, since it would fuck up my stock if I burned it. It is insured, but I think they might call it a suspicious fire, don't you?"

"I'll tell you anything."

"How did you keep the snake alive?"

"There wasn't any snake. Hull didn't make any snake. He was a nut. I was there when he opened the jar. It was just full of goo. I got the snake from a roadside zoo near San Antonio, because I thought it would scare you."

"There wasn't any snake?"

"You didn't believe that shit he wrote about, did you? The guy had gone off his rocker. All of his books and so on he had written years ago—they just didn't start selling till now. All of that magic stuff was an attempt to jump-start his writing. He made a lot of money this year when he optioned that baseball book."

"How do you know what he wrote? He used codes and ciphers."

"Codes and ciphers my ass. He worked on that little notebook every night. He would whisper the words aloud while he would encipher them using these charts. He would have to say the word a bunch of times so he wouldn't get lost. He'd be saying shit like 'Edgar Allan Poe perhaps Edgar Allan Poe perhaps Edgar Allan Poe perhaps Edgar Allan Poe perhaps Edgar Allan Poe perhaps,' as he worked the cipher. I just hung around in the garden and listened to it."

"What made you think that I would figure out the cipher?"

"Your whole fucking life is books. Cut you and you would bleed ink. I figured you would make it up there and have some great death scene. Instead, I had to finish him off."

"Yeah, I know, I made it eventually."

"And you weren't smart enough to see it was all bullshit? Man, he was bug-fuck crazy."

"Then why did you kill him?"

"To save him from disappointment, man. Just like what I'll do for you. I'll give you a fiery death so you'll be ashes just like your wife."

"Where are my wife's ashes?"

"I really don't know, or I would have brought them. He hid them somewhere in Doublesign. He moved around a lot. I tried to make him tell me at the end, but he wouldn't. He told me that the Work would go on even if he died."

"If the 'Work' wasn't real, what is the deputy?"

"That cocksucker? He was crazier than Hull. He just showed up one day. He didn't come out of no jar, that was just full of gooey shit. I think Hull gave him some kind of drugs. Hull was half off all the time. A lot of those incenses he used were drugs."

Matthew glanced at his watch. It was past time for John to be there. Something was wrong.

"Why did you kill him the way you did?"

"It was in one of his books, the *Chymical Wisdom Booke*, that a wizard can only be killed by a stake through the heart, lest his body be suitable for another to raise up. He loved that shit. It was real to him. I made him really happy when I killed him, because that was the way he wanted to go."

Matthew began unscrewing the top of the gas can.

"Are you crazy? This isn't that way I want to die! You are not playing by the rules!"

"Out here in the boondocks there aren't any rules. I tell you what, if you lie real still I'm going to the front office and call the police, but if you move, I'll fire at you." Matthew poured some gasoline over the bookcase and onto William. "You know I don't have to hit you with a hot bullet to start the blaze. Now you be real still."

Matthew walked away, as though going to the front office, then ducked out back through the whole in the fence. He ran to the Diamond Shamrock and called nine-one-one.

"My name is Matthew Reynman and I'm at the Turkey Buzzard Self-Storage on North Parmer. I have a fugitive, William Delaplace, caught. I am holding him at gunpoint, but I don't know how long I can hold him. I'm at the back of the lot."

He hung up and began running back to the lot. Halfway there he had to stop for a moment, as a coughing fit overcame him.

Then he heard a WHOOSH! and screams.

Screams.

Screams.

And as he was getting through the hole in the fence, the screams stopped and there was only the sound of burning and the smell of gasoline and paper and meat.

He pushed through the hole and saw that the inside of the unit had become a fireball, and that fire was spreading to the second unit as well as beginning to lick at his station wagon.

He couldn't even make out the overturned bookcase, but he had no doubt that William had been trapped by it judging from the expression on Mason Aldones's face.

The deputy was wearing street clothes, and he looked as though he had lost about forty pounds, still heavy, but not looking so dangerously overstuffed. His clothes and face were smudged. He turned and looked at Matthew.

"Well, Mr. Reynman, it looks like your troubles have gone up in smoke. I knew that if I watched you, I would find him, and I had a debt to settle. Now I am a free man."

There was none of the madness that had been in his voice in Doublesign. Mineral calm.

Behind him running up the path was John.

Matthew could hear sirens in the distance.

Mason Aldones turned to face John.

John said, "Mason. It is you, isn't it?"

The ex-deputy said, "Only a reasonable facsimile. A better version now that I had a chance to burn my past out of me. Don't worry, John Reynman, I will travel far away from your life. Travel well, friend."

John fainted.

The deputy walked to his car, parked a few units away.

He was pulling out as the police, ambulance, and fire trucks came in.

22 The Finale Rack

On the morning of July 4, Matthew had breakfast with John and Camilla Reynman and Cassilda Jones at the Lost Weekend. They were their disgusting post-orgy selves, all smiles and grins and full of hope. Oh well, Matthew was pretty full of hope these days too. There was a show to do with Falconer Brothers Pyrotechnics in Doublesign today. It would probably be their last Doublesign show. They were jobbing for Titan Pyrotechnics doing a ten-thousand-dollar show—which is as big as a hand-lit show goes. Next year, they would get into the big bucks, which meant an electronically fired show, so Doug and Rodger could do it by themselves.

Breakfasts at the Lost Weekend were good. Bildad's special omelette with turkey, broccoli, and a Parmesan sauce was an especial favorite of Matthew's.

The women were outrageous and John was beaming. Nothing other than usual.

They still believed.

They believed that Rex Hull had done strange alchemical experiments in Austin and Doublesign and that William's gasoline-soaked confessions were meant to hurt Matthew. This was a sign, Matthew was sure, that their brains had been addled with too much sex. But worse still was John's belief that Mason Aldones had been lying dead a year before in John's house. Matthew at least drew hope that neither Saul nor Paul Reynman seemed mad, and that perhaps whatever John's problem was, it wasn't hereditary.

"I finally translated the last section," said Cassilda. "Actually I did weeks ago, but you were pretty busy with the sale and training your new staff."

"Thanks," said Matthew. "What does he say at the end?"

"I'll give it to you. I think at the end he was pretty grim. It's a hand copy of some little squib that appeared in a magazine called *Twice Rejected Tales*. It's about the end of the world. I think he was expecting to go out with a bang and a whimper."

"A sad guy," said Matthew.

"Not too bad perhaps, just deflected," said Camilla.

"What do you mean?" asked Matthew.

"Well, alchemy is about the Royal Art of Being More Than You Seem," Camilla began, and everyone could hear the capitals in her speech, "so it's not about who you are to start with, nor about what you own. Hull was just an average American that got lost in the quest for a trophy wife and a fancy car. If he had made himself better, he could have attracted the woman he wanted."

"Instead of going through wives like socks," said Cassilda.

"Well, he paid for the attempt. Most people that burn themselves out for a better life than the Joneses—no offense—die, but without broom handles in their chest," said Matthew.

John said, "Pretty close. Most American vampires die of heart attacks."

Camilla said, "I'm just sad that Matthew didn't get to see the Albedo."

Matthew gestured for her to continue to show off her arcane knowledge, or perhaps for the waitress to refill his coffee.

"In Alchemy there are three regions. There is the Nigredo, which is black and full of rot and disease and snakes. Then there is the Rubeo, which is full of war and gold and blood and trumpets. Then there is the peaceful synthesis—the Albedo, the region of reflected light."

"Maybe I'll find that with time," said Matthew. "I could use a peaceful region."

Rodger and his daughter Heidi picked up Matthew. It was going to be a great show for Heidi; she was eighteen and now could light the shells. She had been looking forward to this for years. They drove up to Fort Worth.

Doug had already picked up the rental truck and the fireworks, cannon, racks, and so forth. He was loading his special touches into the truck when they arrived—water fire extinguishers, flashlights, goggles, earplugs, and the big American flag that the Falconers always flew at their shows.

They all had a soda with Janet, and helped load lawn chairs into Doug's sport utility vehicle.

There would be a few other people meeting them on site, Doug's adopted son and his wife and a team of social workers that the son worked with who wanted a team-building exercise.

Matthew rode in the rental truck with Doug. He loved riding in a big rental truck with the words DANGER EXPLOSIVES on the side. He liked being able to look down into people's cars, and seeing the response the truck brought at gas stations.

There were the usual patriotic music programs on the radio.

After about an hour's chat, the truck was comfortably quiet and Matthew read the last chapter of Hull's magical notebook.

ח

I oddly can't think of anything to write today. My self-questioning has been a sham. It hasn't led to the Purification that such exercises are supposed to lead to. I am not any wiser, I don't seem to have developed any siddhis, I don't even have a more clear picture of what it is that I am supposed to do. I remembered last night, that the last piece of writing I did (at the end of my marriage to Caitlin) was about fireworks. It scares me that I had forgotten this. It was published in Albert Greenspan's Twice Rejected Tales. *Maybe it was my last really magical moment. I got it out of the pile this morning. I think I might have been telling myself something.*

A Little Cracker
by
Rex Hull

It's always the same dream, Doc. Always the same. I find myself behind the wheel of a large antique car. A pearly white Duesenberg speeding down Highway 66. Oppressive gravity wind in my hair. The white stripes and the crooked fence posts speed by, a confederacy of barbed wire guarding fields of a cereal crop wasting away in summer heat. I pull the great white car off the road to a highway stand. It has lengths of bright lights—Xmas lights rendered superfluous by the sunlight.

An incredible assortment of fireworks stand on whitewashed shelves. A small Chinese man, a whimsical elfin wizard, smiles with friendship. His stand smells of myrrh, like the Phoenix's nest. Behind his neatly coiffured head: 100-Shot Thunderbuzzer, Large Happy Lamp, Golden Fish Vase, Saturn Missile Battery, Lady Fingers, Black Cats, Sparklers, Red Rats, Smoke Bombs, and a huge tube in shiny red white and blue foil—The Reality Annihilator. Like a dealer in jade he sees my pupils dilate when I spot the long tube. He picks it off the shelf, setting it like a great treasure before me. Confucius says in the Li Chi *that a courtier should bear the imperial scepter as though bowed down by its weight.*

The middle-aged Chinaman stands so the cylinder is perfectly reflected in both eyes. With an almost im-

perceptible bow, he speaks with gentle voice like peach pie, "The Reality Annihilator pride of my shop. Made at the Beijing Fireworks Factory with many colorful star mines inside. Entire Aurora Borealis plus strictly noise for the connoisseur. Makes for beautiful finale."

"How much?"

"Only $10.99. Where else can you get so much sound and color so cheaply?"

I reach in the pocket of my ice-cream suit, pulling out a slender Moroccan leather wallet. A ten and one exchanged for a penny and The Reality Annihilator. A small brown bag for my prize, the dealer in fireworks supplying a punk stick for free. I return to my vanilla auto, setting the small bag next to a larger one on the red leather upholstery. I speed back to my hotel. The Holiday Inn. Innkeeper to the World. Begun by a Bethlehem hosteler in the reign of Augustus Caesar. I walk in seedy and furtive in the hot afternoon sun. My room is on the second floor, a hot climb up the wrought-iron staircase. The carpet of my room is orange, matching the neon Vacancy sign.

*I carefully array my treasures on the dark low table. Twenty in all, 19 from the large sack and one from the small. An octagonal 61-shot Beehive; 2 cubic Thunderstorms; 3 Giant Planes Flying at Night (small green tubes with wings); 6 Westlake Rockets made in Jiangxi, China; 1 giant Vertical Wheel; 3 Outer Space rockets made in Deerfield, Ohio; 3 Twisting Tornado buzz bombs; and the red*white*blue Reality Annihilator. I go to the nightstand, open the top drawer, take out my box of Ohio bluetip matches. I pull my small camera from atop the red vinyl Gideon Bible.*

I sprinkle the matches around the fireworks. A beautiful pyrotechnic tableau. I place a full-length mirror at one end of the coffee table. I shoot an entire roll of film—"Fireworks and Man in Mirror." I wrap the film canister in lead foil to protect it from cosmic rays.

I carefully read the instructions on each of the tubes, fountains, cones, bombs, and repeaters. Class C fireworks. Flammable. Caution: emits showers of sparks. Caution: shoots flaming balls. Place on ground, light fuse, and get away. Use under adult supervision. See warnings on back. Made in Kwungtons, China. Made in Shoshone, Ohio. Made in the Plateau of Leng.

I check my golden turnip of a railroad watch. It is 4:15, just past teatime. I know I'll have to be quick. From a monogrammed case I assemble Mr. Gysin's Dream Machine. Flicker will be necessary if I am to round up all of my second attention.

Noise will be necessary for the information overload. Regretfully, my Hieronymus machine was confiscated somewhere, perhaps Uganda, where I used to smuggle DDT.

I turn on the thoughtfully provided radio. KJKK with Wailin' Willy and his Wild Boys. Country music is as near to white noise as I can manage. I assume a lotus position, my back comfortably touching the back of a blue overstuffed chair. My interior monologue vanishes as flicker plays over my eyelids. I feel an itching, pulling sensation in my midsection. Small lines of force, the manifestation of my will, appear as tentacles from my navel. They begin to assemble a visual manifestation of my third attention. A small black crack appears in the air. It opens an oval crack of nothingness. The cosmic vagina. A window to peer into eternity from time. I spring up, my bones cracking, and light the punk stick. I gather my crackers and light them one by one. I toss each into the coatl's hole. Small holes blown in the fabric of time itself.

*The lessons my body has learned play themselves out like an endless string of pearls. I stand in the dark hole already being flattened by the Eagle's crushing attention. I light the last firework, the red*white*blue Reality Annihilator made on the Plateau of Leng. Before I'm flat-*

tened, accelerated, and purified by the Eagle I blow a good-bye kiss to the most expensive firecracker I've ever bought. A violet spume of sparks is already blowing from its top. Then the whole picture shatters like a mirror and each piece falls away into the void below.

Then I wake up. What do you think it means, Doctor?

I'm all better—really? That if I get rid of reality I won't have any more trouble with it? I'm being discharged today? The keys to your car, Doctor, I couldn't. A white Duesenberg? Really wow! Discharge money and suit just like old-time movie prisons. Gosh, this is great, Doc. I just love the Fourth of July.

Boy, thought Matthew, Freud would have had a field day with this.

The last few minutes of the drive into Doublesign Matthew and Doug discuss Western Winter Blast. He and Janet had picked up some pretty powerful Roman candles, and he thought about setting ten or so off at the beginning of the show, along with the salutes. It would look pretty. He was also going to pull out a four-inch and a five-inch red shell to light when they got to the "rockets' red glare" part of the show.

They drove into the city park with the old sheriff waving them on, arriving at the site at two.

The village had helped them out by digging a ninety-foot trench, so that they would only have to pack earth around the cannon. The rest of the team was there and they got the truck unloaded fast. It was going to be a scorching afternoon, the temperature near a hundred degrees. There were several hunks of limestone lying around, fossiliferous limestone, thick with oyster shells—a brown- and cream-colored souvenir of Texas's days as a shallow sea—a lazy dinosaur pool.

Soon everyone smelled of sunscreen.

Janet got the soda and iced tea brigade going as they buried the cannons.

Cannons are 18-inch lengths of pipe. They had six 3-inch, six 4-inch, six 5-inch, and three 6-inch pipe cannons, and two 8-inch single-use cardboard cannons. Each had to be buried standing straight up.

Heidi put the American flag on a light pole near the site. This was not only patriotic, it told the shooters how much the wind was blowing.

Doug gave the team a safety talk. To dramatize things he lit a four-foot strip of quick match, which burned in a second.

They took a break about four.

Doug told a joke. "There was this linguistics professor, and he was lecturing on how in English the double negative makes a positive, but that in some languages, such as Russian, the double negative is still a negative. 'However,' said the prof, 'there are no languages in which two positives make a negative.' And a voice from the back of the lecture hall said, 'Yeah. Right.' "

Matthew swallowed certain fears and walked over to the Kuntry Kitchen.

Orfamay was not in evidence. The magic cake was no longer on the menu.

The new waitress was impressed that he was part of the fireworks crew.

"Is it dangerous?" she asked.

"Oh yes," he said, "very."

This was a patent lie that impressed the crowds and kept them off site—it could be very dangerous to the uninitiated.

Matthew had coffee and a sandwich.

He learned that the deputy had quit his job, and really slimmed up. Waitress couldn't figure out how, all he seemed to eat was "that cake." Seems he got to be a likable fellow. So likable that he and Orfamay ran off together. They had gone down to the library and spun the globe. She put her finger on Tasmania, and off they went.

Matthew asked if people were still getting rich.

People were still getting rich, there was a lot of money coming into town after the trouble. She clearly did not know what the "trouble" was and Matthew had no desire to explain his part in it.

When he got back to the site, they were separating the shells for the ready boxes. Shells come from three sources—American, Chinese, and Japanese. The Japanese shells have very poetic names—Silver Flower in Night. The Chinese shells have very descriptive names—Yellow Flash with Blue Sparkles. The Chinese shells always have misspellings. Matthew had seen a video of the plant in China where the shells were made. They used donkeys to provide some of the rotary power for grinding the coloring minerals.

Heidi and Rodger were taping road flares to wooden pickets. These served as fusees, the device the firers—Doug and Rodger—would use to light the shells.

Matthew and Doug's son began assembling the finale racks. The racks are ten 3-inch cardboard cannons that are tied together in groups of four. There are strings of ten 3-inch shells that are put in the racks—one shell to a cannon. The four strings are tied together with quick match and go off near the same time—filling the sky with forty shells at once. They had three racks of four. Doug asked Matthew if he would light two of them. Matthew had always been a little scared of the finale rack, but said he would.

They took another break about six and walked around the shallow lake to the picnic tables, where they got free barbecue, potato salad, peach cobbler, and Coke.

By eight they were back on site.

There was a musical program, some patriotic, some gospel, some country. Then a few speeches.

Matthew was—as always—moved by the speeches. He had an abiding love of America, despite its warts. He viewed it as the only real triumph Idealism has ever had. That was considerably more magical than Mr. Hull and his potions.

Janet passed out the earplugs and the safety goggles.

Then came the national anthem, with two red shells marking the rockets' red glare.

Then Doug lit ten Roman candles.

Matthew and a couple of others loaded the first line of three-inch cannon with titanium retorts. Those make a big white FLASH and a deafening BOOM. It always gets the attention of the nouveau-huddled masses. When the first retort goes off, every car alarm in two miles goes off as well. Pretty neat.

Heidi began lighting the shells, and so it began.

Thirty minutes of fast show, which meant that there was no black space in the sky.

Matthew would grab a shell, cradle it to his body so that none of the falling burning paper would set it off, and run like mad to the cannon line twenty-five feet away from the ready boxes. Approaching the cannon he would swing the shell by the fuse over the cannon mouth. You don't want to ever have any part of your body over the cannon. Then he would drop the shell. Meanwhile shells were exploding out of nearby cannons, each blast hitting his chest like a soft fist. You don't get to watch a show you're doing, you have to keep running, keep running, keep running back and forth from firing line to ready box.

Everything increases in drama. First the three-inch shells, then the four-inch, and so forth. Each larger shell goes higher in the air and has a bigger explosion.

Finally Doug and Rodger were lighting the eight-inch shells.

Matthew had lit his fusee. He lit first one rack, then the other, then ran like hell. About twenty feet from the racks, he dove to the ground, rolled over, and watched the sky filled with 120 fireworks of all colors.

Then somebody in the audience yelled, “Great Show!” and there was hootin’ and hollerin’ and clapping. It was wonderful.

Matthew took off his safety goggles and earplugs and told Heidi what a great job she had done. The crew was high-fiving each other, and Janet walked over with the count.

There had been two duds.

You have to find duds. Shells are two separate explosives. One explodes in the cannon lifting the firework in the air—roughly a hundred feet for each inch of the shell’s diameter; the other explodes in the air, sending burning metal salts that make the palm trees, the Saturns, the comets. These inner shells look exactly like giant fireworks. A dud occurs when the outer shell has exploded but the fuse to the inner shell has not lit. So somewhere on the ground there were two giant firecrackers waiting for a kid to find—and light. A fireball from fifty to two hundred feet in diameter might be a surprise in a backyard.

Matthew got a flashlight and went looking. He had found a dud a few years ago, and that had made him the dud finder. The flag was pointing toward the northeast, which was in the direction of his aunt’s former house.

The city was turning on klieg lights at the site and the cleanup had started. The finale racks had to be undone, the cannon dug up, the paper and burnt-out fusees collected, and so forth. Matthew was glad to be away from it.

The moon was nearly full; it was beautiful on the lake. Its shimmers on the small lake created a world of imagination that is at home in the dark. The sounds of cars driving away, the people leaving the viewing area, the birds still quite disturbed by the show, all of these things blended, and were held together by the silver metal of the moon like jewels in an armband.

Matthew walked through the low brush and uncut grass, alarming white rabbits and large-winged moths with the arcs of his flashlight's cone. The light of the flashlight began to grow yellow and flicker. Perhaps this had been put away after last year's shoot. It blinked twice and was gone.

The light of the moon now that Matthew's eyes had grown large was sufficient to spot something as large as a dud. It would look like a black rock, a fist-sized stone of trifling value.

He walked on enjoying the reflected light of the moon. It wasn't the pure white of ice cream or church paint. That virginal, impossibly pure light that humans sully by the mere act of being human. No, this reflected light was invitation to fantasy, to make a bush a bear, or to see the low-flying birds as shimmering saucers.

Matthew begin singing his uncle Lullaby Reynman's signature song, "Deep in the Heart of Texas." The stars *were* big and bright, here in the Heart of Texas, and reminded him of the one he loved.

He kept walking further and further into the moonlight, leaving behind the business of the last few months.

He found himself on the lot where his aunt Martha's house once stood. It was late he realized, already the fifth.

For a moment he was surprised by the shiny pool, and then he realized that was the metal cap to her old well, that Rex had put in as a community gesture.

Wait.

That makes no sense. Giving people the magic cake, now that was a community gesture. Giving money to the library, that was a community gesture.

But capping a well?

Was this well such a threat to the commonweal?

William Delaplace was afraid of water.

Wouldn't a well be a good place to hide Haidee's ashes?

Rex could have put one of those large glass tubes down there, bubbling with who knows what strange concoctions.

Matthew pried off the cover.

Within was only darkness. The angle of the moon shed no light. He would come back tomorrow, he still had to find the duds.

He turned.

Then he heard something. Glass cracking? Some small animal moving in the well?

No.

A young black woman was trying to crawl out of the well.

Could it be? He smelled the foul smells of the clinic, her skin glistened wet with jelly in the moonlight. Could it be? Would she remember?

Then she spoke.

And he Knew.

About the Author

Don Webb—fireworks operator, SF writer, author of nonfiction books on the occult, maker of great chili, diabetes advocate, rock song lyricist—is a seldom-spotted recluse in Austin, Texas. Although they show up for the "Books, Beverages and Blasphemy" series at the notorious Fringeware Store in Austin, Texas, this shy, soft-spoken Southerner and his intelligent, sexy wife (and other companions) are held by many to be merely creations of Texan folklore, as lacking in ontology as the jackalope or the furred trout. Don has a large presence on the World Wide Web. His works have been translated into ten languages. Close friends describe him as "quiet, conservative, and lazy—a Champion of American Middle Class values—no wait, that's the guy across the street. Don is—um—well, you know."